12-30-0?
1#—? 14-02-05

FIRST TIME IN PAPERBACK!

RONICKY DOONE'S REWARD

MAX BRAND

Author of Millions of Books in Print!
"Brand's Westerns are good reading and crammed with adventure!"
—*Chicago Tribune*

A writer of legendary genius, Max Brand has brought to his Westerns the raw frontier action and historical authenticity that have earned him the title of the world's most celebrated Western writer.

In *Ronicky Doone's Reward,* Doone arrives in Twin Springs and finds himself in the midst of a deadly feud between two rival families. The stakes are high—honor, revenge, and rich ranch land. Though the townsmen favor the Jenkinses, Ronicky is drawn to the Bennetts, especially beautiful Elsie Bennett. Only Doone has the power to restore peace—but he may take a bullet trying.

W9-AHB-581

RONICKY DOONE'S REWARD

LEISURE BOOKS **NEW YORK CITY**

RONICKY
DOONE'S
REWARD

CHAPTER I

ENTER, BLONDY

The rider shot down the street, swung out of one stirrup, and rested all this weight on the other; then, when his pony flung back on braced legs, still traveling with great speed, he leaped down and ran up the steps to the hotel. His eyes were shining. He whipped off his hat and beat the dust from the crown against his leg, a great cloud of it rolling lazily down the wind.

"Boys," he cried, "what d'you think's up? Old Steve Bennett's new man has come to town!"

This announcement was greeted with such a roar of cheers that even Ronicky Doone turned his head. He was seated at the far end of the veranda, stretched low in his chair and so posed that the keen, hot sunshine fell upon all of him, saving one shoulder and his head, above which his arms were thrown for greater ease. He was taking a sun bath which might have set a lizard boiling, but Ronicky Doone enjoyed every instant of it. As he turned he literally flashed with color, turning from sunlight into shadow. For Ronicky was one of those dandies of the mountain desert who adopted the gaudiness of the Spanish-Indian habits. No band but one of carved gold could surround his sombrero. No ready-made boot could surround his ankles and slope with glove-fitted smoothness about his feet. The red of his bandanna was glowing scarlet and of the purest silk. Silk also was his shirt, though of a heavier and coarser make. What vain, and almost womanly, vanity had made him have such gloves worked to order? The leather was as thin as a fine tissue, it seemed, and clothed his hand so that it hardly impeded the movement of the fingers in flexing. Even his cartridge belt, that symbol of all the grimmer side of the cow business, could not be allowed to remain as it had come from its maker. No, the webbing must needs be taken to some Mexican silver worker who wrought upon it, with infinite patience and skill, figures of birds and beasts and the strange flowers of cacti.

He stretched himself in the shadow now, as if he enjoyed the coolness fully as much as he had enjoyed the heat. He showed, as he turned, a rather lean, handsome face, dark of skin and hair and eyes and with a singularly youthful look. The strangeness of those youthful lines came out of the contrast with a certain weariness which, now and again, dulled his eyes. Just as one was about to write him down as a half-breed for his luxurious laziness and his olive skin, one caught a glimpse of that time-tired look in his eyes, and there was a suggestion of sadness beyond words.

It came and went in his face, however, so quickly that the observer could not be entirely sure. So he lounged in his chair, for he had appropriated to his uses the only long wicker chair in that vast county. It creaked with shrill voices whenever he stirred.

As for the rider who had dismounted in such haste to rush upon the hotel veranda with the tidings that old Steve Bennett's new man had come to town, he had stepped back, laughing and still dusting clouds out of his sombrero and nodding his head to affirm his tidings, as the cow-punchers yelled.

"It's the blond-headed kid," he repeated. "He's come in to look us over, maybe."

This remark provoked a yet heartier chorus of mirth, and Ronicky Doone thrust himself slowly into a more erect position.

"Who's the blond-headed kid?" he asked. "And who's Bennett?"

Now, as a rule, people west of the Rockies avoid direct questions and prefer to learn by inference and by patient waiting. He who bluntly asked to find out what he wishes to know, instead of trailing the information stealthily to the ground, is usually put down as a greenhorn; or else he is an established man with a known reputation, a man born and bred in the West and possessed of sufficient fame to free him from the danger of being put down as a blockhead.

The man to whom Ronicky Doone had put the question had never seen his face before that day, nevertheless, no matter to what other conclusions he may have come, he decided that the olive-skinned youth was not a tenderfoot. The smile of cold derision and aloofness faded instantly from his lips, and he returned: "You're new to these parts, I reckon?"

"I'm plumb new," admitted Ronicky.

"Bennett is the old gent tried to put Al Jenkins out of business thirty years back. But now Jenkins has come back after making a stake in Alaska gold. He sunk that gold right back in the oil range land, bought in the acres that Bennett had robbed him of, and now he's giving Bennett some of his own medicine. And Bennett don't like it. This blond-headed kid—well, I dunno. Every now and then Bennett gets some new hands, and they try to hold down jobs for a while on the ranch, but sooner or later they got to come to town. Well, partner, when they come to town they meet up with the boys, and the boys give 'em a pretty rough ride. You watch the way they handle 'Blondy' when he sails in. Maybe he'll sashay into town as a peacock, but before he leaves Twin Springs I reckon some of the starch will be took out of him!"

He twisted himself from side to side in the ecstasy of his emotion.

"Yes sir, something is sure going to happen to that gun fighter!"

"Gunfighter?" echoed Ronicky. "You know this Blondy, then?"

"Sure I don't. But I know that everybody out on Bennett's ranch has to know that when they wander into Twin Springs they're going to have a rough ride. And the ones that come in, come because they're all set for the party. They know well that the man that can ride into Twin Springs off'n the ranch of old Steve Bennett and get out without having his guns and his spurs took from him, is quite some party!"

He set his teeth to prove the strength of his own convictions on the matter.

"Why," continued Ronicky, forced to raise his voice because of the gathering clamor, as new men came out from the interior of the hotel to hear the tidings, "why should the whole town be agin Bennett and for Al Jenkins?"

"That's easy," responded his informant. "It works this way. The money that Al Jenkins sunk into Twin Springs is what brung it to life. You'd ought to have seen this here town a few years back. Any respectable junk dealer would have laughed himself to death if he'd been asked to make a bid on it. There wasn't a piece of a board in it that wasn't rotten. There wasn't a nail that wasn't rusted in two. Why? Just because the old toll road had been allowed to go bust. That's why! When the railroad picked out The Falls as the place it was going to run through, why everybody in Twin Springs just sat down and folded their hands and said: 'Here's where we slip off the map and get all rubbed out!'

"And that's what was happening, too. Twin Springs done just that same thing. It begun to die like a tree when the taproot's cut. The old toll road was allowed to go to pieces. The rains of a couple of winters put a crimp in that roadbed and made every teamster take chances on cross-country rather than use the old toll road from here to The Falls.

"Well, then along comes old Al Jenkins that Bennett had run out of the country a half lifetime before. What did he do? Did he sit down and fold his hands in his lap like the rest of 'em? No, sir!

"'If the old town is dead,' he says, 'we'll bring the old town back to life,' says he.

"And that is what he's done, just as sure as if you'd read about him in the Bible. He climbed down into his purse and come up covered with gold and greenbacks. He spilled money everywhere, and everything that money touched turned green and begun to put out shoots like springtime. Yes, sir, he was like irrigation. Old Al Jenkins, the first thing he done, was to send out a gang to work on the toll road, and he got that back into better shape than it ever was before. It cost a sight of money but he slicked it up as smooth as glass. He got all the old-timers that had used to team on it before the railroad went through, and he got them to tell him every good feature of the old road. After they'd told him, he went ahead and

10

fixed up this road just the same and better. He got it so good that not a one of the old boys could drive over it without admitting that that road couldn't give a man a bump in the worst wagon that was ever made.

"And when the road was fixed, Twin Springs begin to come to life. The railroad went to The Falls, sure, and so Glendon Falls now is a real city. But we ain't dead any more, no, sir. We're alive and coming! Look down the street. You see all those new houses? Well, they mean new folks and folks with money and folks that are making more money and spending it right where they make it, improving Twin Springs, all because Al Jenkins has put faith in 'em that Twin Springs means good business next year as well as this year. Yes, sir, the railroad is a long way off, and stuff has to be hauled to it, and Twin Springs is a good halfway point. So they all stop here. There's blacksmith shops for shoeing the hosses and fixing the wagons; and there's saddle stores and harness shops; and there's them two eating houses. And—well, everywhere along the line you'll see the signs of what Al Jenkins has done for the town."

"And he done it all for charity?" asked Ronicky Doone.

"Why should he do it for charity?" asked his companion hotly. "No, sir. What he done was to show his faith by buying up a lot of the old folks around here that had let the town die on their hands and the result is now that he owns pretty near all of the ground that the town is built on and——"

"H'm," chuckled Ronicky Doone. "I call it good business, partner."

"I call it public spirit!" asserted the other stoutly.

Apparently that was the interpretation which the townsmen and those from the adjacent country wished to place upon the conduct of old Al Jenkins, and it was folly to argue with them. This man's eye lighted to fiery earnestness the moment he suspected that the intentions of Jenkins were being questioned. And Ronicky at once shrugged his shoulder and turned his head away. It made small difference to him what the opinions of this or any other man in the town might be on this or any other subject, but, just as he was sliding back into his old mental languor, he heard the voices near him hushed, and then a warning murmur: "What yourselves, now. Here comes Blondy. Make out that you don't know who he is or where he come from."

CHAPTER II

THE TIME MATCH

Unable to remain indifferent when such a crisis had come, Ronicky turned his head again to observe.

What he saw was a youth in his early twenties, riding jauntily down the exact center of the street, sitting his pony straight and tall, with one hand dropped in careless self-assurance on his hip and the broad brim of his sombrero furling back from his face. It was a handsome, clean-cut face. The sun and wind had tanned him deepest brown, and out of the tan looked two clear eyes, ready to exchange glances with any one in the world.

His horse, also, though hardly above the average diminutive stature of cow ponies, was rather smaller in the head and more shapely of neck and quarters than the general run of such animals. This was one point on which Ronicky Doone was an expert. He read the capabilities of a horse at a glance, just as some master minds are able to penetrate to the character of other men. And this horse he knew to be a speedster of the first water. Instinctively his glance turned to the side where his own mare stood under the shed, a silken-flanked bay running to black points and with a white-starred forehead. As if she felt the power of his glance, she jerked up her head and whinnied to him softly. He replied with a low whistle which, it seemed, contented her as much as speech would have contented a human being. For she lowered her head again and resumed her occupation of worrying at some shreds of grass.

Ronicky looked back. The youth had brought his horse to a halt before the hotel and was now making a pretense, having dismounted, at tethering the animal. Yet it was only a pretense, as Ronicky's accurate eye could see. The reins were wrapped around and around the crossbar, but they were not slipped one above the other to form a fast knot. One strong jerk was all that was needed to free those reins and set the horse at liberty to run.

Plainly, then, the blond-headed rider expected that he might have need of making a quick exit from the village. Mentally Ronicky Doone sat up. When both sides were prepared for mischief, it would be strange indeed, considering the metal of which they were made, if the sparks did not fly.

Blondy was a big fellow, strongly made around the shoulders, narrow of hips, long and lean of legs—in short, the beau ideal of the cow-puncher who must live so large a portion of his life in the saddle. Ronicky himself, an athlete from his head to his feet, looked with suspicion upon such a build, but he knew it was the height of good opinion.

The moment Blondy turned from his horse Ronicky knew that the youngster had courage. His head was still high. His cheek had blanched a little, to be sure, as he approached the long line of prospective enemies, but his eye was still bold and unabashed. And he walked with an unshortened stride.

And something about him—his youth, his boldness—appealed strongly to Ronicky. He lunged forward until he was erect, sitting lightly on the very edge of his chair and ready to jump into action in any direction.

Whether the courage of the stranger was the courage of mere dare-deviltry which makes a man ready in taking up a dare, for instance, he could not guess. But something told him that it was well for Blondy that the test he was meeting was merely to pass through the village rather than one which demanded a long stay under fire in it. There was something immensely attractive in this proposition to Ronicky. If Blondy could stay here on the veranda of the hotel for the length of time needed to pass a few words about the weather, for instance, and then step back to his horse and ride on out of town, all would be well. He would have accomplished the thing which the men of Twin Springs had sworn that no hired man of Bennett could ever do.

But, before he had been ten seconds on that veranda, it was very probable that about twenty different kinds of trouble would start happening to the tall cow-puncher.

He advanced magnificently up the steps, however, waving his hand in careless good cheer to the waiting line. And when he reached the top of the steps he said to the nearest man, smiling: "Mighty hot day, partner, eh?"

Much, much would depend upon the manner in which that question was answered. If the person addressed acquiesced with a nod, all was well. But he might make some impertinent answer which, to be sure, would draw danger upon his own head, but which would also insure him the enlisted support of all the other men on either side of him. Ronicky listened breathlessly.

The man addressed was little. He was wiry and sundried in appearance. And he had two yellow streaks of mustaches which dripped down past his mouth. He took some moments in answering.

"I dunno," he said at last. "It might be hot to some and cold to others. But I always been taught: If you don't like a place, leave it!"

This had been uttered in the unmistakable accent. It was surcharged with scorn. But the point was that the old man had not been able to find a remark stinging enough to force Blondy into a sharp retort which, in turn, would have precipitated action of one kind or another. The best that the old cow-puncher had been able to find in his mental armory had been a remark which might have its point turned in the manner in which it was taken, and this was exactly what Blondy proceeded to do. He took off his hat, nodded, and laughed good-naturedly.

"That's just what I've done, you see," he said. "I was hot in the sun, so I've come into the shade."

And so saying, he slowly and deliberately turned his back upon the other and stood resting one shoulder against a pillar of the porch.

It had been very well done, Ronicky decided. Blondy had acquitted himself with just the right edge to his voice. He had not been sickeningly acquiescent. Neither had he been stupidly defiant. But with a nice twist of the wrist he had avoided the full brunt of danger and still retained

14

his dignity. And now, behold, his broad back was turned full upon the others!

The beauty of this maneuver actually filled Ronicky with awe. It was, he decided, perfect. They could not strike a man from behind. Neither could they find it very easy to think up insulting things to say to that same back. Ronicky Doone clasped his hands around his knees and rocked himself back and forth in a silent ecstasy. He was delighted.

And now he saw Blondy slowly produce cigarette papers and tobacco. He saw the cigarette manufactured; he saw it placed between Blondy's lips; he saw the sulphur match separated carefully from the rest of the pack; he saw the cigarette lighted; he saw the handsome head of Blondy wreathed in thin blue-brown smoke.

And every other person on the veranda was following every act with similar exactitude of interest and observation. For they had instantly seen the throwing of the gage. The unspoken challenge of Blondy, as plain as words could have stated it, was this: "I shall stand here calmly upon the veranda, roll my cigarette, light and smoke it, and then depart. And if I am able to do this in peace, then I shall consider myself at liberty to go forth into the world and tell other men that I have bearded the citizens of Twin Springs and come off unscathed."

This was all understood. Not only that, but it drew a scowl of rage from the stupidest of the men on the veranda. They were challenged, and yet they knew not how to rise to meet the challenge. Of course some one could arise and, striding forward, shout an insult. But this would make Blondy, if he were half of the man that he seemed to be, whirl upon his heel and pump a stream of leaden slugs at the other. And gun play was not what was desired. The rules of the game required that Blondy should be taken in hand and disciplined for his folly. But the rules also required that he should not be fatally injured unless he really made himself obnoxious. Certainly that should not be done when such tremendous odds were arrayed against him.

The quandary grew. The perspiration poured down the faces of those horny-handed sons of battle. Not a man there but would have sooner died than be shamed. But would could they do?

Ronicky Doone, fairly quivering with excitement, leaned forward and scanned the line of faces. He saw hands go convulsively back and grasp at gun butts and then drop,

15

as though ashamed of the impulse. He saw jaws thrusting out, as the rage for battle grew. But still there did not arise any young Napoleon to show them the manner in which they should strike in honor. One giant-limbed cow-puncher half arose from his chair, as though about to stride up to Blondy and call to him to turn.

His shadow fell across the feet of Blondy, and Ronicky saw the hand of the youth tremble, so that the thin line of smoke rising from the tobacco quivered also. He was afraid, but it was no wonder. If the test were hard on the many, how stern it must be for the one?

But the big man settled back in his chair with a faint sigh and a great creaking of the chair, as it felt his weight. And now the cigarette was half consumed!

"Good boy!" thought Ronicky. "Keep it up!"

He literally hurled the strength of his good will as a guardian cloud around the form of Blondy. He shifted a little, so that his holster hung well clear of the edge of his chair. If any one should make a mistake and attempt to take a cowardly advantage of the fact that Blondy's back was turned—well, the mistake would never be regretted, because the man would not live to repeat!

But there was no question of fair play. The cow-punchers were simply combing the air for a courteous means of making Blondy turn upon them. But if they could not find that, they would not bully him into a fight. The cigarette, however, which was the time match of that strange trial, was now almost burned out, and in an excess of careless confidence Blondy stretched out his hand and snapped the cigarette with his middle finger.

Alas, he struck it too hard. Not only were the ashes jarred off, but the burning tobacco was loosened from the paper as well, and it dropped to the floor of the veranda and fumed there. Not only that, but the loose tobacco also streamed from the butt and left only a seared, fluttering wisp of paper in the fingers of the big man.

The crisis had come. Would he dare to wait to roll another cigarette? Or would his little accident give the slow-witted cow-punchers a clew to some means of baiting Blondy?

CHAPTER III

BLONDY'S BLUNDER

He had not long to wait before there was an answer to the question. The big man who had first risen, as though about to stride up to Blondy and attack him, now sat forward again. No word had risen in his dull brain, but he contrived to bring forth an immense laugh which fairly shook the pillars supporting the veranda. More than all, that laughter broke the spell. It dissolved the bewilderment of the other cow-punchers and made them capable of action. It roused their brains until they could function smoothly once more.

"Hey!" cried a man directly behind Blondy. "Hey, big fellow!"

Blondy did not turn, did not answer. Instead he drew forth cigarette papers and tobacco, and again the heart of Ronicky Doone went out to him. He was taking the hardest way out. He was going to try to stay there on the veranda until he had smoked a second cigarette clear down to the butt.

"He don't know his name!" called another cow-puncher cheerily. "Ring a bell for him. Maybe that'll bring him."

"Maybe he's like a hoss—he sleeps standing!"

But these rough jests apparently had no effect upon

Blondy. He took out a cigarette paper. He held it with thumb and forefinger ready to sift the tobacco into it. The tobacco fell in a small brown stream, some grains caught by the heavy, warm wind and sent winking away through the sunshine and into the shadow to the feet of Ronicky Doone. And he felt as though they bore a message and an appeal to him, as the one fair-minded human being present. But how long could it be before big Blondy was forced by the taunts to turn and face the crowd, or else lose his honor and self-respect by enduring the baiting? And, once he turned, they would probably make for him and swamp him in a real old-fashioned rough-house.

Yet his nerve was iron, this tall, yellow-haired youth! He stood as jauntily, as easily as ever. For only that one instant had his self-control been shaken, when he struck the other cigarette too strongly and knocked off both ash and fire. Now his hands were steady again.

Ronicky saw the cord of the tobacco sack caught between the teeth of Blondy and the top of the sack pulled shut. He saw the tobacco and the papers stowed away in the shirt-breast pocket. And now with a deft twist the cigarette was rolled. Ah, but just as Ronicky felt like cheering, came a second calamity. Those fingers were under a hard-forced control. They tore the paper in a deep rent. In vain Blondy strove to moisten the paper so that it would hold. For when he lighted the cigarette, it refused to draw, and presently from the torn place a few grains of tobacco fell.

It brought another roar of laughter from the big aggressive puncher.

"What sort of a puncher are you, bud?" he bellowed. "Ain't you been raised to roll your own? Hey, gents, here's one that was raised with a silver spoon in his mouth. He had a greaser hired to roll his smokes for him, he did! Ha, ha, ha!"

Again he roared with laughter, joined by the entire assemblage on the veranda, and Blondy turned suddenly on his heel. And when he turned his face was a revelation. It was as gray as dust. The mouth and the eyes were framed in deeply incised lines. That mouth was pressed straight, and the eyes were shadowed by beetling brows. All the energy of Blondy had been exhausted in fighting the silent battle, with his back turned to the crowd. And now his strength was gone. He was weak. The only way he could maintain his honor was by rushing instantly into action. If he waited any longer he was afraid that he would become a trembling coward.

And Ronicky Doone, who had seen men crushed and made worthless vagabonds through mental pressure alone, set his teeth at the sight of Blondy's face. Even the cowpunchers along the veranda sensed that the matter had passed beyond the realm of horseplay and tomfoolery. There was a sudden change. Tragedy was in the air. Every laugh stopped short. Now, if Blondy had been calm, all trouble could have been averted. But he was not calm. He dared not wait any longer. He was afraid of what he himself would do, and that is the most horrible fear in the world. It makes men run from a shadow; and it makes men storm forts.

"And I'd like to know," cried Blondy, "what in thunder all this talk and this laughing is about! Can anybody tell me?"

No one answered. But there was a settling forward in the chairs, as every man there came to the swift and melancholy realization that this affair must end in disaster. Open insults were being cast in the face of the town of Twin Springs. Such things could not be tolerated.

"You, there," went on Blondy, pointing out the big man. "Seems to me that I've heard you make some kind of remark while my back was turned. Well, it ain't turned any more. I'm looking right at you, friend, and I'm waiting to hear when you talk up. Am I going to have to listen long?"

The big man did not stir. At last he sighed. Was he going to back out of the quarrel? Ronicky Doone and the others looked with sick anxiety at him, for it is easier to watch a man die than to watch him accepting a shame. But the big man was not going to be shamed. It was needless for his neighbor on the right to whisper: "Great guns, Oliver Hopkins, say something!"

For instantly he spoke: "I sure dunno why you're talking to me, you nester. What you mean by talking up loud while they's growed men around?"

"Growed men around?" cried Blondy, trembling with anger, as the fear was converted into fighting rage, to which he gave the rein until it galloped. "Growed men around? Why, I ain't seen that kind of men around these parts. They tell me that they don't have that kind of men around this town of Twin Springs!"

It had come. There was no turning from that remark.

It had to be answered with the pulling of a gun. Ronicky Doone marked the companions of the big man drawing away to the right or the left, to keep clear of the bullets when they flew. And he decided that he would do his best to stop the murder, or murders, before they took place. He rose and stepped between the two combatants, turning his back to the big man and his face to Blondy.

"Blondy," he said, "I guess this here has gone about far enough. There ain't any need in you two boys making a killing party out of what ought to be only a joke!"

He was a slender, boyish figure standing between those two mighty men of war, as Oliver Hopkins rose from his chair to confront Blondy. But though the spirit of the whole group had been expressed by Ronicky Doone, it was by no means possible to stop Blondy's course of anger through mere words. He was wild with rage.

"And who in hell are you?" he roared at Ronicky.

"A gent that means well by you, Blondy," said Ronicky gently.

"You talk too smooth to mean well by anybody. You sat back there and laughed at me a minute ago."

"I didn't laugh at anyone," said Ronicky; and though he set his jaw, he continued to smile.

"You lie," said Blondy.

Would Ronicky Doone draw a gun? No, no, he was no hair-trigger man-killer to shoot at the first opportunity. He merely raised a protesting hand.

"You can do the talking now, Blondy," he said. "You and me can find plenty of time to argufy about these things later on. Right now we had ought to talk hoss sense, and hoss sense means for you to sit down and me to——"

But the big man felt that he was being stifled with words. He brushed all kindness away.

"I don't know you," he roared. "Who are you?"

"Ronicky Doone," said Ronicky.

At that announcement two or three of the watchers pricked up their heads and gasped. But the name had no influence with Blondy. He merely shook his big head and scowled more heavily than before.

"Get out of my way," cried Blondy. "These boys want something out of me, and they're going to get it. They've been raising trouble too long, right here in Twin Springs. It's about time that somebody stepped up and asked 'em what was what. And I'm the gent to do it. Stand out of the way, Doone, or I'll knock you out of the way!"

"Blondy!" pleaded Ronicky.

"Curse you, then. Take it!" shouted the madman and smashed out with his great right fist, a blow made quick as the stroke of a snake's head by the loosing of his power of anger. In vain Ronicky Doone cast up a guard. The blow smashed through his blocking forearm, brushed that guard aside, and thudded heavily on his forehead. He was bent almost double backward and fell with a shock that made the floor of the veranda shake. And, as he fell, the blow to the back of his head so paralyzed him that he lay stretched out, incapable of movement, but still his mind and his eye were clear.

The striking of the blow had been enough to clear the brain of Blondy. He gasped in amazement at the prostrate form of Ronicky, as though he were waking from a dream. Then he whirled on his heel, strode to his horse, jerked the reins loose, and flung himself into the saddle.

A deep shout of protest and excitement rose from the men on the veranda at this point, half of them clamoring that he should not be permitted to get away, and the other half saying that there would be another day to make up for this, and that there was no need in staining the repute of Twin Springs on account of a fist fight and some foolish words.

They even tried to drag Oliver Hopkins back, as he started forward. But here they could not prevail. Slow to have an idea seep into his mind, he was, nevertheless, sure as death, once he was started. Now he cast away men from either arm and leaped to the ground beyond the veranda, a magnificent figure of a man, straight, sinewy, active in spite of his great bulk.

"Look here," he cried, "nobody can fight my fights for me. I don't need to have anybody do it. Blondy, you got to get off that hoss and talk business to me for what you've done!"

"I'll see you in China first," cried Blondy.

"You've said enough. Blondy, get off that hoss, or I'll——"

He gripped his revolver as he spoke, but before the barrel had been jerked clear there was a wink and flash of steel in the hand of Blondy, as the latter made a lightning draw. The gun exploded, and Hopkins cast up both arms, hurling the revolver far from him. As it fell

21

in a shining arc, Hopkins whirled and toppled forward upon his side. Ronicky, drawing himself up upon one hand, looked down from the edge of the porch and saw the big benumbed face and heard the fallen giant gasping: "It hadn't ought to have happened—it ain't right! It was all because of an accident that——"

And then he fainted.

CHAPTER IV

RONICKY SADDLES LOU

It caused a yell of mingled horror and anger from the men on the veranda, that revolver shot and that fall. For it so chanced that there was not a man in Twin Springs more popular, and justly so, than Oliver Hopkins. He had been born and raised in the vicinity; and his course of life had been as honest as it was dull and stupid. Half a dozen guns winked in the sunshine to avenge his fall, but they had reckoned without big Blondy.

The latter snapped his cat-footed horse around and shot him about the corner of the building and out of sight as the first brace of wild shots hummed after him harmlessly. The entire crowd lunged for the side of the house to open fire, but, by the time they reached it, Blondy, flattened along the neck of his horse and whipping and spurring for dear life—in all the meaning of that phrase—had placed many a priceless yard between him and the guns of the townsmen.

Instantly they sent a rattling volley after him, but one discharge of shots was all that they could manage; for in the very next instant he had whipped out of sight behind the corner of the first house down the street from the hotel and was sliding away toward security. It seemed incredible that he could have vanished so soon.

A wild rush for the horses and the beginning of the pursuit followed. And, as they swung into the saddles, they saw the familiar form of the bald-headed old doctor run out of the hotel and drop upon his knees by the side of big Hopkins. Then he started up from the fallen man and raised high in the air two hands which were incarnadined.

"He's dead, boys!" he shouted. "Poor Hopkins is dead! Get the skunk that done this!"

And that announcement sent the whole troup away with yells and wails of rage. They had seen a fall, and they had seen crimson stains, and now there was sad need of haste and help for big Blondy. For the best fighting men of a fighting community, mounted upon horses as durable as buckskin, were upon his trail, and a death trail it must prove unless the unprecedented happened.

Ronicky Doone, glancing over his shoulder, saw the gang shoot away into a flurry of dust, man after man swinging into his saddle and plunging away in that direction with a yell, as he got under way. And Ronicky himself drew a deep breath of sobbing rage.

Would they catch him before he arrived? Ronicky hurled the saddle on the back of the bay mare, "Lou." And then the cinches were made literally to fly into place. An instant later he was off, riding like a jockey and calling the name of the mare softly, softly in her ear. Down his face, as he rode, streaked the crimson of the cut on his forehead, where the knuckle of the big man had split the skin. And that crimson stain touched his mouth.

Brushing his face with the back of his hand, he saw the stain and cursed. There are some men whom the sight of their own blood throws into a panic, some whom it horrifies, and others, again, whom it drives into a frenzy of cold rage. And Ronicky Doone was one of the last-named kind. He was ready to kill now. He had attempted his best in the interests of big Blondy, and he had been struck down as a reward for his pains. Moreover, the lightning speed with which Blondy had whipped the gun out of its holster and the sureness of his shot were ample demonstration that he was an expert in the use of the weapon. And the thought of that expertness, instead of appalling Ronicky, filled him with a fierce, warm exaltation. This was game worthy of his own hand, he declared to himself, as he urged Lou forward.

So fast did she shoot down the street, that the cry of men running out of the houses, as she passed, were blurred and mixed together. Once he glanced over his shoulder to see yet others mounting for the pursuit.

Then he plunged out of the town and into the open country with a full view of the chase. What he saw was the horse of Blondy streaking up the trail, with a rapidly increasing advantage, while behind him the posse lost ground at every stride. Ronicky Doone showed his teeth in the fierceness of his satisfaction. He only had one regret, he told himself, as he sent the mare on: that was that the men of the posse would not be near enough to witness the action when he killed this man!

In the meantime, whether a poor rider, or simply over-confident in the ability of his horse, Blondy was sending his fleet pony away at a heartbreaking rate. Perhaps he wished to shake off the crowd at once, so as to be able to double around and cut through the country. But Ronicky laughed exultantly to himself as he held in Lou. There was no need of her bolting away at full speed up this killing grade. Never yet had he seen her speed matched over such country as this. Though there might be horses who could best her on the flat he would challenge the world in a run over hill and dale.

Already the leading horses of the posse began to draw back to him, and when they topped the first long slope rising out of Twin Springs, he was neck and neck with the two leaders. They were two hardy veterans of the cow country, he could tell at a glance, and by their greeting he guessed that they both might have heard of him before, for they called: "Pull your hoss in, Doone. Give us a chance at the fun, too, won't you? Don't hog it all. We're Twin Springs men, and it's up to us to be in at the death."

But, instead of obeying, he merely waved his hand and let Lou drift easily away toward the lead; and so she shot down the road and twisted around the next turn.

The gray pony of Blondy was no longer racing in front. Far to the left down a gulley went the speedy little streak of horseflesh. Lou herself did not relish the plunge in pursuit, but, after shaking her wise head as one in doubt, she dipped over the edge of the ravine and went down, sliding like a dog.

The rest of the riders from Twin Springs milled for a

time on the verge of the drop, and then a few began to go over, but they went so slowly, and so many of the horses refused, even when the riders were willing, that Ronicky, glancing back when the opportunity came to him, could see at a glance that the race was ended, except between him and Blondy.

He was in no haste to make up ground going down the sharp declivity. The limbs of Lou were more precious to him than his revenge. And when they came to the killing angle of the far slope, he again let her take her time, talking kindly to her and bidding her find the best way. And she, big heart that she was, alternately laid an ear back to listen to the voice of the master and again pricked it, as she examined her course. She could judge ground with the wisdom of a very Solomon. She knew at a glance, or so it seemed, when a rock might roll under her weight, and when an apparently loose slide of gravel was in reality cemented to solidity. And therefore, of course, she was invaluable to Ronicky in his careless cross-country cuts. For he scorned beaten trails and was accustomed to strike across country with the freedom of a bird picking its way.

Now Lou gained the crest of the slope, and they entered upon better ground beyond. It was still not a well-beaten trail, but it was well enough defined by cattle to give Lou good footing. And here she commenced to gain in real earnest. For the early burst of speed had told sadly upon the wind and strength of the gray pony, and now, though he still ran gallantly and would so run until he dropped, he had not his first fire and edge for a dash. And Lou began to walk up on him, hand over hand. Ronicky Doone began to enjoy the ride for another reason, a rare and a cruel one. He began to feel that it might be amusing to allow this man-killer to trail along a little distance ahead of him, playing with hope, and then to strike him down at last, at the very time when the big man began to feel truly secure. That savage determination grew fixed and strong in the mind of Ronicky. And he checked Lou back and let her creep up on the gray only by inches.

As for the rest of the posse, they were out of sight, out of sound. Indeed, why so bold a man as big Blondy did not turn and give battle to his solitary pursuer, was more than Ronicky could understand unless it might be that the fugitive, not being able to see any distance behind

26

him, made up his mind that Ronicky was only the fore-runner of the rest, and that if he turned to fight there would be a whole cloud of horsemen on him at once.

At least Blondy showed no inclination to turn, but held straight away on his course, sometimes casting hasty glances over his shoulder, always followed by fresh spurring and whipping to drive the brave little gray forward. And still Ronicky gained as he pleased, not in great leaps, but in terrible inches, each inch eating up the distance between them. When would the big man turn?

Blondy had turned into a steep-sided ravine now, with a strong river rushing and roaming in the bottom; the walls were sometimes sheer cliffs of rock, and again they were long slides of gravelly ground. On this heavy going, along an obscure trail which had been eaten away by the action of the river and the weather, the gray began to labor more and more; for the great weight of his rider, combined with the nature of the ground underfoot, placed him under a sad handicap. In five minutes, at any time he wished, Ronicky felt that he could close on the fugitive.

And then it was that disaster overtook him, and it came with terrible and startling suddenness. He had darted around a curve in the ravine when the side of a whole bank melted away under his feet, and Lou was pitched down toward the river.

CHAPTER V

CLEAN FROM THE
HEART

The desperate scrambling of Lou twisted her around so that her head pointed up the bank away from the trail, but that same twist, coming almost instantly after the plunge down and to the side, had the effect of the snapping of a whip. And Ronicky, fine horseman that he was, was taken by surprise and jerked out of the saddle.

He himself would have been flung into the boiling current, but, whirling over and over in the soft ground, he managed to clutch a projecting shrub, and there he clung, groaning with despair, as he saw the bay lurch down into the rush of the river. She was more to him than any friend had ever been. She was more to him, he often thought, than any human friend *could* be. Because in all the time of her service she had never once failed him in his need, saving on this sole occasion, when her failure and her death were apt to come together.

He saw her go down into the water. He saw her rise again. When, looking straight down the stream, he perceived the explanation of the heavier roaring down the valley. The floor of it dropped out of view, and the river with it. Here there was a waterfall, and that waterfall, unless she were stopped in the meantime, must be the death of poor Lou. For, gallantly though she swam, her ears pricking through the foam, she could make no headway toward the shore in that terrific current. She could only keep her head up the stream, fighting with all her power to gain the bank.

Assistance must come from the shore, and already she was rods down the stream toward the fall. Ronicky rose and labored toward the top of the slope, for he could not progress along the shore of the stream. He must first gain the firmer footing above, on the trail from which they had fallen. He gained the top, or nearly the top, when a treacherous stone slipped under his foot and rolled him down again; when he recovered and stopped his fall, he was halfway toward the water.

He looked in a horror of fear toward the mare and saw at a glance that it was too late. He could never reach her in time to save her. Should he shoot her rather than let her be mangled in the rocks below the fall? He jerked his gun into his hand and poised it, but the sight of that gallant head in the water, where she labored still with undaunted courage, unnerved him. He put the gun away and with a breaking heart turned to climb the slope again, knowing it was vain to attempt to come to her, and yet unable to endure the inaction of waiting for her death.

So, groaning and panting with the effort, he staggered up to the trail and whirled to race downstream. But the current was even more terrible in its speed than he had suspected. Lou was struggling, so it seemed, on the verge of the falling water, where the current was pulled out slick and flat, without a fleck of foam.

He saw that in the first glance, and the second look was called up the bank by a heartening shout. He could not believe that which he saw. Yonder down the trail stood the little gray horse, his head hanging from the terrific labors through which he had passed. And now, down the bank slid big Blondy, with his rope coiled in his hand. He was giving up his own chance for life and liberty for the sake of rescuing the horse from the water. And the heart of Ronicky Doone literally stood still.

He saw the big cow-puncher reach the edge of the water, saw him plant and brace his feet on the rocks, and then the rope shot out from his hand toward the head of the mare. It struck true on its target, but the current swung it on past the head of Lou.

Ronicky Doone closed his eyes. When he looked again,

expecting to see an empty stretch of water and the horror ended, he was amazed to see the courageous mare still near to the verge, but not yet swept over. Perhaps she had struck shallows and was dragging at the yielding sand with her hoofs. At any rate now was her last moment.

The rope shot again from the hand of Blondy. It poised in the air at the end of the throw, then it shot down. Heavy with the water, the noose struck true around the head of Lou and disappeared under the surface. And then Blondy began to pull back. At once the rope was whipped above the river; the noose had tightened around the neck of the mare, and she was saved.

Saved, at least, if they could draw her to the bank before she was drowned or strangled.

It seemed to Ronicky afterward that his feet were rooted deep in the ground, and that he could hardly move in that nightmare, and run to the help of big Blondy. As a matter of fact he literally flung himself over the intervening distance and reached the bank and the side of the rescuer.

Swiftly, with their combined strength, pursued and pursuer, tugged on the rope and swept the bay closer to the shore, dragged her in the lee of it to still water, and then of one accord they both leaped, found the water not higher than their breasts, loosed the strangling knot from the neck of Lou, and raised her head above the water.

And for a moment, deafened by the roar of the waterfall, they waited until they were sure. But it was only an instant before the glazed eyes cleared and the breathing recommenced. And the two opened their mouths and shouted with all their power, a faint, small sound in the infernal uproar of the fall.

After that they turned their attention to getting her up the bank, but this proved a smaller matter than they had expected; for Lou was quickly herself again, and with her own unaided strength she clambered up to the dry land, shook herself like a dog, and then struggled up to the trail above.

She was touching friendly noses with the gray when the two weary, dripping men dragged themselves to the same place and faced each other. And not until that moment did they realize what had happened—the fugitive with the charge of murder on his head shaking hands with one of his pursuers whom he had insulted mortally with words and with a blow.

"Partner," Ronicky Doone was saying, "I've seen gents do some fine things in my time, but never one that was cleaner from the heart than what you done right now."

"It's nothing," Blondy was answering. "You'd have done the same if you'd seen my 'Jack,' yonder, in the same sort of a mess."

"I dunno," said Ronicky. "I'd like to think that I would, but if I was streaking it with a bunch like that behind me I——"

He paused, and big Blondy drew back. They had both remembered all that went before, and both their faces had darkened, Blondy's with pride, and Ronicky Doone's with savagery.

"Doone," said Blondy, "I ain't ashamed out here by ourselves to say that I'm sorry I knocked you down that way when you were stepping in to keep me out of trouble. But I was seeing black and——"

"Listen, son," answered Ronicky. "You've saved my hoss. And that makes up for the words you said. Yes, it more'n makes up. But it don't make up for the fist you hit me with."

He quivered with a sudden influx of wrath.

"I've been over quite a pile of country, Blondy. And I've had dealings with a whole pile of folks, but I never had anybody do what you've done to me." And he touched the wound and the swelling on his forehead.

Blondy glanced up the mountainside and made out that there was no pursuit in sight.

"Do what you please," he said coldly. "You don't have to bust yourself wide open to thank me for getting the mare. I done that for her sake, not for yours!"

"Partner, I'll write that down and remember it," said Ronicky. "If you——"

"I'd like to stand and chatter with you," said Blondy scornfully, "but I ain't got the time. If you want to do something about that knockdown, start it right now!"

There was an instant when Ronicky was on the verge of accepting the invitation, and then it was that the bay mare touched his shoulder with her nose. And he relented.

"I can't do it," he muttered. "You go down your trail, Blondy, and I'll go back down mine. You start streaking, because the boys will sure be along this way before long. Ride like the wind and get shut of them and this whole section of the country, Blondy. After you've done that,

31

then you can start worrying about me and what I might do."

"Thanks," said Blondy, still sneering. "I ain't ever formed the habit of worrying about any man and what he might do!"

"That's because you're a kid," said Ronicky with more calm.

"I aim to be about as old as you, Doone."

"Years ain't what count. But let that go. Start on down the trail, Blondy. But, after you've got out of this section, you can lay to it that I'm going to come after you; and when we meet up there'll be trouble to pay. Understand? I'm going to have you where you had me—lying flat on your back, bleeding and helpless. The only thing is that I won't do just the way you did—I'll tell you I'm ready to fight when the time comes and give you a chance to get in shape to protect yourself."

The blow told, for the big man flushed hotly, seemed on the verge of attacking Ronicky, and then changed his mind and swung into the saddle on the gray, which had now had a chance to catch a second wind.

He hesitated again.

"Doone," he said, "will you tell me if that gent is going to be laid up long with that slug I sent into him?"

"Kind of long, said Ronicky coldly. "He's dead."

"Dead!" gasped Blondy. "My God!"

He lost all vestige of color, rubbed the back of his hand across his face, as though the blow had numbed him, and then turned the gray horse down the trail. His head was sagging. He was as spent in spirit as Jack was spent in wind.

CHAPTER VI

RONICKY REFLECTS

After he had watched the other out of sight, Ronicky then sat down to wait for what he knew must happen. First he stripped Lou of the saddle and turned it up so that the wind and sun might begin to dry the blanket and padding. Lou herself found a grassy place for rolling, and in a trice she was dry and, stripped of both saddle and bridle, had wandered up the slope and was nibbling here and there.

So carefree were they, Ronicky smoking at his ease, and the mare roving as her pleasure dictated, that no one could have surmised that a few moments before poor Lou had been struggling at the very door of death. But now and again Ronicky would turn and look fondly after her, or with a low whistle he brought her to him, as readily as a dog answers a call.

There was a fine, free spirit in the mare. She carried herself with the nonchalance and the gayety and good nature of a man who has no heavy burdens on his conscience. So she would play around Ronicky Doone, and he followed her with a lazy and contented eye through the drifts and hazes of his cigarette smoke. She was all that he wished in the line of horseflesh. And, as he often said to his friends, she was better than most company because she never lost her temper and started talking back and thinking for herself in a crisis when he needed coöperation. So it was with her on this day. And when she strayed near him, his hand would go out and pass in a caress down her silken neck.

They had idled there for some minutes before the sound of hoofs, for which he had been waiting, came up the ravine toward him, and then, around the corner of the valley, there pounded half a dozen riders, all that were left from the horde which started out of Twin Springs. They shouted at the sight of Ronicky Doone, and in another instant they were halting their horses around him. They wanted to know, in a burst of questioning, exactly what had happened, and he told them, while they wondered.

When he ended, they wanted to know why he had not fought it out with the murderer before the latter left. Because, they declared, saving the life of a horse was one thing, but taking the life of a man was quite another, and so completely did it outbalance the former that it ceased to exist on the books. But Ronicky Doone was not of that opinion. And when they asked him if he were not going to saddle and continue the trail with them, he rose and made his answer briefly and to the point.

"Gents, I'd sure like to see the insides of big Blondy. But I'd rather be plugged myself, I guess, than to have another gent do the opening of him. No, I ain't going to ride down that trail any more, and if you ask me straight, I don't mind saying that I'm plumb set against any of the rest of you riding down that trail. Is that clear?"

They could hardly believe him. For upon his head they could see still the crimson imprint which the fist of big Blondy had made. And yet here was the enemy barring their way!

They shouted furiously at him to step aside, but he remained firm in their path.

"In the first place," he told them, "I've promised Blondy that he ain't going to be followed after to-day, and that he's going to have a chance to get clean of this section of the country. And I aim to do what I've said for him. In the second place, boys, before you get all riled and boiling and ready to eat me up, you can lay to it that you wouldn't never catch him even if you went on ahead. That little gray hoss of his has a pile of running in it still. It could take up with the best hoss in your whole bunch and run the legs right off of it."

"D'you think," they roared, "that we're going to turn around and go back and tell the boys that the six of us got scared or tired of following the trail of the gent that killed poor Oliver Hopkins?"

"What I think you'll do," said Ronicky, diplomatically, "is to go back to Twin Springs and tell the folks there that when you come up with me and seen what Blondy had stopped and done for my hoss when it was drowning, you just nacherally didn't have it in your hearts to go after him any more that day. Besides, he was too far ahead of you anyway! That'll sound good, and it'll give all the boys a fine warm feeling, like they'd had a good drink or just finished the reading of a pretty story."

He grinned as he spoke, and the others were forced to agree with him. There was nothing else for them to do but bring their horses about and journey slowly, wearily back toward the little town, and this finally they did. But all the way the bay mare, Lou, with the dried saddle bound once more upon her back, danced along among the jaded horses, as though she had not that day run down one good horse and looked death in the face.

So that they all agreed, as they neared the town of Twin Springs, that there was never a horse more honest and fleet of foot than Lou. Moreover, there was no particular sting of shame in having been blocked in their pursuit by Ronicky Doone. As a matter of fact he had simply warned them that if they continued on the trail of Blondy, there would be trouble in great chunks ahead of them. But he had said it in such a manner that they were fairly certain he would never make what he had done a subject of boasting. There was nothing insulting in his attitude, as they returned. He picked up with them the subject of Blondy, and he agreed with them that for what he had done that day Blondy must die. It merely happened that on this occasion Blondy's horse had been good enough to outfoot the pursuers.

"And yet," they admitted, when they cantered back into Twin Springs, "ain't it a shame that a game gent like Blondy has to be plugged because he done what any one of the rest of us, being in Blondy's boots, would have done."

No sooner were they within the confines of Twin Springs, however, than they began to learn new things with great rapidity. In the first place they were greeted by a crowd of men at the hotel, where, as at the seat of knowledge, the crowd was assembled to await bulletins which would give them the latest information from the battle front, so to speak. And when the little host learned that big Blondy still rode unmolested over the hills, there was a howl of rage.

The reason for their sorrow was a strange one. For it was discovered that Oliver Hopkins was not dead—he was not even seriously wounded; for the bullet had simply taken a glancing course around his body, and what had seemed mortal had been no more than a stunning and surface injury! Oliver Hopkins was not dead, and therefore there was no reason for killing the victor. But there was another angle from which the case had to be viewed.

When it was thought that Oliver was dead, the whole affair had taken on a somber and gloomy atmosphere. What had started as a prank had resulted as a killing, and only grim and joyless duty forced the riders along the trail of Blondy. But now it appeared that Hopkins lived, and the infuriated townsmen knew that they had been insulted, slapped in the face, and baffled!

It was enough to spread a thick layer of shame over two generations, such an event as this. The cow-punchers ground their teeth. All sympathy for Blondy was conjured away into a thin mist immediately, and in its place there was fury. Law had now nothing to do with it. The insult had been to the entire town. It became known that that morning Blondy had loudly boasted of how he intended to ride into Twin Springs, show his undaunted face wheresoever he pleased, and then return unscathed and thereby break the spell of dread with which the cow-punchers at the Bennett Ranch had come to regard the village.

What was more, old Bennett had tried to dissuade him. And pretty Elsie Bennett, so they said, had followed him clear to his horse, entreating him with tears in her eyes not to take such a terrible chance.

And how had he answered? He had laughed loudly as he sat in the saddle, and, waving his hat to her, he had cried that they didn't make men big enough in Twin Springs to keep him from riding peaceably into the town and peaceably out again.

And he had done what he promised!

In the completeness of their rage the foiled townsmen could not devise future punishment terrible enough to satisfy their spirits. Some suggested tar and feathers when they caught him. Others would have been content with riding him on a rail and kindred amusements. But here Ronicky Doone murmured his belief that the fugitive would never come back to face them. They laughed him to scorn. Short as was the time Blondy had been on the Bennett Ranch, it was an open secret that he was devoted body and soul to gay little Elsie. He would return to her as inevitably as iron must go to the magnet. As a matter of fact, they swore, he had simply undertaken this daring feat to make himself out a hero in the eyes of the girl.

And Ronicky left them, while they were still devising ways and means and grinding their communal teeth, so to speak. He went up to his room in the hotel and sat before the window to watch in solitude the coming of the sunset.

He was in a gloomy humor. The mention of the girl had, for some reason, poured salt into his wounds. Here was young Blondy starting on a career of glory for fame and for the lady. And there sat he, Ronicky Doone, with the thin fingers of a thousand ghostly deeds plucking at his memory, but nothing left of all he had done! His life had left no solid body. The revolver at his hip, the rifle on his saddle, the horse he rode, the gay clothes upon his back and a pittance in his pocket—this represented the total gain of his labors.

With a sad pride he told himself that at least he had never debased himself to win money or reputation. He had labored for others more than for himself. And yet these were small consolations. The mere name of the unseen girl, linked with the thought of Blondy, tormented him. Blondy and Elsie Bennett would someday, he felt by premonition, be happy together. And he, Ronicky Doone, could never reach that wished for goal. He knew it with all the greater certainty, as the brilliance of the sunset faded out, and there fell over the town the partial night cast by the western mountains. Out of the past he carried nothing, he kept repeating—he carried nothing! Such a monody, drumming into the ear and the spirit of a young man is not good for the soul, and Ronicky Doone finally dropped his head on his fist in a joyless study.

It was certain that he could not leave the community until he had confronted big Blondy, and yet he longed with all his soul to leave the town and the men in it behind him and ride on. That had been the course of his past years—riding on and on, from one set of acquaintances and from one community to another until there was behind him a wild and swiftly shifting host of recollections— no fixed group of men and women and events such as make up the background of our average life.

Here he was surprised and startled by a heavy knocking at the door, delivered so strongly as to suggest that the door had been kicked with the boot rather than struck by the hand. Ronicky rose in some anger.

CHAPTER VII

AN INVITATION TO
JOIN UP

He had no more than time to rise and turn, however, when the door opened, and it opened in such a way as to indicate the manner in which the knocks had been delivered. It flew wide and folded back on the wall with a crash, and the foot of the man in the hall was stretched forth in mid-stride. He had announced himself by booting the door. And now he had kicked it open and stepped in before Ronicky, at the same time turning carelessly and waving toward some people on the outside.

"I'll be down in a minute, boys. Start eating, and tell 'em that it's on me tonight. Everybody eats free on Al Jenkins!"

And with this introduction he made a back swipe with his heel, caught the edge of the door with his spur, and slammed it shut as violently as he had opened it, the rowel cutting a visible gash in the wood. Then he advanced upon Ronicky.

He was a man of middle height, though so stoutly built from head to foot that he seemed much less. Ronicky was surprised to find the eyes of Al Jenkins almost on a level with his own, and he hastily recast his first conception and mental measurements of the man. Truly Al was a mighty man. It would have been inappropriate to speak of his fifty winters; summers was the word for Al Jenkins. For there was a bloom and gloss to his cheek like the cheek of an apple when the leaves begin to bronze, and the apples shine on the bough. His eye was as bright as his cheek. His teeth when he smiled—and he was always smiling—were polished and white. He had a hand as big as two, and his foot was well nigh in the same proportion. So that Ronicky Doone could hardly repress a smile at the thought of such a man as this setting siege to the heart of a pretty girl and making and wrecking his life because of her.

Yet he had once been other than he was now. His hand was made gross with flesh, whereas it had once been simply wide and strong. His waist, too, was unduly corpulent, and in a leaner youth those shoulders and that chest must have swelled with a suggestion of herculean power. Even at fifty he was a mighty man. Not only was he mighty in muscle, but his personality struck Ronicky in the face and made him look down.

The great hand was stretched toward him.

"You're Ronicky Doone?"

"I'm him," said Ronicky and gingerly intrusted his fingers to the bone-breaking possibilities of that great paw. To his surprise the grip of Al Jenkins proved to be as gentle as the touch of a girl, and it told Ronicky, more strongly than words could have done, that Al Jenkins was as considerate as he was powerful. In a flash he understood the popularity of Al in the town. Money alone could not have purchased such a repute west of the rockies.

"Been hearing about you," said Al Jenkins.

"I been hearing more about you," said Ronicky.

"That's a lie," said Jenkins. "Because the gent that told me about you can tell more in a minute than another man can tell in a year. I mean old Sam Tompson. Most of what he says is lies, but he strings his lies together pretty well. He makes 'em look good. The only thing I balked on about you is when he told me that you was a mass of scars from head to foot, and that you done all he said you'd done and are still shy of twenty-seven. Turn around here and let me have a look at you!"

He had a great proprietary, possessive air which was not really offensive. Now with one hand he turned Ronicky Doone around. With the other hand he struck a match and lighted a lamp and then held the light high, so that in the dusk he could examine the face of the youth. In another man it would have been intolerable impertinence, but in Al Jenkins it was simply an idiosyncrasy with which Ronicky for one was quite willing to put up. He even broke into laughter, as Al Jenkins stepped back and lowered the lamp, shaking his head in bewilderment.

"What plumb beats me," said Al Jenkins, "is how he can keep a straight face when he tells them lies, that Tompson! He said that you—why, half of the things that he said about you would have filled a book, Ronicky. How much of 'em are straight? What's all this about you being a fire-eating, man-killing terror? Is that the truth about the time when you——"

"It's all wrong," said Ronicky instantly. "I'm the most gentlest, peaceablest, law-abidingest gent you ever seen, Mr. Jenkins. You can lay to that! I dunno where old Tompson got hold of his yarns about me, but——"

"He got 'em down south. Says that once on the Staked Plains——"

"Oh, he don't know what he's talking about," said Ronicky calmly. "There ain't no use talking about what he said."

"For the first time I begin to think that there's something in what he told me," replied Jenkins.

He now folded his arms above his stomach and planted his legs well apart. "Doone," he said, "I guess this is a lucky day for both of us."

"I hope so," said Ronicky politely.

"Well, I'm going to *make* it so!" boomed the big man. "Hope is all well and good. But it's better off when it's left inside the covers of a book. It ain't a good word for a man to use. He's got hands to make things and to take things with. That's better than a dreamer's head to hope!"

He brought his sentence to a conclusion by crashing the flat of his hand down upon the table, so that that flimsy article of furniture sagged sadly to one side with a great groan. Al Jenkins straightened it with a jerk that set the lamp to dancing, and the flame to leaping in the glass chimney's throat. But Jenkins allowed the lamp to stagger unregarded. He was already pacing up and down the room, now and then coming to a pause in front of Ronicky and directing the full power of his resonant voice and his bright, clear eyes upon the younger man.

"Here's what I'm driving at," said Jenkins. "You been

in town long enough to know what I'm doing around here?"

"I got a general idea," said Ronicky, fumbling to find the words which would most gently approach the truth. "They tell me that you're sort of interested in road building and real estate and that you are buying a good deal of land."

"Thunder!" burst in Jenkins. "They tell you a lot of rot. What I'm after is old Bennett, and, if they talked to you about me at all, they told you that first off. I'm here doing things for the town, and maybe some of them are done because I *do* like the place. But right down in the bottom of your heart you can get to the real facts, which I don't try to hide: that I'm in here helping Twin Springs because I want Twin Springs to help me. And why do I need help? Because I'm smashing Bennett —because I'm smashing him root and branch!"

As he spoke he crashed his fist into the palm of his other hand repeatedly with force enough to have knocked down an ordinary man. The energy of the rancher was amazing. No wonder he had succeeded in tearing wealth out of the frozen land of Alaska. He put enough effort into five minutes of conversation to have enabled another to run a mile.

"H'm," said Ronicky, "I see. Well I did hear a little about that."

"And you thought I was a mean old scoundrel for doing it, eh?"

"Why——"

"Don't deny it! That's what you thought! Well, there's no harm in thinking what you please. This is a mighty free country, son, and I want it to stay free so far as I'm concerned. Think what you please, Doone, but just listen to me while I talk sense to you. Ronicky, I've got a need of you. I want you on my side!"

Ronicky Doone regarded him with wonder.

"You got the wrong idea about me," he said. "I ain't floating through here aiming to get into trouble on one side or the other. Matter of fact all that I want to do is to get even with big Blondy, and then I'll be traveling along, I guess."

"Sure," said Al Jenkins hastily, waving his hand in large agreement with this statement. "Don't I know what's going on inside of your head, boy? You're plumb peaceable. All you want to do is to finish up Blondy. But,

Ronicky, I aim to tell you that before you've finished up Blondy you'll be a mite older than you are."

Ronicky shook his head.

"I finish my business quick," he declared. "Either he gets me, or I get him. That's all there is to it. As soon as he finds out that Oliver Hopkins ain't dead, he'll be back on the Bennett place as big as life. So I guess it won't be long before him and me meet up."

Al Jenkins shook his head.

"Son," he said, "I'd like to trust you to do the right thing, but I can't. You go to kill Blondy—don't shake your head and cuss because I say that. You're going to fight him, and the only way you can stop one of Blondy's kind is to kill him. I know! But when you go out to the ranch, nine chances out of ten, the person you run into will be old Bennett, with a tongue slicker than a snake's tongue. And he'll talk you around onto his side quicker'n you can wink. Oh, he's a fine talker, old Bennett is. Why he picked a job where he'd have to talk to cows instead of to men, I can't make out! He could steal a baby out of the arms of the judge, if he was a lawyer, and have the jury weeping and swearing that the kid belonged to him, all inside of the shake of a lamb's tail. That's the sort of a pizen gent this Bennett is!"

"But I'm not going out to talk," said Ronicky. "I——"

He might as well have tried to stop the rush of an un-damned stream. Al Jenkins when he began to talk kept on until his mind was empty of ideas.

"Or if it ain't the old man, then his girl will get you. Have you heard anything about his girl?"

"Only that she's pretty," said Ronicky.

The older man stared at him in disgust.

"What kind of men do they breed nowadays?" he roared at last. "I'll tell you all about Elsie Bennett, son. She's the living image of her mother. Oh my, oh my, oh my!"

He brought out the exclamations partly as devout sighs and partly as groans.

"Know what that means? That means that she's one of them deadly blondes. She's one of them kind that got hair that's a sort of a palpitating gold. Pale gold, you see, with the sun in it, is what her hair is. She's got blue eyes. She may be thinking up more kinds of deviltry than there are underground, but all the time she'll have a look in her eye that makes a man think of heaven. She's got a dimple tucked away in one cheek and a sort of a little crooked smile. That smile always seems to be *at* you as much as it is *with* you. She ain't got one of these tissue-paper skins with color in her cheeks like it was slapped on with a paint brush—one of them skins that fade and wrinkle up by the time a girl's thirty, in this here climate. No, sir. Her skin is just sort of creamy, with a look like it had been rubbed and sponged till it was fresh and clear as crystal. D'you foller me, son?"

He had changed his tone wonderfully in speaking of the girl. He stood with his head thrown back, so that the immense column of this throat was exposed. But out of that great throat came a voice soft and deep and tremulous with an edging of emotion that cut to Ronicky's quick.

"Oh, lad," said the big man, "a girl like her hadn't ought to belong to no one man. Why, she should be private property. She'd ought to be taken around where everybody could see her and be happy looking at her. A sight of her is better than good news. And a picture of her smiling, or the hearing of her laugh, is like striking gold in the desert."

He raised his head again and scowled at Ronicky Doone.

"Why ain't you standing on tiptoe, champing and chawing the bit to get out and see her, you young rapscallion?" he roared.

"I can get along tolerable well without seeing her," admitted Ronicky Doone.

"Bah!" said Al Jenkins. "You maybe think that you're in love with some other girl, but you ain't! It ain't no ways possible for a man to be really in love except with a woman like she is, or her mother was before her! Why, I got more reasons for hating Bennett and the Bennett stock than a spider has got for hating a wasp. But I don't dare get within range of that girl. All my hate would wither up. I'd soften up like a sponge. I'd begin to grin and gape at her. And I'd be lost, and she could do what she wanted with me. Inside of a minute I'd be signing over half of my land to that skunk of a father of hers. That's the sort of a girl she is!" He concluded with another explosion of sound.

"And you think that you'd be safe if you went out to shoot Blondy and met her instead? Bah! She'd make a fool of you. You'd crawl around on your hands and knees begging for a chance to work for her and fight for her!"

"How does it come," suggested Ronicky, "that she doesn't have the same effect on the other men around these parts? Why doesn't she get a whole army of 'em for her father?"

"I'll tell you why: folks are blind to what they grow up next to. I was born by the sea. And I never seen nothing in it. I come west and went plumb batty with a case of desert fever, and here I stick. And do you hear them that are born on the desert talking a lot about it? No, you don't. They're too used to it. When you take 'em away from it after a while, they may begin to mourn for it. But it's the things you ain't never lacked that you can't appreciate. Same way with the young folks around here and that flower of a girl, Elsie Bennett. They've growed up in the same schools with her. They've seen her playing dolls with other little girls and putting on long skirts to play grownups. They've seen her get into the feet-hands-and-elbows stage, when all girls look plumb ugly. They've seen all that, and no wonder they don't know what she is! One or two have rubbed their eyes and waked up and found out the truth and gone batty about her for a while, but she gives them the cold shoulder when they come talking marriage, and they wander off some other place to keep from busting their hearts. That's why they don't know what she is."

Ronicky had listened with the most profound interest, not so much caught by the warnings and the pictures of Jenkins, but intrigued by the revelation of the old man's character.

"But why are you so set on getting me?" he asked at length.

"I'll tell you why. Because things ain't now the way they used to be. I don't mean to speak light of you, Doone, after all that I've heard about you. But I just want you to know that twenty years ago I wouldn't have given a shake which side you joined, because with my money and my men I could wipe out old Bennett any time I took a mind to it. But them days ain't no more! Them days ain't no more! They're gone!"

He groaned bitterly.

"When Bennett wanted to run me out of the country twenty years ago, what did he do? He simply hired a bunch of men and run off my cows in a gang. He didn't

45

waste no time thinking and planning. He scooped what I had and left me busted. Easy for him! Oh, curse his hide! But when I come back with some money of my own and find him down, times have changed. A gent can't come in and do what he pleases. No, sir; he's got to wait around and see what the public sentiment is. Like as not, if he lifts a hand, he'll get hanged for it. So I've been laboring here these years working up my case against Bennett. I have things all worked up fine and ready to squash Bennett when along comes this big Blondy and makes this play of his. Well, folks didn't take him none too serious before. But they begin to now, and they take Bennett serious along with Blondy. And now if you go in and join up with Bennett—why, it'd be a mighty serious thing, and it might stall me altogether! You got brains, both you and Blondy, and you're both born fighters. And if you teamed it on the same side you might bust up my little game for me and spoil things all around."

His frankness made Ronicky gasp. Certainly there was an old-fashioned honesty underlying the malignant hatred with which Jenkins pursued Bennett.

"Talk straight out," he said finally. "I don't mind saying that I like you, Mr. Jenkins, and I'd like to please you. Just tell me where I could fit into your plans, and I'll see what I can do for you."

"That's talk of the right kind!" cried Al Jenkins. "It's taken a long time to get around to it, but I seen when I laid eyes on you that I couldn't get you in a second. Ronicky, d'you ever ride the range?"

"That's my regular way of making a living."

"Are you aiming to take a job pretty soon?"

"Maybe."

"Then line up for a month under me, Ronicky. I just want to make sure that you ain't going to be against me. I ain't buying you, and I ain't offering to, because I know that money couldn't do it. I'm just saying: Will you come out and hang up your saddle in my bunk house for a while?"

"And if I don't?" asked Ronicky.

"If you don't, and particular if you line up with Bennett, it's going to go hard with you. I'm ready to close in on them, son. I've got public opinion switched over my way. We're a long, long ways from the law. And if I should clean up Bennett's beef now, the way he done with mine, I don't think he'd have much of a chance to prove anything against me and my men. What d'you say, Ronicky?"

"I'm going to take a ride around tonight," said Ronicky, checking himself on the verge of agreeing. "When I come back I'll let you know."

"Right!" said Al Jenkins. "A gent that thinks before he does a thing is a gent that don't change his mind afterward. Good-by!"

CHAPTER VIII

A CRY FROM THE SHRUBS

After Al Jenkins left the room there were still a few moments during which Ronicky Doone sat by the black square of the window, staring out on the shadows of the street, broken by the bars of yellow lamplight. The acrid scent of dust impregnated with bitter alkali floated toward him in thin drifts from time to time, after a horseman had lurched up or down the street, his hoofbeats muffled to soft thuds by the thick layer of dust through which they struck. While he sat there, letting the peace of the village steal over him and all the quiet of the mountains, he revolved in his mind what Al Jenkins had said to him, and the more he pondered the stranger the position seemed to him.

Yet what Jenkins wanted was understandable. He had reduced Bennett to such a point that he could soon crush his rival. But the addition of the slightest strength might unbalance the scale and postpone the destruction of Bennett for an indefinite period. One more daring deed performed in the name of Bennett, as Blondy had performed his deed this day, would convince the men of the village that Bennett had under him something beside a number of tramps. Public sentiment might swing mightily toward the opposite side. Therefore Jenkins had tried to make doubly sure of Ronicky.

As for Ronicky, the old urge to go on and on and on which whipped him remorselessly through the mountains, was now dying out. Twin Springs was becoming a focus around which his thoughts gathered and centered. Just in this fashion men find a new place strange and desolate which, after a little living, seems to become the center of the world, all their lives moving within its bounds. And Ronicky, looking out of the window, felt that he was looking into the heart of the town and the country around it.

Necessarily he must join the forces of honest Al Jenkins, if he stayed. And he must stay to fight big Blondy. And if he stayed to fight Blondy he must be with those who were opposed to Bennett. What could be more logical than this strain of reasoning? And yet, because he hated alliances of all kinds, he delayed and determined to have that ride before his mind was made up.

When he went down to the veranda of the hotel a score of heads—for the porch was well filled—turned toward him at once in greeting. That day's work had got him known. More than that, those who had heard of him had been about buzzing the rumors which they had picked up. He was a known man, indeed.

He stepped down through a murmur of greetings and went out to the shed, where Lou was stabled. He groomed her by lantern light. For, though she was one of the tough mustang breed that live as happily without brushing as with it, yet it was a custom which Ronicky had started and could not stop. He worked until the red bay was a shining velvet, with high lights from the lantern splashed along the silk of her flanks. Then he saddled her and swung up in the stirrups.

She slipped out from the shed, as light of foot and eager on the bit as though she had been in pasture for a month. Truly she was made of watch springs and leather, a tireless mechanism! At the trough he gave her one swallow of water and then sent her across the country. He picked the course at random. East and west rose rough-sided mountains. He did not wish to break the heart of Lou with such work. They were out for a pleasure walk, so to speak, not for labor. To the south the hills separated in uninteresting monotony. But to the north a valley lay like a funnel into the heart of the mountains. And into this funnel he sent Lou.

There might be no road at all. But for that he did not care. Straight across the country fled Lou, running among shrubs, with a smoothly wavering line, just as a dry twig is floated down among stones by the current of a brook, twisted here and there quickly, but with never a jar. When a fence rose before her, she rose and cleared it in lovely style, tucking up her heels beneath her in the most approved manner, which a trained hunter might have envied. Over the meadows she struck a hotter pace; in the rough ground she went more slowly, but still fast enough. And all this while the rein was dangling loose on her neck!

Yes, once the direction was given to her, it was not necessary that he concern himself with the course she picked. She would keep on in the line selected, diverging here and there, as the lay of the land forced her to do, but swinging always back to the original direction, as the needle swings toward the pole. She kept her head high, for the sky was made darker than usual by a high-flying sheet of clouds, which were swept rapidly across the heavens by a wind not felt in the valleys. That high head enabled her to pierce the dimness for some distance and plan her course with fair accuracy. And all the while she was enjoying her work just as much as Ronicky Doone enjoyed his ride.

Lou had so beautifully free and elastic a stride that by her way of going one would have guessed her to be ever on the trail for home; yes, one would have thought that she was every minute passing familiar landmarks which called into her mind the old home and brought the very scent of the sweet hay and the warm barn into her nostrils. This night ride was to her a frolic and more joyous than to her master. As for Ronicky, he had only to half close his eyes, as the deliciously cool air whirred against his face, and let his mind wander where it would.

He did not rouse himself into full consciousness of his direction until he felt Lou throw up her head with a little start, such as she always gave when there was before her a problem which she felt might better have the attention of the master. At the same time she quickened her stride, settling down toward the ground a little, in the manner which unmistakably betokens a leap to come.

Ronicky looked up barely in time to see before him

a wide, still stretch of water, shining faintly in the darkness of the night. Where a star, looking through the swirl of dizzy clouds above, peered down at the water, there was a point of light. He saw that and measured with a sudden concern the width of the leap; then Lou rose like a swallow against a sudden gust of wind and sailed high in the air.

He could tell by the convulsive effort with which she flung herself up and forward that she knew the leap to be close to the limit of her ability. And, as she passed the apex of her spring and began to shoot down, it seemed to Ronicky a certain thing that she would dip in the water. But she shot on, and her forehoofs landed on the dry ground, and her hind toes scooped up a spray of the water, but the next moment she was cantering on, only laboring a little in the heavy going which the water of the creek had impregnated. But she had hardly taken a stride—indeed, it was almost simultaneous with her landing across the water—when there was a faint cry and then a shrill one from some shrubs to Ronicky's right. At once he whirled the mare toward the voice.

CHAPTER IX

IN THE DARK

It was a woman's voice; the first sound coming as though she was half choked by surprise, and the second shrill with terror. Ronicky ranged his horse behind the shrubs, just as she darted out, an indistinct figure in the night. He halted her with a shout, at the same time peering on all sides to make out the light of her home, but there was no such light in view. She seemed to have been standing there in the thicket by choice. Ronicky had heard, however, of female tramps, though even in his wide wanderings he had never seen one. But such she must unquestionably be.

"Look here," he said, "there ain't any call for running. I ain't going to harm you. Who might you be?"

She paused at the side of a tree, more distinctly visible to him, now that he was able to fix her with his eyes. Moreover she was wearing a dress of some light color which helped to define her in the night.

"Who are you?" she asked in turn. "And what are you doing here, off the road?"

The first sound of her voice convinced Ronicky that he had been wrong in his surmise about the female tramp. Never in the world could there be a wanderer of the road with such a voice. He could guess at other things, too, having once heard her speak. She had courage, or her voice would not have been so even. She had surprising courage considering the youth which her voice suggested, and the lateness of the hour and the midnight dark.

"Me?" answered Ronicky, with as much daylight good humor as he could manage to throw into his voice, "Why, I'm just a stranger out riding for the sake of the ride."

She remained silent, as one who did not believe what she had heard, but who considered that it would be bad policy to dispute with the unknown.

"I might be asking you," said Ronicky, "what you're doing out here at this time of night—away from the road?"

"Oh, I'll tell you how to reach it," she said, not answering this question. "You start over to your right and keep going till you reach a fence. Then ride down the fence, turning north until you come to a gate. That gate opens onto the road to Twin Springs. I suppose that's the place you're trying to find?"

"That's the place I've just left," said Ronicky, "and I don't worry about the road. My hoss and me—we sort of get along where there ain't no road to speak of."

Again she was silent, but what little she had spoken left such a pleasant impression on Ronicky that he paused and hunted through his mind for the means of prolonging the talk.

"I'd an idea," he murmured at length, "that maybe you was lost yourself, being out here alone in the night. You see?"

Still she did not speak, and he could see by the increasing dimness of her figure that she was slowly drawing back from him. All at once Ronicky Doone began to laugh.

"Lady," he said, "it's sure a queer thing what the sun does to us. If this was by daylight, you wouldn't think nothing of meeting me here, but because it's night, you figure that there's danger. Is that it?"

"There's no danger of course," said the girl, her voice as steady as ever, in spite of her retreat. Then suddenly she was laughing, also. "Who are you?" she asked.

"My name," he answered, "don't matter particular. I'm just drifting through. Most like I'll never be in this valley again. What might the valley be, lady?"

"If you'll never see it again," she answered, "I don't suppose the name matters much."

"Oh, if you're going to put it that way," said Ronicky, "I'll tell you. My name is Ronicky Doone."

"Ronicky Doone!" she gasped, and then again she repeated: "Ronicky Doone! You're the man that Charlie Loring——"

She stopped short, but Ronicky continued for her in perfect good nature. "Is that big Blondy's name? Yes, I'm the man that Charlie Loring knocked down and beat up, and then he got away clean, and I didn't do a thing to him!"

"But, oh," she broke in, "you're the man whose horse he saved from the river, so you bear him no grudge, of course!"

"No grudge?" asked Ronicky. "Well, he saved the hoss right enough, but he also knocked me flat when I'd done nothing to him. For saving Lou I'd sure like to save a dozen hosses for him, but for knocking me down—but women can't understand things like that."

"Can't we? But we do! And you've come up here trying to find him in the dark because you don't care to face him in the daylight. Oh, how cowardly!"

If she had struck him suddenly in the face Ronicky Doone could not have been more surprised. He fumbled for an answer, found no polite rejoinder, and was still, a silence which she instantly interpreted as a confession. Certainly if she had been afraid before, all fear now vanished, as she came swiftly toward him and only halted when she was under the very nose of the mare. And she stood there, regardless of the fearless and inquisitive muzzle which Lou poked toward her. For the bay mare had the trust of those animals which have never endured pain from the hand of man. In her fury, however, the girl paid no heed to that reaching head.

"Before you can do what you hope to do," she said fiercely, "you'll have to be ten times the man that you are. Oh, I know what stories they brought out—about Ronicky Doone the gun fighter and the man-killer, but no man who hunts in the dark and sneaks around to strike from behind can ever beat Charlie Loring. No man!"

She stopped. He heard her panting with her rush of anger, as she waited for his retort, but he only said, light breaking in on him: "I guess this is Hanshaw Valley? And you're Elsie Bennett?"

"What of that?" she asked.

"Only that I won't be bothering you no more," said Ronicky Doone dryly, and he turned Lou away into the darkness.

"Wait! Wait!" she cried after him, but Ronicky had had enough of facing such guns in battle. He sent Lou away at a brisk canter and shot away out of view over the next swell of ground, and the calling of the girl died out behind him.

No sooner was the rim of the hill between them, however, than he turned about and slipped back in the direction from which he had come until his head was just above the edge of the hill. There he paused: scanning the shrubbery beside the water carefully, he was able to make out the dim outlines of the upper part of the body of the girl, as she stood among the bushes with the flat surface of the pool behind her.

There was only one reason why she should be standing there, it seemed to Ronicky, and that was to meet Blondy. It had occurred to him as soon as he guessed her identity. This was a secret meeting place which she and the big fellow had agreed upon, and now that he was in trouble she was waiting out for him here, confident that he would come, if that were possible, and then she could tell him the good news, without which he might wander on for days and days, unknowing. She could tell him that death did not hang over his head after all, for big Oliver Hopkins had recovered. And then they would go happily back to the house together. And on the way she would tell him how she had met his enemy, Ronicky Doone, and how Ronicky had slipped away into the night.

If all of these surmises proved correct, then that blind ride into the darkness from Twin Springs had taken him directly to his enemy. The thought warmed his heart. There was only a matter of a few minutes to wait now, before he received verification of his suspicions. For in the distance he heard the sound of a jogging horse. And then, as that sound approached, he made out the shadowy form of a horseman who approached the stream and the wide pool from the farther side. This traveler presently halted his horse and sent a low-pitched, wavering whistle up the hill, which was immediately answered by another from the shrubs by the water.

The heart of Ronicky leaped, as he saw that his guess had been perfectly accurate. Now the rider urged his mount, so it seemed, straight into the water, though Ronicky shrewdly guessed that he was riding out on a firm sand bar, from which the easiest leap would carry him safe to the farther shore. Presently the rider was in the shrubs, off the horse, and beside the girl.

So hushed was the night air that Ronicky could hear the murmur of their voices distinctly. Then after a moment or two they began to walk toward the hill, with the vague form of the gray horse drifting along behind them. No matter how queenly Elsie Bennett might be—and from the description of old Al Jenkins she must be a heart-stopping beauty—she had apparently made her choice. The handsome form of big, blond-headed Charlie Loring was her selection as a husband, it seemed. For surely only love could keep a girl waiting in such a place at such a time, alone. Indeed it must be an affair of long standing, comparatively speaking, or they would not have agreed so perfectly on their meeting point and on their system of signals.

In the meantime Ronicky must remove himself from their course. For they were making straight for the hill, and he must take care that Lou moved softly, since the wind was blowing down to them and would carry every sound a considerable distance. So Ronicky leaned and whispered in the ear of the bay mare, at the same time bringing the most careful pressure to bear on the reins. The result was astonishing, for Lou was converted in a trice into a stealthy-stepping cat. Crouching a little and gliding with such a delicate foot-fall that the grass was hardly disturbed underfoot, she slipped away to the shelter of a low line of trees. Behind these Ronicky Doone turned her and there cautioned her once more in a whisper to which she listened with her ears pricked anxiously forward. Having been warned in this fashion, nothing could make her betray their position with a neigh.

In fact the girl and the man, with the staunch little gray horse dragging wearily in the rear, passed within fifteen yards without giving a sign that anything was suspected. Just as they were by, however, and Ronicky was congratulating himself that the maneuver was so successfully accomplished, the gray tossed his head and neighed. Ronicky ground his teeth, as the girl and her escort stopped and turned with exclamations. But the gray was too tired to continue his whinnying. They apparently took it for granted that the little outburst was simply due to the fact that the hungry horse sensed his nearness to home and a well-earned portion of grain; for they went on almost at once and faded into the darkness.

No sooner were they a glimmering, almost invisible shadoow ahead of him, than Ronicky Doone sent the light-footed Lou out from the trees once more, and so he stole along on the trail of the two.

CHAPTER X

IN THE BARN

He felt somewhat as he would have felt had he been eavesdropping, but now stealth was necessary, for he had to make these people his guide to the house which, beyond doubt, was their destination—that of Steve Bennett. There the girl would probably go inside the house, while Charlie Loring went out to put up his horse, and Ronicky could stop him on the way. Or perhaps they could finish their argument by lantern light in the barn. Why not?

All turned out as he hoped. Before long, as they worked their way up that rolling, pleasant valley, he saw from the crest of a rise the yellow window lights of a house which, as he drew nearer, assumed large dimensions. For the wind had shifted in the past half hour or more and had scoured the sky clean of clouds, and the big house was distinctly drawn across the stars. Beyond it stretched the usual array of barns and the gloomy network of fences around corrals which goes with the Western ranch. In the starlight, too, it was easily possible to trace the movements of the two by the gray horse. Ronicky stayed just within sight of that spot of color, trusting that the drab color of Lou would not be visible.

For a moment they paused at the house, and then the gray horse and the man went on toward the barn, alone. Ronicky at once dropped out of the saddle, threw his reins to make Lou keep to that spot until he needed her, and hurried on after Blondy. It was not exactly a joyous occasion for him. He had no feeling of personal animosity against Blondy Loring. But it was necessary in the strictest sense of the term that he should clear his honor. For he could not leave that district until he had finished with Loring. And now was as good a time as any, or better.

Vaguely he wondered what would happen. He would not shoot to kill, if it had to come to a gun play, as it probably would. But if he did not shoot to kill, there was a vast probability that Charlie Loring would. This, however, was a problem which he had faced before, and he was not unnerved by it now. He saw the door of the house open and let out a shaft of light which framed the black form of the girl and glimmered in her hair. Then the door closed, and Ronicky hurried on until he picked the barn into which big Blondy Loring and the gray horse disappeared.

Here, before resuming his pursuit, he paused a moment to take his bearings as accurately as he could. And, as one long familiar with danger, he now worked most coolly, jotting down in his mind an elaborate sketch in which the position of the house, the fences, what seemed to be the bunk house, and the outlying sheds were all marked. When he left that barn he might be in considerable haste, so that it would pay him to know exactly in what direction he had best race to get to the mare. He would start her toward him with his alarm whistle, as soon as he left the barn, and they would meet midway.

With his retreat thus cared for, or at least carefully considered, he turned his back resolutely on the past and fronted the work just before him. And, so doing, he settled himself into a strange attitude of mind which an ordinary man could never have achieved.

Carefully he cut out and threw from his attention all his past. And of his future nothing was left to concern him except the events of the next few instants. He was about to confront an antagonist who had given the most conclusive proof that he was a foeman worthy of the steel of even a Ronicky Doone. For that reason the heart of Ronicky began to rise. On times before this he had been forced by public opinion into battle with men who were beaten before the fight began. But this case was distinctly different, and he rallied himself to meet it.

He found something to rejoice in. There was war ahead of him. He could turn himself for the nonce into a wild man. The law would not strike him down even if he killed. And, though he would fight to conquer, not to destroy, this was a consolation; they would consider this battle as a duel.

When he reached the entrance to the long barn, at the side where the gray horse had entered, Ronicky was high of head, almost smiling, and with a fierce joy keeping him tensed and keen. In the darkness of the barn he saw a match struck, a sharp line of blue leaping out, as the match was drawn over the trousers of Blondy. Then the head spurted into flame. Next, as that flame gathered strength, it showed the hand, the intent, tired face of Charlie Loring, and the glass of the lantern he was lighting. The head of the gray horse was shown, also, and the light rudely outlined the forms of two or three other horses. But this was the season when most of the stock would be running on pasture.

As soon as the lantern chimney was drawn down into place, shutting off the wind, the flame steadied, and the light was multiplied tenfold. Blondy hung the light at the side of the barn and, after tethering his horse, climbed into the mow and threw a quantity of hay into the manger. In the meantime Ronicky turned and looked back toward the ranch house. There was only one lighted window when the place was looked at from this direction, and that light was bleared to a greasy effect, perhaps by cobwebs and other dirt. Yet it gave Ronicky the effect of an eye overlooking him from behind.

And might they not come out of the house toward him? No, the great chances were that the girl had stolen from the house without telling anyone of her intention of meeting Blondy. Her father would not have permitted it. Besides it would have revealed the secret meeting place, and that no girl could have consented to. So it stood to reason that she had gone out secretly after supper, and now she was secretly returning. So that there was no danger of an alarm being spread among the men to send them out to congratulate big Blondy on his escape of that day and his epic achievement in riding into Twin Springs. Such an errand would have brought them squarely upon Ronicky Doone.

This decision heartened Ronicky still more. He had waited just outside the door, and now he stepped in, as Blondy swung down from the manger and came whistling toward the lantern. Certainly he was a magnificent man! The lantern threw a giant shadow behind him, blotching the far side of the almost empty haymow, and yet there was no need of shadows to exaggerate the size of those wide shoulders. He was as huge as two ordinary men rolled into one.

Just as he was reaching for the lantern he saw Ronicky and with an oath sprang back.

"By Heaven," cried Blondy Loring, "she was right!"

What that meant Ronicky did not pause to consider, for his mind was stunned by perceiving that the gun belt had been left off, and that Charlie Loring was weaponless before him! So thoroughly was he prepared to see Loring armed that he had not been able to see the truth until he waited for the big man's hand to go for the revolver. Then he discovered the truth. Loring stepped back and folded his arms.

"You've got me," he said. "You've got me I guess, Doone. Going to make it a cold murder, eh?"

"Don't talk like a rat," answered Ronicky, very angry at this insinuation. "You know that I ain't that kind of a hound. If you don't know it, it's time that you did. I ain't going to take advantage. I've come here for a fair fight, Loring. You come up here where you left your saddle and your gun; then put your gat back on. Then we'll have it out, fair and square. Does that suit you?"

"Right in here—where we'd scare the hosses?"

The nerve of big Blondy was a fine thing to see, and Ronicky grinned in whole-souled appreciation.

"It sure goes against the grain," he told Blondy. "But I've done what I could to pay you back for saving Lou. I've kept 'em off of your trail, and I gave you a chance to find out the truth. I don't aim to say that that makes us even up, but I hope it shows that I mean right by you, Blondy."

"But I mean right by you, too," said Blondy, still chuckling, as though the outcome of the battle were a foregone conclusion. "I mean right by you, and I'll see that you get a fair and even break out of his, Ronicky. I'll bury you in style when this is over, and I'll do up your coffin all in velvet. What you say to that?"

Ronicky smiled again.

"Help yourself," he said gallantly, and stepping back, as Loring drew near, he waved toward the gun belt.

As he did so he saw that Blondy was very pale. Yes, there were even little beads visible, as the lantern light struck aslant upon his forehead. It astonished Ronicky so much that for the moment his mind was dizzy and refused to act. Still Blondy was smiling, and yet the smile, which had seemed so real at a little distance, was a stiff, carved image of a smile, now that it was seen at close hand. Indeed it looked for all the world as though Blondy was in a blue funk.

That, Ronicky knew, could not be true. He had tried the courage of Blondy and believed it to be faultless. He had stood by and seen Blondy draw a gun with a nerve and hand as steady as though he were at target work.

"Go ahead," said Ronicky, as the big man turned toward the saddle. "You don't need to worry. I ain't going to shoot you in the back, Blondy!"

Blondy shuddered and jerked about. His face was now positively ghastly. He had seemed a carefree boy a few moments before. Now he was a gray-faced old man.

"How do I know?" he snarled, grown suddenly vicious.

Ronicky Doone blinked at him. He could not believe his eyes.

"How do you know? Why, because you know that I ain't that kind!"

Blondy ground his teeth. He seemed for all the world like a man striving vainly to lash himself into a temper.

"I know nothing about you," he said.

"Then I'll stand back as far as you want," said Ronicky coldly. "But if——"

He got no farther with his offer. Blondy, turning as though to listen and consider the new proposal, now continued his turn until he was directly facing Ronicky, and at the same time he leaped out and hurled his whole great weight at Ronicky. Quick as a cat's paw works, Ronicky side-stepped, but he was too close to have a chance at maneuvering. The great left arm of Blondy shot around him. In another moment the other arm of the big man got its hold, and Ronicky was lifted from the ground in arms which constricted like shrinking bands of hot steel around him, threatening to break every bone in his body.

CHAPTER XI

BLONDY'S BASE MOVE

It seemed at first, by the savage and animal-like snarling of Blondy, that this was indeed his purpose, to half strangle Ronicky in mid-air and then finish the work by dashing him upon the ground. Never had Ronicky dreamed that a mere man could possess such herculean powers.

"You rat!" breathed Charlie Loring, and then, as though the surety of his victory restored his mental balance to some degree, he turned and strode forward through the door of the barn, still bearing Ronicky securely trussed in his arms.

It was in vain that Ronicky kicked and squirmed and struggled to be free. He was of average weight and of vastly more than average strength and activity, but caught unprepared, his agility neutralized by the surprise attack, he was perfectly helpless, and now every struggle only served to make the grip of Charlie sink more deeply into his body.

Then Ronicky went sick, almost fainted, as the sickening degradation to which he was going to be exposed was revealed to him. It was the purpose of Charlie Loring to take his captive straight into the big house and there, before Bennett and Elsie Bennett and whatever hands might be on the place, show Ronicky helpless in his hands!

Every step of the way the certainty grew until at last, as they reached the door of the house, Ronicky gasped: "Blondy, if you take me inside like this, you'll have to kill me; because if you don't I'll get you sure for this."

"Bah!" answered Blondy. "When I get through with you, Doone, you ain't going to be able to lift your hands as high as your head for a year. Just lay to that and keep your mouth shut. I'm running this little party from now on!" And he kicked open the door and strode into the house.

The room in which he entered held both Bennett and the girl. There was no chance for Ronicky to steel himself against the shock. But all in a flash he found himself before them, and then he was crashed down into a chair with a force that stunned him, and his gun belt was torn from him. After that, Blondy stood behind the chair, with a revolver jammed against Ronicky's neck.

And the latter looked miserably at Bennett and the girl.

Of course they had risen, as Blondy entered, the girl with an exclamation which identified her, if identification was needed, as she whom Ronicky had encountered near the brook so short a time before. And now that he could see her in the full light of the room, he felt that Al Jenkins had not exaggerated in his description of her. Blue, starry eyes and lighted hair of gold and features modeled with exquisite nicety, Ronicky had never before seen such a face in all his wide wanderings. Scorn and anger now made her eyes wide.

"That's he!" she cried to a whiteheaded man. "That's the man who spoke to me, I know! Oh, Charlie, I was right! He was sneaking somewhere near, and he followed you!"

"The hound!" growled the old man, shaking his venerable locks in detestation of such rascally work. And he folded his arms across his thin chest and glowered at Ronicky. He looked like a picture of a type—that type which is supposed to be represented in the gentlemen of the South, with fluffs of hair grown long, and wide mus-taches made to bristle out in spikes or tufts, according to the fancy of the wearer, and nicely pointed beard. They have weary, droop-lidded eyes, these men of the fanciful Southland; they have erect, martial bearing, and their manner can rise to great heights of pomposity.

Such, in every detail, was the picture of Stephen Bennett who had conducted the long war again Al Jenkins. He had won at first, but now he was fallen on declining fortunes. The room in which he and his daughter had been reading, showed unmistakable signs of the loss of money. It had at one time been furnished with some elegance, for that section of the country. But the upholstery on the chairs was now sadly worn. The very pictures on the wall seemed to have faded. And only under the shelter of the great round center table did the carpet retain the pristine vigor of its color and design.

In the costume of Steve Bennett the same disrepair showed. He was wearing a long Prince Albert of faded cloth which went most inappropriately with the rather unclean riding boots on his feet and the much cheaper trousers. But he wore that Prince Albert in the way that *makes* one address the possessor as "colonel"; and he thrust out his breast as though it supported a row of medals.

In this fashion he looked down upon Ronicky Doone, striding toward him so brusquely and towering so high and so close above him that Ronicky would not have been surprised if the bony old fist had been dashed into his face.

In the meantime big Blondy was telling a strange story. He was pouring grain into the feed box of the gray, he declared, when he heard what was much like the sound of a stealthy footfall behind him. He had waited cautiously for a moment until he made sure that he who approached was close to him; and then he had whirled and discovered Ronicky Doone, stealing up with leveled revolver.

In the same motion with which he had whirled, he struck the weapon from the hand of the astonished Ronicky, and the next moment the would-be murderer was helpless in his arms. And here he was. He, Blondy, wanted to turn the hound loose and kick him off the place after disarming him, but he decided that it might not be well to leave such a sneak to wander near the premises. And for that reason he had decided to bring him in and allow Steve Bennett and Elsie to have a chance to pass judgment upon the villain.

This astounding story he told with the utmost fluidity and even with an air of indifference. It was not, he insisted, because he had the slightest desire to persecute this treacherous rascal, that he had brought him here. But something should be done as an example.

It was typical of father and daughter that, when the sordid recital was ended, the former drew closer, and the latter drew back.

"To think that I was within arm's reach of him to-night!" breathed Elsie. "And—and that I thought his laugh was frank and manly! Oh!"

Words failed her. Her father spoke.

"This—this vermin," he said, "ought to be tried in the courts of the law, Loring. But we ain't got courts of law around Twin Springs."

He shook his head and took a turn through the room, with one hand thrust into the breast of his coat and the other crossed upon the small of his back.

"Yes, sir," he said, "the damnation truth—pardon me, Elsie—but it *is* the damnation truth that there ain't justice to be had in the courts where the influence of that snake, Jenkins, reaches. There ain't any justice, and there ain't any chance of justice. He's got folks so much in the palm of his hand that they can't put him and wrong-doing in the same sentence, or even in the same day. Because he spent some money on a road, they got him worked up into a saint. I never seen anything like it! And more than that, if he wants to back up a man, there ain't any power that dares to put out a hand to stop the man that Al Jenkins has picked. And all that Jenkins would need to do to keep this murderer of his——"

"Father!" cried the girl. "Do you really think that he sent this—this creature to kill Charlie Loring?"

"Do I think it? Bah! I know it! I know the workings of his reptile mind! And what can we do? If we harm this man seriously we'll have to answer for it in the courts which Jenkins controls. If we don't harm him, a flock of Jenkins' other assistants of the same sort will be out here and after us! No sir! It ain't any trouble to Jenkins if I have just a bunch of worn-out tramps working my range for me, men that'll close their eyes when the rustlers want to run off some cows. That don't mean nothing to Jenkins, but when it comes to letting me have a real honest-injun man like Charlie Loring, why, that's a different yarn altogether. He's going to get Loring away from me. If he can do it with fair play, well enough; but if he can't he'll try dirty means. So he's sent this hound out here. Charlie, I near forget myself when I think of it!"

He fairly swelled with a poisonous anger. But the detestation in the face of the girl was what bowed the head of Ronicky and crushed his spirit. It made little difference that this was all blindest injustice. What mattered was that she should be able to scorn him so utterly. Out of that pit of wretchedness he could never climb to good esteem, he felt.

"Which all narrows the thing down," said the rancher, "and leaves us only one thing to do, namely, to call the boys together at breakfast to-morrow and turn Ronicky over to them. Just let Charlie Loring stand up and tell 'em what he's told us, and then let the boys be alone for five minutes with this Ronicky Doone. When they're through with him, I guess he'll be punished enough!"

He rubbed his hands violently together. The perfect thought grew upon his mind and entranced him.

"There'll be justice done!" he cried.

And Ronicky Doone looked in horror at Charlie Loring to see if he would protest, but the handsome face of the big man was set and hard, and his eyes were glittering. No doubt remained that the mind of Loring was made up. The greatest possible evil that could be inflicted upon Ronicky Doone was, in the eyes of Loring, the greatest possible good. Only the girl cried out in a protest for which Ronicky could have blessed her.

"But father!" she exclaimed. "That's worse than death, almost, if they mob him! You know what happened to that man of ours when he——"

"I *do* remember," said Stephen Bennett, "and that's just exactly why I propose to see to it that the same thing happens to Ronicky Doone. Our man very foolishly tried to steal a cow. This man tried to steal a human life. Does that answer you, Elsie?"

And Ronicky knew. Three or four times he had seen such things happen, though luckily his hands were clean of guilt. But he had seen the lynching of a horse thief, and more than that, he had seen the mobbing of a sneak who attempted a murder—not a fair fight, gun to gun, and man to man, but a shooting from behind, just of the nature of which big Blondy was about to accuse him. What had happened to that man had been so terrible that Ronicky had never dared recall the picture in its entirety.

And now he was in the same situation. The full and consummate cruelty of the rancher struck home in his mind, and he merely bowed his head still lower.

Of what use were words?

CHAPTER XII

OLD-FASHIONED IRONS

He would never forget what followed. Old Steve Bennett left the room, was gone for a minute, and then returned with an accompanying sound of clanking iron. When he reappeared he carried manacles in his hand.

"Old-fashioned irons, but strong," he told Charlie Loring. "Like a lot of old-fashioned things, they don't look as good as they really are." And he snapped them over the wrists of Ronicky. Here the girl protested again.

"Charlie—father!" she exclaimed, coming between them and Ronicky. "There's something wrong about all this. He—he might have something to say. Why don't we give him a chance to talk—to explain—perhaps to put forward his side of the story."

Charlie Loring fired into a rage at once.

"D'you think there *is* another side to the story?" he asked.

"No, no! Don't lose your temper, Charlie. I only mean that he should have a chance to talk. Men have that right in a law court. Why shouldn't we give him that right here?"

"Nobody's stopping him from talking," said Charlie Loring, but the scowl with which he turned upon Ronicky was thunderous in blackness. "Go ahead and tell your little lie, Ronicky. We ain't stopping you!"

He stepped back, his face working and pale, and the fingers with which he rolled his cigarette were uneasy at their work.

"Look at him!" said Ronicky Doone. "Does he look like a gent that's just finished telling the truth, or like a liar that figures his lie might possibly be found out?"

"You——" cried Charlie Loring. He crushed the cigarette to shapelessness and stepped a long stride toward Ronicky, but Elsie Bennett faced him and pushed him back with the lightest pressure of her hand.

"Why, Charlie!" she cried, and again, "Why, Charlie!"

"Al Jenkins is right," thought Ronicky in the depths of his miserable heart. "She's an angel! She'll look right through him!"

Charlie Loring was facing the girl in desperation.

"You weren't going to strike him when his hands are in the irons?" she asked, wonder and a tinge of scorn giving her voice an edge.

"I—I've stood a good deal from him, Elsie," said the big man. "I saved his hoss to-day and might have throwed my life away doing it, with that posse of madmen spurring down the trail to get at me. And after doing that for him, he comes and tried to kill me from behind. Ain't that enough to make a gent forget himself?"

"I suppose it is," said Elsie Bennett and turned toward Ronicky, with a peculiar mixture of loathing and curiosity. He met her glance. His own eyes widened to meet it. For a moment they stared steadily at each other, and with all his might he was sending the message to her through that glance: "Don't you see that I'm an honest man?"

Some of the loathing finally passed from her expression. She came a little closer and no longer held her skirts together, as though in touching him they might float against a permanent defilement.

"Talk," she said. "Tell us what you have to say to explain yourself!"

Ronicky Doone smiled and shook his head.

"I tell you seriously," said the girl, "that if you don't talk you'll be given to-morrow morning, a terrible punishment for what you've tried to do."

Again he shook his head, again he smiled faintly, and Steve Bennett said angrily: "Don't you see that he ain't able to frame a lie to fit? That's the only reason he ain't wagging his tongue this minute, girl!"

She turned troubled eyes to her father and then looked back to Ronicky.

"I don't know," she whispered more to herself than to the others. "But you two know so much more than I do. Surely you won't make a mistake!"

"Make a mistake? Of course not! The hound knows what he's done, and he knows what he has to expect if he's caught trying to do it. He'll have the nerve to take his dose without whining beforehand, I hope!"

This from Charlie Loring, and again Ronicky Doone favored the big man with an eloquent glance. The girl had stepped back again, but still she studied the prisoner, as if her mind were not yet entirely made up, as though she still leaned toward mercy.

"If there *is* a mistake," she said at last, as Ronicky rose in obedience to a command from Loring, "it's a most terrible one. I warn you of that, Charlie!"

Charlie Loring turned at the door.

"What's the matter, Elsie?" he asked. "Good Lord, if you almost believe his silence, what would you do if he started *talking*?"

But she made no answer, merely bowing her head in thought. And the last Ronicky saw of her, as he went through the door, was the gold of her head against the blue-gray of the faded wall paper.

Then he turned his eyes to the front and followed old Steve Bennett, as the latter mounted the steps, with a lamp raised high above his head and the lamplight brilliant in the edges of his white and misty hair. Just behind him followed Charlie Loring, revolver in hand.

"Watch yourself every minute," Charlie advised Steve Bennett. "This fellow is apt to try some snake trick almost any minute."

Ronicky plodded on. He might cast himself suddenly back down the stairs and trust to luck that movement would surprise Loring. But he had a shrewd idea that if he tried such a maneuver a forty-five slug would tear through his vitals. He slowed up, thinking of this problem, and was prodded in the small of the back by the muzzle of the big gun. Yes, it would not do to attempt a surprise movement while Charlie Loring walked behind him with a gun. In the upper hall they turned aside into the first room, and there the lamp was placed on the floor.

There was no other place for it. The room was denuded of all furniture. Dust was thick on walls and floor, and an atmosphere of unutterable desolation pervaded the apartment.

"You make yourself comfortable here," said the old man with a grim humor. "Just take as much room as you want. And if you got any requests, holler."

He turned his back to leave.

"Are you going to leave this light here?" asked Charlie Loring.

"Why not? Or would it be too much comfort for him if he could have the light to see by?"

"The thoughts he has to think ain't going to be much more pleasant in the light than in the dark," chuckled Charlie. "But the hound might dump the lamp over and trust to luck that the flames would bite down through the floor, and so he could get loose. We'll leave him no light, I guess. What about the window?"

"There ain't nothing that he can climb down by without using his arms. If he tries to get out that way, we won't have to bother the boys with him in the morning."

This thought pleased Steve Bennett, and he continued to chuckle the rest of the time that he was in the room. This was not long, for Charlie said that he wished to have a moment alone with Ronicky, and the rancher obligingly stepped out of the room. When he was gone, the big man stepped over to the prisoner, holding the lamp high. There he waited, his forehead covered with wrinkles of doubt and thought which were deeply outlined in shadows which struck up from the lamp in his hand. And his whole face in that manner was made older in appearance.

"Ronicky," he said very softly, "I hate what I've been doing. I hate it like death. But I had to do it. And now I've got in so deep that I've got to go through with it."

"You think you will," said Ronicky, "but you'll change your mind. You'll change your mind when the morning comes, Charlie. That's why I didn't talk downstairs, I wanted to give you a chance to work out of this all by yourself, because I know you ain't snake enough to do what you're trying to do."

Charlie Loring waited and said nothing. A hundred things seemed to be pressing toward the tip of his tongue, but none of them was formed into words.

"Good Heaven!" he muttered at last. "I only wish——"

His wish was never expressed, but turning hastily on his heels, he literally fled out of the room and slammed the door heavily and locked it behind him.

Ronicky heard his steps descending the stairs, and a little later he could make out the voices, as the girl and her father and Charlie talked. And by the sharp sounds he knew that a hot argument was in progress. For a time he strained his ears to make out the words, but after a while he abandoned that effort, because each syllable was sufficiently removed to blur.

This continued for some time, and after that he heard them go off to bed, Charlie Loring remaining in the house. This struck Ronicky as odd indeed. The report had it that Charlie was a new man on the Bennett ranch, but while the other cow-punchers slept in the bunk house, which he had distinguished by its lights, he, the new hand, was given the privilege of sleeping in the owner's house. And the granting of that privilege showed what a poor judge of human nature Bennett was. It was enough to raise a revolt among self-respecting cow-punchers. Only tramps and loafers would submit to the making of such distinctions, no matter how necessary Charlie might have made himself to Bennett, or how agreeable to the girl.

He heard the voices of Charlie and Elsie now mount the stairs until they reached the hall just opposite his door, and now he could understand the words they spoke.

"Stop thinking about him," Charlie Loring was saying to her. "You just stop worring about him, will you? What he gets won't be more'n what's coming to him."

"If I could stop thinking about him, Heaven knows I would. But it was his silence, Charlie, that unnerved me, and that calls my mind back to him now. I can't forget it—that and the way he had of looking at me."

"Hush, he may hear you."

"What difference does it make if he hears?"

"I know, but—Elsie, are you really angry?"

"No, no, I'm trying not to be. Good night!"

"Wait!"

But she did not wait. Her steps hurried away down the hall. The heavy stride of Charlie Loring carried his two hundred and more pounds of flesh a little way after her, and then he turned and went slowly in the opposite direction, a door finally closing that sound away.

CHAPTER XIII

DELIVERANCE

The knowledge that the others were awake, even though they were unseen and no matter how hostile to him they might be, had kept Ronicky company, as he lay in his dark room. But, as the voices died out and all the house finally slept, he passed into a new state of alertness. It was something as sharp as that emotion to which he worked himself when he was preparing to step in and fight Charlie Loring to the death. But where there had been a fierce joy and excitement in that prospect, there was only a dreary feeling of doom in this.

Yet it was not a dull surrender. His mind kept fighting against the facts for a time and striving to contrive a means of escape. But when he got stealthily to his feet and went to the window, he saw that the rancher had spoken the truth, so far as he could make out by the starlight. There was no sign of a ledge beneath the window on which he could have secured sufficient purchase for his feet. So he returned to his place by the wall, where he sat down cross-legged and resumed his black reflections.

The time would not be very long, now, before the morning came and the tragedy with it. It might not be actual death that he would come to, but it would be something closely akin to death. He would be nearly a murdered man before the cow-punchers were through with one whom they would be led to consider a treacherous man-killer.

His hope had been that Charlie Loring could not carry the thing through. He would be forced to repent before the moment came to execute his diabolical plan.

And, as he thought of this he was brought back with a shock to the consideration of Loring and his impulses. For what could be the reason underlying and explaining the big fellow's actions? Nothing could have been finer than the actions of Loring in Twin Springs earlier on that same day, when he faced the crowd for the sake of an idea—and Elsie Bennett. No doubt the consummate loveliness of the girl explained part of the reckless gallantry with which Charlie Loring had ridden into Twin Springs and flirted with death. But the beauty of Elsie Bennett could surely have nothing to do with the generous and big-hearted carelessness with which he again risked his safety in order to ride down the slope and save Lou from the waterfall.

The memory of that act increased the rhythm of the pulse of Ronicky Doone. It had been as fine a thing as he had ever witnessed. And now could he believe that such a man, capable of such actions, was the cunning trickster and dastard which Charlie Loring had shown himself to be on this night.

Now the wonder of it appalled him, and he bowed his head.

There was only one thing remaining for him to do, and that was to accept the villainy of Charlie Loring as an accomplished fact and, putting this and all hope behind him, turn toward the morning and the dangers which loomed before him. He must steady his nerve until it was iron. He must be ready to endure the most horrible tortures of shame and of actual physical agony when he faced the cow-punchers. And for this he already began to set his teeth.

Indefinitely the silence of the night had worn on when Ronicky heard another sign of life in the house, just loud enough to be audible above the night whispers which went to and fro in the big place. This sound was a light creaking in the hall, a creaking which advanced slowly, but regularly, toward the door of his room and stopped. It occurred to Ronicky that some of the cow-punchers on the place might well have heard of his capture, and that they had made up their minds to kidnap him from the house of the owner and take him out for a lynching, or for an ordeal nearly as terrible. So he waited breathlessly until the door opened, and through the opening a strong, cold draught blew over him. But with the wind he heard a rustling of garments at the door.

When it was closed he knew that Elsie Bennett was with him in the dark. But there was no striking of a light. Only the whisper of her gown told of her progress across the floor. She came straight to the center of the floor and paused there, quite close to Ronicky.

"Ronicky Doone!" she called, for there was a quality in her whisper that made it like a cry of alarm.

"Here!" he answered in the same tone.

He could tell by the breath she drew and the flutter of skirts that she had drawn suddenly away from the sound of his voice.

"Be quiet!" she cautioned him. "It is I, Elsie Bennett. I've come to do you no harm. But be quiet—make no noise, or it will be the worse for you."

In spite of his situation he could not help smiling. There was so much frightened childishness in her caution. *She* had not come to harm him!

A match scratched, and presently a long, trembling flame grew up from a candle. She shielded it with one gleaming hand so that her own face was thrown in deeper shadow, while a pale glow fell upon Ronicky Doone, as he rose to his feet and stood frowning at the light. No doubt he looked villainous enough, but he set his teeth when she gave back from him in manifest fear. She began to talk rapidly, to get the message with which she had come out of her mind, so that she could be gone.

"Ronicky Doone," she said, "I've come to save you— you understand? I've come so that you may be let loose —on condition."

"All right," said Ronicky.

"On condition"—and here a forefinger was raised in stiff caution—"that you give me your solemn word of honor that you will never harm Charlie Loring on account of all that has happened between you two. I have a key here which will fit the irons that are on your wrists, and I'll set you free. But only if you promise never to hurt him!"

Ronicky stared patiently at her. It made him feel sadly wicked and ancient to witness such innocence. He waited until the last sound of her vibrating and eager voice had died away from his ear, for it seemed to cling there. It was odd that he should feel so detached. It was as though he stood in the distance and looked in upon this scene, noting down coldly the questions and answers. And always, as they talked, his glances were prying past that single gleaming hand and the pale circle of the candle glow and trying to get at the reality of her face; and he could never succeed.

"Why don't you answer?" she asked suddenly. "Are you sick? Or do you think I don't mean it? I tell you, here is the key!"

She held it up. It came to Ronicky that in spite of his manacled hands he could leap at her, knock her down, tear the key from her, and unfasten his own bonds by using a little dexterity of wrist and fingers. But the thought was a distant and unreal picture to him. He could never use violence against her. The danger even could not persuade him to a serious consideration of that possibility.

"You're wasting your time," he answered her finally. "I won't give you that promise, ma'am."

The jerk of the hand which held the light and the corresponding flutter and leap of the flame, told how much she was startled by this announcement. She could not speak at once. Finally she said: "But I'm not joking with you. I'm offering you your liberty—really. Otherwise your promise wouldn't mean anything."

"I can't give it," said Ronicky.

"But," she went on, "you don't understand. They might even kill you in the morning. They are going to be told how you stole up behind Charlie Loring and tried to—oh, when our men hear that, they'll be simply mad with rage, Ronicky Doone. Keep that picture in mind. Our cow-punchers are rough—very rough!"

He watched her steadily. She had come a little nearer. People always do when they are persuading.

"Yes, I know that they're rough," he replied, "but still I can't promise."

"Why not?"

"I couldn't hold up my head if I did. A man has one thing that's worth more'n his life, lady, and that's his honor."

"Honor!" gasped Elsie Bennett. "Honor—from you!"

She recovered at once.

"I didn't mean to say that. I didn't mean to hurt you unnecessarily. But a man who would slip up with a revolver behind another man—and still worry about such scruples as—"

She paused.

"I'm sorry," said Ronicky. "But I told you before. You're just wasting your time!"

She passed a hand across her forehead. This time she came so close that he could make her out quite distinctly. And in that dim light, against the velvet darkness, she seemed to Ronicky as lovely as a jewel and as radiant. And he felt again the sense of awe with which he had first looked at her, though then that emotion had been covered with a more profound feeling of shame.

"I try to make out what can be in your mind and behind your words," said the girl faintly. "But I can't. You bewilder me. You seem to be throwing away a—"

"Miss Bennett," said Ronicky, "I figure that you'll have to work it out this way: that if you believe everything Charlie Loring said about me, you never can understand."

"You ask me to put him down as a liar?"

"I don't ask that. Only—maybe he's mistaken."

"Ah, yes. I'm foolish to say so, but I can't help it. I was interested from the very first. It was hard to believe of you all that my father, for instance, believes. And I'm half prepared to sympathize with any good explanation you can offer. You had no chance to talk downstairs. Will you talk now—to me?"

He was sharply tempted, but he shook his head.

"Words ain't going to help me none," declared Ronicky. "Nope! What's needed is a little action. When I've done a few things, maybe you'll be willing to take another think. But if I talk to-night, Blondy Loring will talk in the morning. And what he says will wipe out what I say."

It was such frank, clear-cut talk that she was amazed and showed her surprise.

"You really don't intend to buy your liberty with a promise?" she asked.

"Look here," said Ronicky argumentatively, "you talk as if a promise I gave might be worth something."

"Of course!"

"Then you figure that my honor *is* worth something. And if it is, I sure can't wait around after Charlie Loring has knocked me down and—lied about me! Miss Bennett, I got to fight back!"

"Then you can't expect me to help you!"

"Why not? I'll give you this promise—that I won't hurt him on this ranch. Will that suit you? And if I ever get the upper hand with him, I'll promise to go easy for your sake."

At this she smiled in frank scorn. It was plain that her mind was unable to grasp the possibility of big Charlie Loring being defeated by any man that lived.

"Very good," she said thoughtfully. "Suppose I let you go and trust to your promise—it seems to me that I'm doing a great deal for a very small return and no security—at least none that a bank would take."

"It'll be the first time," said Ronicky, "that I've had this sort of a favor done me. But wait and see. In the end, maybe, I can pay you back."

She bit her lip and looked down at the floor, and by that he knew that she would do as he wished.

"I'm going to take your word and let you go," she said at the last. "And your word is simply that you'll never come back to the Bennett Ranch to hunt down Charlie—and lie in wait for him on the range."

He nodded, and Elsie Bennett without another word unlocked the handcuffs and stepped back from him, a little frightened by the possibilities of what he might do. He reassured her with a smile and by chafing his wrists to restore the circulation. Then, as she backed toward the door, he followed her to it.

She put out the candle before she stepped into the hall. There, swallowed again in the gloom, they exchanged some whispered words.

"I suppose it's for the sake of your name that I'm doing this," she said. "But there's such a fine free swing to that name—Ronicky Doone—that I couldn't hold all the evil against you that my father does, for instance."

"I've noticed it before," said Ronicky Doone, "that a good woman don't need any long list of reasons for doing a good thing. God bless you for this one!"

She could literally feel the quiver of the gesture with which he jerked his liberated hands above his head and shook them at nothingness, rejoicing in his freedom. Then he turned down the stairs, but with his foot on the first step he turned back again toward the dim form in the hall.

"And when they start in damning me to-morrow and the days that come after," he said, "will you keep a place in the back of your brain where you cache away a couple of good, man-sized doubts? Just wait to be showed?"

"I think I shall," said the girl. "At least I'll honestly try to!"

"Then—good-by!"

"Good-by," said Elsie Bennett, and he felt her leaning above him in the darkness, as he glided down the steps.

The consummate noiselessness of that descent roused the old alarm and suspicion in the heart of Elsie Bennett. She hurried to her own room on the front of the big house and leaned out the window to watch her freed prisoner depart. She had a great and swelling desire suddenly to rouse the people in the house and endeavor to reclaim the fugitive. It seemed madness, this thing she had done. It was sending danger of death to hover over the head of Charlie Loring.

And then, out of the night beneath her window, she heard a faint whistle. It was keyed so high that it pierced to a great distance. The whistle was repeated. Ronicky Doone was standing beneath the window waiting—for what?

There came a rapid beat of hoofs. The form of a horse glimmered in the night, and Ronicky Doone swung into the saddle and disappeared at a rapid gallop.

With a beating heart she watched him fade out.

"He can't be all bad," said Elsie Bennett. "He can't be all bad when he has a horse that comes to his whistle."

CHAPTER XIV

JENKINS GETS A JOLT

Of all the winged things in the world, there is nothing that flies so fast as rumor, and of all rumors there is none so fleet as bad news.

Ronicky Doone reached Twin Springs late, very late. And he slept till noon at the hotel. When he wakened he found that the town knew more about his adventure of the night before than he knew himself. He could tell by the first face he confronted down the stairs that all was known—at least from the viewpoint of Blondy Loring.

Another man would have lost all appetite for the day when he confronted that expression of sneering disgust on the face of the hotel keeper. But Ronicky Doone merely drew the belt of his trousers tighter and walked into the dining room for lunch.

He ate it in profound silence. Not a man spoke to him except one or two who happened to catch his eye full upon them, and they favored him with a muffled grunt. Plainly he was in the deepest disgrace into which it is possible for a man to fall; at least in the West.

He finished his lunch slowly, however, admirable testimony that his nerve was as cold as steel in a crisis, and he looked up unabashed when the proprietor of the hotel paused at his table in his round of the room to inquire after the comfort of his guests.

"Look here," said the proprietor, looking out the window above the head of Ronicky, so that he might not be forced to encounter the eyes of the despicable gunman who stole upon his victims from behind. "Look here, Doone, I got a terrible rush of business coming, and when I looked over the list I seen how I'd reserved all the rooms. I'll have to use your place to-night, so I guess you'll be moseying along to-day." And he turned his back without further explanation. But the hand of Ronicky shot out and touched his arm.

"Turn around," said Ronicky.

The other turned a quarter of the way.

"Look me in the eye," said Ronicky.

Reluctantly it was done.

"I'll stay till I'm good and ready to go," said Ronicky. "You write that down in red and start betting on it. I'll stay here till I can't pay for my room no more. That's final."

The proprietor started to hurl a loud protest upon Ronicky's head. But apparently he found something in the eye of Ronicky that was in sharp contrast with the reports of Ronicky's meeting with Blondy Loring, which had been retailed throughout the town during the morning. At any rate the host retreated to a corner, muttering like a dog over a bone.

And Ronicky rose, stretched himself, carelessly picked up every disgusted, scornful eye that dwelt upon him, and then sauntered out of the room.

As on the day before, he selected the one, large, easy chair on the veranda and bore it to the edge of the shadow, where he stretched out luxuriously in the sun; and while the heat seeped through his tissues and filled him with a pleasant drowsiness, he smoked a cigarette and watched the smoke drift up, blue-brown in the sun, rising sometimes a considerable distance until it vanished in a touch of the wind.

In the meantime Ronicky was thinking, buried in the most profound reflection. He was picking up one idea at a time and turning it and examining it, as an expert raises and turns a jewel, criticizing every tiny facet. And all this he did with a sleepy face. For the brow of a philosopher is never wrinkled.

The other men began to troop out. He heard the jingling of their spurs as from a great distance. Loud laughter somewhere jarred on his ear; and the murmur of other voices made a smooth current bearing one on toward sleep. Ronicky Doone regarded them not. He was forgetting the village of Twin Springs rapidly. He was totally occupied with the more vitally engrossing problem of how he could draw to him big Blondy.

For it stood to reason that Charlie Loring would never come to meet him. For some reason the big fellow had wished to avoid a man-to-man conflict with Ronicky. No matter what that reason was—and Ronicky could not discover it—if it had made Charlie take the risk of being shot while he sprang barehanded upon Ronicky in the barn, it would make him resort to other and stranger methods to avoid the conflict. Since Ronicky could not hunt him down on Blondy's own range, Ronicky must induce his quarry to come to his place.

He was still struggling with this great problem when a heavy foot crunched on the boards near him, and a cloud of smoke billowed across him. Ronicky turned and saw big Al Jenkins standing there, and the look on Al's face was by no means an invitation to cordial talk.

"I been hearing things," was what Jenkins said, "and the things that I been hearing about you, stranger, is enough to turn a man's hair gray. It seems that you ain't Ronicky Doone at all. It seems that you just been wandering around and using his name promiscuous without being him at all!"

Ronicky covered a yawn. He turned his head a little and considered Jenkins with solemn gravity. But he did not speak, and this silence caused the lower jaw of Jenkins to thrust out. He even made a motion with his big hands, as though he were about to grasp Ronicky and break him like a stick of kindling. He gathered himself into control after a moment, and he went on: "I suppose that that don't mean much in your life, son. But around Twin Springs we're a queer lot of people. And we take every man for what he says he is. That's why, when we hear that a gent has been telling a flock of lies about himself, it riles us, son—it sure riles us terrible!"

And he waited, grinding his teeth with increasing fury. Here Ronicky Doone yawned again, and this caused Jenkins to stamp with such convulsive energy that the board beneath his heel cracked loudly. He had to shift to one side to avoid a possible fall through the broken flooring.

"D'you hear me talk?" he roared at last. "D'you hear what I'm saying to you?"

"Yes," said Ronicky gently.

"And what d'you think about it?"

The voice of Ronicky was more gentle than ever.

"You're too old," he said, "for me to tell you what I think. That's all."

Al Jenkins, the fearless, the battle-hardened, the man-breaker, was struck purple. His face swelled. Dark veins stood out on the temples.

"You insulting young rat!" he thundered. "I got a mind to tear the hide off of you and—"

He paused. Ronicky Doone had swung to a sitting posture. It was amazing to watch him. A cat does not glide from deep sleep to wakefulness more suddenly or completely. One second her eyes are dull; the next they are balls of baleful fire. And the change in the face of Ronicky Doone was hardly less.

"Back up," he said. "You're right on the edge of a cliff. Back up and start pawing for a good road," said Ronicky. "Now tell me what you want."

In fact the rich man gave back a short step in his astonishment. He had had much to do with men of all kinds, and cowards among them. And he had more use for a mangy dog, he often said, than for a man with a streak of "yaller" in him. Yet the actions of Ronicky Doone were not at all such actions as one would ordinarily attribute to a coward. His eye did not waver. His voice did not shake. And the hand with which he removed the cigarette from his lips was steady as a rock.

Also, it was to be noted, and be sure the glance of Al Jenkins did not fail to note, that the hand which held the cigarette was the left hand, and that the right hand dangled carefully near the hip of the youth. Jenkins glowered at him uneasily. Literally, he was mentally and physically upon one foot.

"I'll tell you what we want," he went on, his voice now somewhat abated in violence. "We want you to get out of this town, Doone, or whatever your name is. There's some here that think we'd ought to make an example of you. But there's others, like myself, that ain't for no tar-and-feather party. It makes too much talk, and Twin Springs is plumb agin' talk. Is that plain?"

"That all sounds like English. Couldn't be clearer if I'd read it in a book," said Ronicky Doone.

"Then start moving," said Jenkins. "We allow you about ten minutes to pack up and start. Lemme see you do something."

"Sure," said Ronicky. "Look all you want." And he turned and stretched out at ease along the big chair.

Al Jenkins gasped, blinked, and then said: "Son, don't make no mistake. We don't want to start no party around here. But if we have to we'll stage one all trimmed in red pepper—one that'll keep you stinging for a year and a day. Are you going to git?"

"No," said Ronicky, without turning his head, "I ain't going to git."

And he drew forth his cigarette tobacco and papers. The head of Al Jenkins spun like a top. Was he seeing correctly? Was this the despicable coward of whom they had been told this morning, who, the very night before, had sneaked up behind big Blondy and attempted to blow off the head of the cow-puncher? Was this that dastardly assassin who had been released from his due and merited punishment by the foolish mercy of a girl?

And staring closely at Ronicky Doone, the rancher saw that the eyes of Ronicky, though apparently fixed straight before him, were in reality inclined a little toward him, and that the lips of the slender fellow were a little compressed, just a trifle compressed and colorless.

Jenkins fell into another quandary. He knew suddenly that this man was either a coward acting a part with consummate skill, or else he was a fighting man who lay there in a wild, senseless passion, inviting the entire town to attack him and rejoicing in the prospect of a kill. So shocking was the very thought of this second possibility that Al Jenkins recoiled a little more and became entirely uncertain. There was one clew to cowardice. Cowards generally try to talk themselves out of corners. And this man was silent.

On the other hand Al was so old a veteran that he knew that there are exceptions necessary to the proving of every rule. And in his wisdom he could not be sure that Ronicky was not a "yellow liver" playing a role. What could he do? Should he call in the townsmen to share in the mobbing of a fighter, or should he kick a coward off the porch, chair and all, and then jump after him and bring him wriggling in his arms back to the crowd, just as it was reported big Blondy had borne the same man into Bennett's house the night before?

Hesitation and too much thought is not the mother of strong action. Al Jenkins sighed, paused, and noticed the slender grace and surety of the fingers which were whipping the cigarette into shape. It was placed in the lips of Ronicky, and now it was lighted.

At this, Jenkins frankly cursed in his bewilderment.

"Hang it, man," he said, "you know what we've heard. Tell us your side of the story. We're willing to give you a hearing."

"Thanks," said Ronicky Doone, but he said not a word more.

Al Jenkins was perspiring with anger and uneasiness. He was a fighter, but no gunman.

"What d'you want to do?" he said.

"Wait here," said Ronicky. "Wait here for Blondy Loring."

He had not thought of it before. It needed the badgering of the rancher to force him into this inspired conclusion and solution of the difficulty.

"Wait for him here? Wait for Loring, the gent that—"

"That'd take a little trouble off your hands, wouldn't it? You and the boys wouldn't have to kick me out of town. You could just wait until big Blondy comes along, and then he'd do the job for you. Ain't that satisfactory?"

Al Jenkins paused. It might be—there was one chance in many—that the youth was not bluffing. And if he were not bluffing, it was a bitter shame that Twin Springs should miss the beautiful spectacle that was promised.

"What d'you mean?" asked Al to draw out Ronicky.

"I mean just this," said Ronicky Doone. "If Blondy Loring was to take it into his head that it'd be a good thing to do to come into town and have a chat with me, I'd be right here and waiting for him, say at noon tomorrow. You might send him word, if you want to!"

CHAPTER XV

CURLY CARRIES A MESSAGE

Two minutes later Al Jenkins, whose word ruled Twin Springs, and whose nod shook it as truly as the nod of Homer's Zeus ever shook Olympus, was busied in the hotel, telling the boys about the agreement which had been made. Ronicky Doone was to stay there quietly at the hotel, while word was sent to Blondy Loring that his enemy awaited him here. It was to be, in a way, a repetition of the incursion of the day before. Then Charlie Loring had cantered into town for the first time, an unknown quantity. He had taken the townsmen by surprise and swept them off their feet. If he came to-morrow he would not have that advantage.

On the other hand, if he came in to-morrow, their hands would be tied. He would be coming for the express purpose of disposing definitely of a man whom he had twice before beaten. And if he did that he could go away, and they were in honor bound not to hamper his going.

So the matter of which Al Jenkins spoke was reviewed from two angles by the crowd, and while there were many favorable voices for it, there were many against it who declared that the town, in effect, ought to wash its own dirty linen. They should kick the pseudo Ronicky Doone out of their precincts and let him do as he would on the outside.

To this Al Jenkins returned the rather pointed observation that if any single man cared to do the kicking, he was welcome to the task, but that he, Al Jenkins, was not at all eager for the task because he had a lingering suspicion that this stranger might be the real and actual Ronicky Doone in person, in which case the kicking was apt to be accompanied with difficulties in the shape of large slugs of lead driven as hard as powder could drive.

The remarks of Jenkins were at least so taken to heart that, though several young men who hankered for a reputation loitered near Ronicky's post that afternoon, none of them ventured to actually disturb the dreamer. And that evening he went into supper, the center of attention once more, even though that attention were hardly as favorable to him as it had been twenty-four hours previous. At least Twin Springs had decided to keep its utter condemnation in abeyance until Ronicky had been given another chance to redeem himself.

In the meantime Al Jenkins had selected from the ranks of his retainers a hardy and devoted servant. This was no other than "Curly." He derived his name from the quantity of hair which was twisted tight around his head in dense, glistening masses of blue-black. Curly had no other name than the one drawn from his hair. He came out of nowhere. He had no past; he answered no questions with the truth. In short he was a big, powerful, round-cheeked, swarthy-skinned, merry-eyed individual who parried all inquiries about his past with lies, the first that came to his mind.

It was impossible to extract the truth out of Curly. Also it was impossible to corner him with a quantity of his own lies and embarrass him. He simply refused to worry. If an old woman asked him about his childhood, he was apt to tell a particularly pathetic tale of a fond mother who died young, of the cruel stepmother who came into the house; of cruel and insidious persecution which finally drove him out of the house to find his own fortune where he might.

If a young woman asked him the same question, Curly answered according to her complexion. If she were dark, he told her of the plantation in the sunny South which he called home, and to which he would some day return to claim his own. If she were a blonde, he related a pretty fable of meadow lands and rich orchards and mighty barns, well stocked; this was the paternal estate which must on a day become his. And to it he would assuredly go, but only when his taste for freedom was dulled. In the meantime he preferred to wander.

These wild yarns of Curly had opened the door to many a lady's heart, but of late years they had accomplished little for him. And when he began to talk men relaxed their minds and their attentions and allowed themselves to revel in the fancies and the cunning inventions of the story-teller. This was the man who started for the Bennett place. Such an errand was not one which Al Jenkins would have easily intrusted to another of his men. For when a Jenkins adherent and a Bennett met on soil which was not neutral, there was generally a crash which started echoes flying through the hills. But Curly was such a good-natured soul that Jenkins felt he could safely be trusted to get to the Bennett Ranch and off again with his message. So he waved him down the road and then sat down to chuckle and wonder how Curly would deliver the message. Certainly that fertile brain would not pass the challenge through his hands without embroidering some new designs unheard of by the creators. But no matter what he said, or how strong he made it, the purpose would be answered by bringing Charlie Loring back into town either to expose the cheat, or to battle with the stranger.

It was a blithe day for Curly. Rocking down the road on his cow pony, he sent his whistle thrilling before him until he came in view of the house of Bennett. Then he hastened his gait and rode on headlong, arriving with his horse in a lather. He flung himself down to the ground, rushed to the door, and beat on it with the butt of his quirt. Two pairs of footsteps came hurrying to answer him. He was confronted when the door was jerked open, by both Charlie Loring and Steve Bennett. And in the distance his quick eyes took in the form of beautiful Elsie Bennett, with a lapful of sewing.

The two men started a little at the sight of an emissary from the hostile camp, but they stepped back to allow Curly to enter. He availed himself of the offer only by stepping into the doorway, so that he could look about the room at leisure, and also appear to the eyes of the girl, framed in the most impressive manner to bring out his size.

"Al Jenkins," began Curly, in the manner of one in great haste, "told me to rush out here as fast as I could and tell you that you was needed in Twin Springs tomorrow at noon." He turned to Charlie Loring directly. "And he says for you to bring your favorite shooting irons with you because—"

There was a shrill cry from the girl. She sprang up and came running toward them.

"You fool!" snarled Charlie Loring at Curly.

The rancher turned to his daughter.

"Keep back," he said. "Don't be bothering us now. It's kind of late for you to be pretending a pile of interest in what happens to Charlie, after you turned loose the rat that Charlie trapped out here. You go on out of the room and don't be troubling us."

She backed toward the door to which he had pointed.

"Oh, Charlie," she pleaded, "promise me that——"

"Later," said Charlie Loring. "I'll promise you later. Just now I've got to talk to this man. Don't worry, Elsie. Don't keep bothering about what happens to me, because——"

Curley looked gloomily toward the girl and big Blondy, as the latter went to escort her from the room.

"She's out of her head about him," sighed Curly to himself. "Curse it, that's what comes of a gent being close around where there's some action in sight. He gets the action, and the rest of us that stays off in the background get nothing but the whiff of his dust, as he rides over the sky line."

These were the reflections which Curly interrupted, as big Blondy Loring and the rancher turned back toward their visitor. But now he was surprised to find that Blondy Loring was not exhibiting the anger which Curly had reckoned upon. Of course it had been a tactless thing to do—this announcement of the danger which impended over the head of Blondy, in the presence of the girl. And of course Curly had made that announcement with a full understanding of what he was doing, and with the purpose of beating the bird out of the bush, so to speak, and discovering what was the real attitude of beautiful Elsie Bennett to the big cow-puncher.

He had now found out and greatly to his own dissatisfaction. And he glowered at Bennett and Loring, as they came hastily toward him, having shut Elsie away.

"What's up?" asked Stephen Bennett.

"Well, I'll tell you," said Curly. "Last night Ronicky Doone comes riding into town with a yarn about how he came out here and licked you, Loring, and made you take water. And when——"

"What!" shouted Bennett and his new foreman in loud unison. "Why, the truth is that——"

But Curly held up his hand.

"I ain't out here arguing, gents," he declared. "I'm just out here spreading the news around. I'm telling you what's been told to us in the town. If you want to talk, go into Twin Springs and do your talking in there. What Doone told us was that he came out here and tried to get Loring to fight, and that Charlie wouldn't fight, and that he stepped up and punched Charlie Loring in the jaw and dropped him flat on his back, and that when Charlie waked up, he didn't reach for his gun but just crawled over to Ronicky, begging him not to shoot. And——"

There was a hoarse cry from Charlie Loring.

"I'll kill him for this!" he shouted. "The dog."

"The yaller hound," cried the rancher. "Why, son, right here in this room I——"

"Oh, I know," said Curly, "you and Charlie know all the facts of the case, and you're agreed on 'em fine and slick. But I ain't out here arguing, as I said before. I'm just circulating with the news of what they're talking about in Twin Springs. Now I've told you, and I'm about through. The next thing that comes, though, is something that you might sort of want to hear. When we up and asked Doone how he'd prove what he said to be true, he said: 'Just go out and ask Charlie Loring if he wants to come in and meet me to-morrow at noon in front of the hotel. I'll be here waiting.'

"And that's why I'm out here, Loring. To-morrow at noon the boys will be waiting and watching for you. Just come in and let your gun talk for you. Good luck!"

He turned, but as he turned, he heard Bennett crying to his foreman: "It's a trap all laid for you, Charlie, but I ain't going to let you go. I ain't going to let you go!"

"Hell," answered Charlie Loring. "I *got* to go!"

"Sure," chuckled Curly, as he swung into the saddle, "he's got to go."

And he rode away with the happy smile of one who is conscious of having performed a good deed.

CHAPTER XVI

JENKINS TALKS TO HIS HENCHMAN

All the way back to Twin Springs, Curly retained that joyous smile, for he had with him the sense of a perfectly fulfilled piece of work. When he arrived in the dusk, he sauntered onto the veranda of the hotel, only to be instantly surrounded by a score of curious men, all anxious to learn the facts of the case as the Bennetts might have retold them. But Curly made sure that his voice would carry to the drowsy form of Ronicky Doone, where the latter lay stretched at his ease, partly in sun and partly in shadow.

"When I went out and told 'em what had happened," he said, "I didn't get no cheers out of 'em. When I told 'em that Ronicky Doone was going to wait for Charlie Loring here at the hotel until noon to-morrow, Bennett and Charlie just started laughing, and they kept on laughing until I looked around behind me to find out where the joke might be. But pretty soon, out of what they said, I made out that they thought that Doone was just bluffing, and that he'd rather stay to see snow in the desert than stay to see Charlie Loring come riding into the town."

There was a murmur from the men, and many heads turned to watch the news taking effect upon Ronicky

Doone. They only saw one slender hand, bearing the inevitable cigarette, rise slowly from his lips, and the white haze of smoke drifted upward, dissolving slowly in the dusky air.

"Pretty soon Charlie was able to talk for laughing," said Curly raising his voice still more, because it seemed impossible that his words could have carried to the impassive form in the distance without bringing forth some sign of life; and he boomed now: "When Charlie could talk after he'd eased up on the laughing, he says to me that when noon shows up to-morrow he'll probably be sliding into town. Not that he expects to find any Ronicky Doone around, but so's he can have a laugh at the dumbbells in Twin Springs that would believe a yarn like the one Doone told us."

This remark brought forth a loud howl of rage from the crowd. They became so excited that they forgot to watch the face of Ronicky. That is, all failed to watch him except Al Jenkins and Curly. And they saw Ronicky close his eyes, as he inhaled another deep breath of the smoke, and then smile, as he blew it forth into nothingness.

Al Jenkins pulled his henchman to one side.

"I don't believe that he even heard what you was saying," he declared to Curly.

"I dunno," said Curly. "I sure was watching him all the time and trying to get some sort of action out of him. But I guess he's made up solid."

"He's a queer sort," said Jenkins. "Either he's a fighting devil, or he's a coward and fine actor. Any way you take him, he's different from anything that we've ever had in Twin Springs."

"Yes, he is," admitted Curly. "I never seen his like except once back in Omaha. I was a young feller, then. I had just come into a little stake that an uncle of mine left to me when he died. It was only a couple of thousand, but it looked good to me. Well, I had my wallet bulging with this loot, and I was walking down the street when——"

"When you met this gent you're leading up to, eh?" snorted Al Jenkins. And he went on, interrupting gracelessly: "Now tell me the truth about what you saw out there."

"Plain facts?" sighed Curly.

"That's what I want. If you can separate yourself from

your dreams about what things might be, and see 'em the way they really are, I'd sure take it kind of you, Curly!"

"Well," said Curly, "she loves him."

"Who loves what?"

"Elsie and Blondy."

A terrific stream of oaths burst forth from the lips of Al Jenkins. "Liar" was the mildest term he applied to Curly for having brought this news to Twin Springs.

"Liar, am I?" cried Curly at last, drawing himself up. "Lemme tell you what happened! When they opened the door the first thing they done was to flip out their guns— it was that nacheral for them to go for their gats when they seen one of your men around. And——"

"Curly, if you lie about this I'll print the lie on hot iron and make you eat it!"

"These are honest truths," said Curly sadly. "It'd make a dog sick, the amount of suspicion I got to live with around these parts."

"Go on, then!"

"Well, when I out and told Charlie that he was going to be waited for with a gun at noon to-day, she let out a screech that you gents would have heard in Twin Springs, here, if you'd yanked the stuffing out of your ears and been listening! Never heard such a holler in my life, not since the time Hugh Tully's wife seen the coyote playing with her two-year-old boy and——"

Here Al Jenkins exploded again.

"You told Blondy that, with the girl inside of hearing distance?"

"Sure."

"You ought to be tarred and feathered, Curly. You got no sense, and you got no feeling."

"I done it on purpose," protested Curly. "I wanted to find out if there was anything between her and Blondy. And I sure succeeded."

Another stream of curses issued from the lips of Jenkins.

"It ain't possible," he declared at last. "She's worth ten like him. She's too good for any man I've ever seen, if she's half as good as her mother, but a big, thick-skulled fellow like that Loring, why——"

He broke off with a groan.

"Go on, Curly. What happened then?"

"She goes and throws her arms around Loring's neck.

" 'Dearest,' says she, 'you'll break my heart if you——' "

"Shut up," bellowed Jenkins. "I can't stand even listening to it. How could you stand hearing it and seeing it?"

"Well," proceeded the truthful Curly, "she was run out of the room by Blondy and her father, and then they come back to me and asked me if I was plumb crazy, because they wouldn't believe that this gent calls himself Ronicky Doone is really going to wait for Blondy to come in to-morrow. Do you believe it, chief?"

"If he's using his right name," said Jenkins, "he'll do that and more."

"Then how come he tried to murder Blondy from behind."

"Maybe Blondy lied about it."

"But old Bennett and the girl both seen Blondy carry Doone into the house."

"Now," groaned Jenkins, "I dunno what to think. All I know is this: that if Blondy Loring rides into town to-morrow and don't find nobody waiting for him, or if he comes in and cleans up on Ronicky Doone, Twin Springs as a town ain't going to have no more name than a jack rabbit around these parts."

Curly nodded.

"They's a worse thing than that," he said. "Some of the boys take to Blondy real strong. They say that if a gent like Blondy will stick to Bennett, Bennett can't be so bad. And, besides, I've heard 'em talking that you're kind of hard on the old man, the colonel, as they call him."

"Colonel nothing!" shouted Jenkins.

"All it needs is a little bit more," Curly declared, "and Bennett can have a fine crew of hands working out on his ranch, and then the rustling stops!"

He lowered his voice and became serious as he said this. Jenkins also glanced guiltily around.

"You talk like it was murder," he muttered at length. "But all I'm doing is what was done to me. Bennett busted me the same way that I'm busting him. Besides he stabbed me in the back when I thought he was my friend. But what I'm doing to him he knows I'm doing."

"Well," said Curly, "you can call it what you want; I'd hate to get caught at it. But you got to step light, chief. You got a bunch of rough customers working for you, and they can scare out a bunch of regular cow-punchers, and they can buy out a lot of tramps like them that are working for Bennett now. But if you was to run into some real fighters on the Bennett range you might have a hand full of trouble."

Al Jenkins nodded. The truth of this was manifest.

"I know that," he agreed. "It's a ticklish business. But, Curly, I'm going to stay by it till I do to him the same as he's done to me in the past. Ain't that fair and square?"

Curly nodded. Such argument seemed to him too clearly established to admit of dispute.

"You got the right of it, chief," he said. "The only thing is that it would look sort of crooked if every one was to find out what's going on. And if some more like Blondy get up on the Bennett ranch, you'll have a lot on your hands."

"No more like him are going to get there," affirmed Jenkins. "One week from to-day I'm going to make a scoop—a scoop that'll clean him out and break his heart!"

And he turned away upon his heel and went off, humming to himself. As for Curly, he stared after his master with amazement and awe. Such hardness of heart was to him something to be admired from a great distance. And yet, as he had told Jenkins, the justice of it was unimpeachable. But how were they to stampede Blondy?

Looking toward the end of the veranda, his eye rested upon the slender form of Ronicky Doone in the chair, a form now barely perceptible against the gathering darkness. Curly shook his head. Such a man as this was hardly the force which should be pitted against big Blondy Loring.

Also his heart ached for the fair town of Twin Springs. Just as Al Jenkins said, if big Blondy were allowed to ride unscathed and defiant into Twin Springs and out of it again, the reputation of those who dwelt in the little place would be down at zero.

"What's on old Jenkins' mind?" asked a cow-puncher, coming near him.

"I'll tell you," said Curly solemnly. "Al took me aside and says to me: 'I mislike having this Ronicky Doone picked to stand up to a man like Blondy in the name of Twin Springs. If it was you, Curly,' he says, 'I'd feel a lot better about it.'"

CHAPTER XVII

WOODEN SLUGS

For Twin Springs the night was a troubled one, as it turned and tossed, full of nervous expectation of the trial of the day to come. For Ronicky Doone, who by force of circumstances had become the champion of the town, the night was long and quiet. For he retired and slept until dawn, the sleep of the blessed. Then he wakened, went to the window, saw the industrious world stirring about its work in the beginning of the cold day, and went back to bed to sleep again. For, as he put it himself: "The best time for sleep is the time you steal for it."

It was. midmorning before he rose from his bed, and when he came down the stairs a little later he was given the attention of a king. On every side of him he found anxious faces. Without a murmur, breakfast was served to him late in the dining room, and by the proprietor himself. A score of times he was asked how he felt, and how he had slept; and the whole atmosphere in which he found himself was one of kindly concern—more than that, there was at times an air of desperate interest! And Ronicky, remembering the day before, enjoyed every scruple of the altered temperature.

After breakfast he sought as usual his chair on the

edge of the veranda, and there he stretched half in sun and half in shade, awaiting the hour of the battle. And the populace of Twin Springs, fast assembling in points of advantage to await the shooting, looked upon their champion with amazement. Al Jenkins, having by common assent been appointed to the position of manager and chief functionary at this shooting, was bewildered.

"Either he's a great bluff," he declared, "or else he's dead sure of himself. But he ain't seeming to worry about the condition his gun is in, or how his nerves might be. He seems to figure that everything is the way it ought to be. I'm going to talk to him a little. The rest of you keep clear of him. Too much talking might be bad for him."

And so saying he approached Ronicky Doone and stood beside him, just as he had stood the day before. Only now how different was his attitude, how different the voice in which he spoke.

"Doone," he said, "you seem to be getting on pretty well."

"Tolerable well," said Ronicky. "Thanks."

"Which I been thinking back to our talk of yesterday," went on Al. "And I been figuring out that I said a lot too much and a lot too loud."

"Forget about it," said Ronicky, "the same as I have forgotten."

Al Jenkins sighed. This was more than he could have hoped. At the same time he reserved a deep suspicion in his brain. These smooth-speaking fellows were apt to carry a poisoned knife.

"I was just wondering," said Jenkins, "if you wouldn't want to oil up your gun and get it warmed up a bit. I got all the ammunition that you want ready and handy for you, and there's a nice clear stretch right behind the hotel where you could unlimber a few slugs, if you felt like it."

"Thanks," said Ronicky Doone. "But shooting plumb jars my hands. I don't do no more of it than I can help. You see?"

Al Jenkins gasped.

"You don't practice much?" he asked.

"I practice a bit now and then," said Ronicky. "But I figure that a gent has to trust a lot to luck when it comes to hitting anything with a revolver."

Jenkins merely turned on his heel and hurried away.

This was an attitude before a mortal combat which he had never before encountered, and which he never expected to find again. He turned into the hotel and in the lobby he sat down panting in the circle of serious-faced men. They became doubly concerned when they noted the expression on his face.

"What's happened?" they asked. "Is Doone losing his nerve?"

"I dunno," groaned Jenkins. "He beats me. He's just different! He says that he doesn't do much practicing because it jars his hands too much!"

His gasp found a score of echoes.

"Anyway," went on Jenkins, "the only thing that we can do is to wait and hope. Here, Curly! You go out and start talking to Doone and telling him some stories that'll cheer him up. Just talk about anything so long as it'll keep his mind off the subject of what's about to happen to him. But I'm afraid that it ain't going to be much good. That gent out there that calls himself Ronicky Doone is just some nut that's got a pet illusion that he's a gun fighter. But go ahead, Curly. Do what you can!"

Feeling that the hopes of Twin Springs were, to no small degree, resting upon his shoulders, Curly sauntered out upon the veranda, tightening his belt as he went and rolling a thousand possible topics in his mind. Actually to be encouraged to talk was a new experience for Curly. After all, the quality for which they so often laughed at him or abused him, they were now coming to applaud as a rare talent.

Going to Ronicky he broached conversation easily on the first topic that came into his head, which happened to be the fine make of boots which now clothed the feet of the cow-puncher. And when Ronicky replied with the usual kindness and quiet of voice, Curly drew up a chair and sat down. He would have passed from the topic of the boots to some kindred vein, but Ronicky rather abruptly stopped him with the question: "What d'you know about this Blondy Loring that I'm going to meet up with to-day, partner?"

Curly scratched his head. He had an idea that the last thing his employer wanted him to do was to talk about Loring with the champion. But a great and evil idea popped into his head. He could not resist it. As a matter of fact, he knew nothing at all about Loring. Neither did any one else in Twin Springs, except that Blondy had come into that part of the country some few weeks before, and that since then he had been the active partisan of Bennett. Other than this, Blondy was a perfect stranger to them all. It was the very meagerness of his knowledge that supplied so powerful a stimulus to the brain of Curly.

He sighed as he leaned back in the chair.

"Blondy Loring?" he said. "Sure I know about him. I used to live across the street from him in his own home town."

"The devil you did!"

"The devil I didn't! Me and Loring was pals together when I started to school——"

"You look eight years older than Blondy, though."

"Blondy? Who said anything about Blondy? I said Loring—Blondy's brother, Jack Loring. Him and me went to school together. But Jack ran away before he got through the third grade and never was heard of again. Sure I know Blondy Loring."

"Well, what d'you know about him?"

"Nothing that's good," said Curly sadly. "I sure don't know nothing that's good about him. He was always a devil from the time that he sicced his dog on my old cat, Jerry, the best squirrel catcher I ever seen. His dog killed Jerry. I never seen such a cat; and while the dog was chewing up old Jerry, Blondy Loring stood right across the street, dancing and clapping his hands together. That's the kind he was when he was a kid."

Ronicky Doone, shifting a little in his chair, turned a keen glance upon Curly. But the face of the latter was impenetrably sad. He had that gift which only comes after years of practice—he began to believe his own lies as soon as he started to fabricate them.

"But kids often change," said Ronicky. "I've knowed the worst kids in the world to turn into good men. And I've seen the best of 'em go bad when they get started out. Maybe it's the same way with Blondy. Have you knowed him since he was a kid?"

"Knowed him all his life, off and on," said Curly curtly. "If I didn't know him personal, I knowed them that was close to him. He's a plain bad one, Doone. D'you know what he is?"

He leaned forward. His face was drawn, his brow puckered, his eyes straining at the grisly truth.

"What?" asked Ronicky, aghast.

"He's a man-killer!"

Ronicky sat bolt erect in his chair. Curly flopped back in his.

"A man-killer!" breathed Ronicky.

"You hear me saying it! That's what he is!"

"H'm," said Ronicky. "Him a man-killer?"

"That's what I said. Why, down in Tuxson——"

But Ronicky Doone had risen from his chair and was pacing up and down the veranda, with short, quick steps. Finally he jumped down from it and disappeared around the corner of the hotel, leaving the narrative of how Blondy Loring killed two men on the same day in Arizona, unfinished behind him. Curly went back into the lobby of the hotel, as the entrance hall with the stove in the center, was called.

"Well?" they asked him. "Why did you leave so soon?"

"He was restless," said Curly. "He couldn't sit still and listen to me talking long. He got up and left."

"What did you talk to him about?" asked one.

"About one time up in Montana I was riding range in the winter for——"

Here a man came running in from the front of the hotel and tossed a cartridge into the lap of Al Jenkins.

"What's that?" he asked.

Al Jenkins looked it over quickly and then looked up with a start.

"It's a wooden slug!" he exclaimed. "Where did you get this?"

"I was around behind the hotel a while back," said the man. "And I seen Ronicky Doone—or him that lets on to be Ronicky Doone—break his gun open and dump out a whole cylinder full of these. Then he loaded up with some new ones out of his cartridge belt, and he kicked the dummies into the dust before he went away. He give a hard look around, like he'd have done a murder if anybody'd seen him. But he didn't get a sight of me.

"After he went on, I sneaked out and picked up that. I couldn't believe my eyes at first. What might he be doing with wooden plugs like that in his gat?"

There was a subdued muttering of comments. But Curly rose from his chair and started for the door. It was his news that Blondy was a man-killer that had made Ronicky load his weapon with real slugs; but what a dauntless courage was his if he had been determined, be-

100

fore that, to fight with fake bullets? Curly reached the door.

"Blondy's coming!" called some one across the street. "He's ahead of time."

CHAPTER XVIII

DOONE DRAWS

And Curly stepping through the doorway saw that it was indeed the truth. Swinging around the bend of the street, nearly at the far side of the village, came a big man on a small horse—at least the rider was so much larger than the average that he made the horse seem small. It was Blondy Loring, and he was coming fast, while at the end of the veranda was Ronicky Doone, stretched again in his usual chair, with his hands folded behind his head!

And Curly, in an agony of spirit, stood undecided. He felt like a murderer. If Charlie Loring were killed in the fight that was to come, he Curly, would be to blame for having deliberately lied about Bennett's foreman. But now it was too late to speak and tell the truth, he decided. In another moment Loring would be upon Ronicky, and the latter's nerves must not be upset by conflicting statements.

He glanced across the street. It seemed that hundreds were in view, crowding windows, placed everywhere that they could be in safety, at the same time commanding a view of the battle to be. He saw women; he saw white-faced girls and round-eyed boys. But there was no one there who felt as Curly did. With all his faults, he had a kindly heart, and now he honestly wished that the place of one of the fighters could be given to him. He saw the dust curling up above the head of Blondy, as the latter came rushing on. But what was the matter with Ronicky? Why did he not arise?

Ah, now he sat up, and Twin Springs breathed a sigh of relief. He sat up, and he was rolling a cigarette. Incredible though it seemed, he was going to smoke while he encountered this formidable foeman.

There was a swish of dust spurting sidewise, as Blondy twisted his horse to a halt and swung down from the saddle. Straight toward Ronicky he strode, his left hand clenched, his right hand ungloved and carried frankly near the butt of the revolver that was exposed in the holster on his thigh. His face was set, almost convulsed with his emotions. Never had Curly seen such battle fury, and he half felt that the story which he had told to Ronicky Doone might after all be the true one concerning Bennett's foreman.

"Doone!" cried Charlie Loring.

Ronicky lifted his head. At the same instant the right hand of Blondy Loring flipped around the butt of his revolver and jerked it almost all the way from the sheath. But the other combatant did not stir. He merely followed the gesture with studious eyes and continued to calmly roll his cigarette, smoothing it into shape as a perfect cylinder. Then he placed it in his mouth and drew out matches. And there was a groan from the good men of Twin Springs. Was this strange fellow about to disgrace the town by taking water from Charlie Loring, as he had been reputed to have done once before?

"You dirty hound!" Loring was crying, so that every one could hear. "You been talking about me here in town. You been lying about me! You know why I'm here!"

"You're talking sort of loud," said Ronicky Doone, mouthing the words with some clumsiness, as he kept the cigarette in his lips and lighted it. "This ain't a high wind, Loring. I can hear you tolerable well even when you speak nacheral. Or maybe you want all of them folks at the windows to hear you, eh?"

In spite of the quiet tone in which he spoke, his words were audible for a considerable distance. For all of Twin Springs was holding its breath, except one irrepressible dog in the back yard of one of the houses. He had been barking most of the morning, barking at the flies that flew

103

past him, barking at the chain which held him. And he barked at this juncture.

At the sharp noise Blondy Loring started a little and changed color, though why that should be, Curly, for one, could not imagine. He noticed now, also, that the red was fading quickly from the face of Loring and turning to a gray.

"I've brought a gun with me, same as you asked me to," said Blondy. "And I see you got one with you. Let's see why you wear it."

"Sure," nodded Ronicky Doone. "There's lots of time for that. But I ain't ready yet. I ain't near ready, Loring!"

"You're going to show the yaller streak again, eh?"

"Maybe you'd call it that, but I'm one of them that like to take things slow and easy. Right now, for instance, I got an idea that you're a sneaking hound, but I'm just letting that idea filter around through my head until I'm plumb certain. Then—then I'm going to kill you, Loring!"

He spoke it softly, but he spoke it with a savage satisfaction, and to the amazement of Curly, big Loring winced. Then Curly began to see some purpose in the delay of Doone. If, indeed, the smaller man possessed nerves of steel, as he seemed to, he was trying to break down the poise of Loring by taunts and by prolonging that critical moment which precedes actual combat.

"I give you ten seconds," said Loring, with a sudden burst of curses, in a voice that was pitched almost femininely high and small. "'I give you ten seconds for getting out your gun and defending yourself if you can. I call on the rest of you gents of Twin Springs to hear me when I tell him. Because I mean business—and business quick!"

But Ronicky Doone merely laughed. It was a fearful thing to watch him laughing in the face of a hysterical fighter such as Loring.

"You're talking plumb foolish," he assured the big man. "We ain't going to shoot according to when you get ready. We're going to have a signal; and when the signal comes, we'll shoot." He jumped down from the edge of the veranda. He stood at ease before Blondy, with one hand draped from his hip and a smile on his lips. And still his left hand was occupied with the cigarette. He seemed to be in the act of casually opening conversation with the big man. And very big indeed did Blondy seem by contrast with the slender, agile form which confronted him.

"You and the rest of 'em have framed some trick," exclaimed Blondy, falling back. "I got odds of a hundred to one against me in here. Before I give you a chance to take advantage of me, I'm going to——"

"What?" asked Ronicky.

The answer was deadly silence, and beads stood out glistening on the forehead of Blondy Loring.

"You listen to me, and I'll tell you what you're going to do," said Ronicky. "You're going to wait right here with me until we hear the yap of that dog behind one of the houses yonder. And when the dog yaps, I'm going to shoot; that's your signal, Loring!"

And he blew out a cloud of cigarette smoke and through it stared steadily at Loring.

The latter glanced aside, and even behind him, and fell back again.

"What's the matter?" asked Ronicky Doone. "Don't you like close attention?" He added: "But I do! I want to get close enough to watch the way your eyes work, Loring!"

And he stepped nearer, smiling.

"Curse you!" gasped Charlie Loring with inexpressible horror and rage in his voice. "Curse you!"

"Watch for the dog barking, partner," advised Ronicky. "That's what we got to keep an ear open for. He's talking to both of us when he speaks again."

The hand of Loring made a convulsive movement. It almost seemed that he was about to tear the gun from its holster without awaiting the signal. And once, but this must have been merely the effect of a gust of wind fluttering his clothes, he seemed to tremble.

Ronicky Doone was saying: "I want you to hark back to what you been saying about me, Loring. I want you to remember what you been saying about how I tried to sneak up behind you and murder you with your back turned to me, Loring. And how, when you turned around and knocked me down, I crawled to you and begged you not to shoot! Keep thinking about that, Loring. Because the rest of the folks in Twin Springs are thinking about it now. They're all thinking; they're keeping it in mind, that yarn that you spun about me. And if they believe it, then I'm a fool!"

Loring moistened his dry, white lips, and he could

not answer. And it seemed to Curly, though the idea was so strange that he never dared to mention it to another soul so long as he lived, that big, blond Charlie Loring was actually in fear; at least his face was the white mask of fear and rage commingled.

Then the dog barked.

Blondy Loring with a gasping intake of breath—a gasp of actual joy, as the moment for action came upon him—grasped at his weapon and brought it out with the skill of one who has practised the movement until the execution of it is perfected to the last detail. But Ronicky Doone whipped out his gun almost carelessly and without even coming to an erect position from his slouching pose. The gun exploded, but Blondy Loring's gun did not.

It was not yet raised to the level when the slug from Ronicky's gun struck him. And with a sweep of his arm he flung his unexploded gun from him, clutched at his breast, and fell.

Ronicky Doone did not stir. He stood staring scornfully down at his victim. When the others ran in they found that the bullet had cut straight through the body of big Blondy. He was no better than dead, to all appearances.

Most amazing had been that fall. And more amazing still were the words which they heard the stricken man murmuring: "Thank God that it's over!"

CHAPTER XIX

WAITING

They carried him into the hotel and placed him in the proprietor's own room. Nothing was too good for a dying man. They brought the doctor, he who had pronounced Oliver Hopkins dead before his time. But on this occasion he did not jump to conclusions. He had been shamed in the eyes of the entire town by his mistake of a few days before. Now he would make certain not to fall into the same error. He would recall what had been drummed ceaselessly into his brain during his first year in the West—that men toughened by a constant life in the wind and all weathers are sure to die hard.

And, while they waited for the doctor's verdict, the men of Twin Springs came around Ronicky Doone and congratulated him, and Al Jenkins apologized frankly and humbly for the insults which in the near past he had heaped upon the head of Ronicky. But the warmth of the townsmen received somewhat of a damper from the bearing of Ronicky Doone. He was smoking again in the most nonchalant manner. He received their congratulations with modesty—with more than modesty—indifference. And such coldness was a terrible thing to see. They began to draw back from him.

In short he was too deadly a marksman to be altogether pleasant company. When a man is so sure with his weapons that he kills another between smokes, without lifting an eyebrow or changing color, he is not altogether a comfortable companion. Yet the utter indifference of Ronicky Doone to the thing he had done continued until big Curly broke through the group and drew Ronicky to one side.

"Ronicky," he said, "if you pull a gun on me for what I'm going to tell you, I won't blame you. Nobody would blame you."

"Go ahead," said Ronicky. "I ain't a gun-fighter every day of my life. Go ahead, Curly."

"Well," said the wretched Curly, "from what I've found out, you were figuring on using fake slugs on Blondy—you were figuring on using wooden slugs that would just knock him down if they were planted right. Is that the straight of it?"

"Who told you that?" asked Ronicky. "Who's been spreading that sort of talk around about me?"

"You were seen to dump 'em out of your gun," said Curly. "I got one in my pocket now. But the point is this—that you dumped out them wooden slugs after I talked to you. And what I want to know, Ronicky, is: Did you dump 'em out because of what I said to you?"

Ronicky paused. Then the cigarette crumpled between his fingers. He caught Curly by the shoulder with fingers that gripped deep in his flesh.

"Curly," he gasped, "don't tell me that what you said ain't the truth. Don't tell me that!"

But Curly dropped his head.

"Being sorry ain't a help—it's that wagging tongue of mine. I can't stop it when it gets started, Doone."

If he expected denunciation or violence from Ronicky, however, he was mistaken. The smaller man merely glided past him like a ghost and fled through the door of the hotel.

"What did you do to bring him to life?" asked some one. "What yarn did you tell him this time, Curly?"

But the miserable Curly went away trailing his feet in the deep, soft dust and answering nothing.

Outside the door of the proprietor's room Ronicky confronted the doctor, as that worthy came out. And there was something ominous in the softness with which he closed the door.

"What's the news?" asked Ronicky sharply.

But the doctor raised his hand, as one who protests against too much noise in a holy place. And the cold dread came to Ronicky that it was the nearness of death which had awed the doctor.

"I fear," said the doctor sadly, "that there is no hope. Where——"

"You lie!" groaned Ronicky.

"Young man?" queried the doctor sternly. "Where, I was about to say, can we get in touch with his family?"

Ronicky started for the door, but the doctor barred the way.

"No one must enter. He is now in a state of coma. If he wakens from that condition, then we may begin to hope. But I fear—I greatly fear he will never waken."

"Carry the news out to the Bennett place, then," said some one softly. "He done this thing for the sake of old Bennett—in a way. Bennett sure had ought to take care of him."

"You don't know him!" snarled Al Jenkins in answer. "But I'll see that the boy is cared for. If there's a bunch of bills, send 'em to me. I ain't no friend to Bennett nor none of them that fight for him, but when they get past fighting for him and are flat on their backs, they'll find that I ain't as hard as they think."

He was as good as his word. Not a penny was another person allowed to contribute to the care of Charlie Loring. In the meantime two men were chosen to go to the Bennett Ranch bearing the news that Loring had fallen in battle.

And Ronicky Doone sat down to wait in the lobby, regardless of the men around him, though nearly all of them strove to draw him into conversation. He was waiting on the reports which were sent out from the sick room. On the whole they told a steady story of decline, or else there was "no change."

Ronicky had paid the doctor liberally to have these ten-minute reports sent out. And once, when the physician himself came out and walked up and down, not displeased at his opportunity to allow the world to see him engaged in the battle with death, Ronicky went up to the good man and inquired again.

"It's just as I sent you word," said the doctor. "There is little use in watching him closely. The bullet entered adjacent to the——"

But Ronicky waved the technical details away. He had heard them rehearsed three or four times before, because the description contained several large words which the doctor was fond of turning over his tongue's tip.

"I don't give a hang about the facts. I just want to know what's in your mind?"

"Facts—you don't care—my mind?" stammered the doctor. "My boy——"

"Listen to me," said Ronicky, and at the same time he stuffed his entire stock of money into the coat pocket of the doctor. "You are going back into that room, and you're going to stick with Blondy Loring until there ain't a chance left for him. And every minute that you're in there you're going to keep hammering the same thought at him; that he's going to get well!"

"But, Doone, he can't hear a word—he's senseless."

"He'll feel your thinking. He can't help it. And, besides, if you go in there to watch a man die, you're going to see him die. But if you go in there to keep a man from dying, you got half a chance in ten of bringing him through. Go on back!"

And the doctor went. It was not altogether the money that persuaded him. His heart was kindly enough and generous enough, but now and then most of us need to be shaken together, so to speak, and brought to a crisper sense of things. And this was what Ronicky had done for the doctor. He sent the good man back in a fighting humor, and for half an hour no message came out of the room.

In the meantime the townsmen were baffled by the change in Ronicky. They had seen him perfectly indifferent one moment and wildly anxious the next. They had seen him sneering at the man who lay bleeding at his feet. And now they saw him pacing nervously up and down through the lobby, throwing himself into a chair, rising, and pacing again, and never stopping movement of one kind or another.

He offered no explanation. And Curly waited wretchedly until he was sure that Ronicky would not speak of the lie which had been told him. When Curly was sure that this explanation was not forthcoming he offered one of his own to the others.

"He looked like he was taking everything easy," said Curly. "He was even rolling a cigarette with Blondy dying at his feet. But all the time there wasn't really nothing going on inside of his head. It was just misty in there. But after a while the mist cleared off. He seen what he'd done. He heard that Blondy was dying, and then he come out of it with a jump and got the way you see him now."

This explanation had to pass.

Al Jenkins approached Ronicky with an excellent proposal to the effect that Ronicky should come out to his ranch with him and look around until he found a place on it that suited him. Then he was to name his own salary.

"And there you'll stay," said the rancher, "until I'm through with Bennett. Maybe you think, lad, that I ain't a man that remembers. But when you knocked over big Blondy you took the wind out of Bennett's sails. He's done for now. And when I clean up the old hound and back him off the range, the same way that he done with me years back, I'll be thinking that you had a hand in the shaping of the game, son!"

But Ronicky refused to listen to him. He thanked the rancher for the offer. But just now, he declared, he could not think and did not wish to think of anything but the condition of Charlie Loring.

"There's a pile of ranches in the world," said Ronicky. "But there ain't another Charlie Loring. I'll talk to you to-morrow, maybe, or whenever there's a decision about Charlie. Up till then my time belongs to him!"

"If you're that fond of him," grumbled the rancher, "why did you ever pull a gat on him?"

But Ronicky turned his back and walked away.

In the meantime the hours drifted slowly, wearily past. And still the condition of Charlie Loring was unchanged. And as every hour passed, the hopes of Ronicky increased. For if Charlie had held out as long as this, might he not eventually recover?

The doctor issued again from the room, but this time it was only for an instant.

He was a wonderfully and sadly changed man. There were pouches beneath his eyes. His shoulders were stooped. His every gesture betokened uneasiness. And when he saw Ronicky his face brightened a little.

"It's a queer thing to see," he declared in a murmur. "It's something I wouldn't believe if I weren't in there

111

watching. But—come in for yourself! He's living in spite of everything. God knows what keeps him up!"

He dragged Ronicky through the door and closed it softly. Then he stole across the room to the bedside. Ronicky, following, looked down, cold with horror, on the face of the wounded man.

For there was a strange alteration. It was no longer the rosy-cheeked Charlie Loring—Blondy—who had dazzled Twin Springs with his courage and his headlong taking of chances. Instead it was a thin-featured man that Ronicky saw. The flesh around the mouth had sagged away, making a ghastly caricature of a smile. The temples seemed to have fallen. The nose seemed sharper, thinner. Altogether there was the appearance of one who had been sick for a long time.

"He's dead!" breathed Ronicky, for it seemed impossible that there could be any life behind that mask of a face.

But the doctor shook his head.

"Still living!" he insisted.

"Is there a hope?" whispered Ronicky.

"No—I think not."

"There is a hope," said Ronicky, "because there's *got* to be."

The doctor made a gesture of abandon. Then there was a light, fluttering tap at the door.

"They've got to stop bothering me," said the doctor. "I can't work when they're holding my hands like this."

"I'll go," said Ronicky. "I'll throw them out, the fools! They'd ought to have better sense!"

He strode to the door and opened it with a jerk, his brow black as thunder, and he found himself glowering at Elsie Bennett.

CHAPTER XX

"ALL AROUND A CIRCLE"

He repaid his scowl with an indignant, scornful glance which said plainly enough, "You here?" And then, as he fell in chagrin and surprise, she stepped into the room. She left Ronicky to close the door behind her. The throwing out of her arms narrowed all the world to what lay before her hands, and that one thing was Charlie Loring.

Ronicky Doone was so fascinated by what followed that he only subconsciously and ineffectually resisted the pressure upon the door from the outside. When the door opened again and another stood beside him, Ronicky made no move to shut out the newcomer. He was too busy filling his eyes with the sight of beautiful Elsie Bennett dropping on her knees by the side of the bed of Charlie Loring. He saw the slender hands cherishing the pale face of Charlie Loring. And Ronicky Doone groaned silently. If they brought a man to this, the work of bullets was not all tragic.

Then he turned his head and saw that he who had just intruded was not Bennett, as he had subconsciously expected, but Al Jenkins himself! The big fellow had settled his shoulders against the door, as though to endure a shock, and with his head thrust forward between his great shoulders he was glaring at Elsie Bennett, as though she were an enemy with a gun pointed at him. Ronicky could see the stiff lips of the man working a little. But the murmur was inaudible. Then the doctor drew Elsie from the bed.

"You're apt to do him harm," said he. "He's got to have quiet. But if you'll stay and help nurse him—if you'll stay and take care of him, that's just what I want. He needs a woman's hands around him. The hands of a man are too thick, too heavy. Will you stay and help me with him?"

"Will I stay?" murmured she. "No one could make me leave!"

She turned and saw Ronicky and Al Jenkins together. There was one flash of anger and scorn for Ronicky, and then her gaze centered bright and wide upon big Al Jenkins. She pointed.

"Who is that?" she whispered.

"You don't know him? That's Jenkins—Al Jenkins!"

"Oh!" cried the girl and buried her face in her hands.

It seemed impossible to Ronicky that she should never have seen the big rancher before. But then he remembered how recently it was that Jenkins had come back to that district, and how his way with Bennett must have kept the two apart, and the mystery was not so strange. It dawned on him in a burst that these two were seeing one another actually for the first time, the girl and her formidable antagonist. Ronicky was struck by the horror in the face of Jenkins, the look as if he were facing a ghost. Perhaps that sprang from the similarity he saw between her and her mother whom he had loved before her.

At any rate she recovered before he did. Jenkins was still leaning against the door, overcome as it seemed, when Elsie Bennett came swiftly to them, flushed with a lofty anger.

"You and your hired man!" she said to Jenkins. "Is there no shame in you? Have you come here to gloat over him? Oh, I've heard of base things, but never anything so base as this! Will you go?"

They looked at one another, as though each hoped the other would be able to speak, and then they turned of one accord and faded through the doorway.

"I'm going up to my room," said Ronicky, when they stood outside, silent and shamefaced.

"And I'm going with you," declared Jenkins.

They climbed the stairs together, but at his door Ronicky turned to his companion.

"I'd sort of like to be alone," he said.

"You think you would," said Jenkins, "but you're wrong. You wouldn't like it a bit. You need company. I'm going in there and get you cheered up."

To this insistence there was nothing which Ronicky could oppose, and they went into the room and sat down. But almost immediately Ronicky was up and walking to and fro. The rancher watched him with a keen and measuring eye. Presently Ronicky spoke.

"Did you ever see such love as she has for Blondy? Did you ever see anything like it, Jenkins?"

He stopped, stared at the wall or vacancy, and shook his head as he remembered. To Ronicky's surprise, Al Jenkins merely shrugged his shoulders.

"It looks like love to you, son. But you never can tell."

"Eh?" cried Ronicky. "What do you mean by that?"

"How old are you?" asked the rancher.

"Twenty-seven," said Ronicky. "But what the devil has that to do with——"

"Twenty-seven! That's about what I thought. You're too young."

"Too young for what?" asked Ronicky, his irritation growing apace under the cross fire of apparently irrelevant questions.

"To young to know anything about women. About ten years is what you need on top of your age, son."

Ronicky merely glared. His face might be youthful, he told himself, but inside him there was a weary sense of age.

"I'm old enough to use my eyes and my ears," he said. "I could see what she did and hear what she said."

"Sure you could," said Jenkins, yawning. "My guns, ain't she beautiful, Ronicky? I've only seen her a couple of times in the distance before. But today when I stood up and faced her in the same room, it was like having a gun shoved in my face. It carried me back twenty years in a second!"

He stopped and sighed.

"But what she did and said don't mean nothing," he declared presently.

"Maybe she's sort of weak-minded?" asked Ronicky fiercely. "Maybe that's why what she says and does don't mean anything?"

This savage sarcasm left Jenkins untouched. He yawned again.

"She's in love with the idea of being in love, maybe," he said at last.

"Now what the devil do you mean by that?"

"She's at the ripe age for it, you see," said Jenkins. "Most likely she's been cramming her head full of stories about love, poems about love, music about love. Understand?"

"I'm trying to follow you," said Ronicky. "Go on."

"And presently along comes a young gent pretty well set up and with a good clear voice and a fine set of teeth and a handsome face. Well, she brings herself up short. This is a man," says she to herself. "He's young; he's handsome; he's a stranger. Why ain't I in love with him?

"Well, sir, if you ask old folks a question the first thing that pops into their heads is to say 'no' tolerable loud. But if you ask young folks they all have 'yes' bubbling right behind their teeth. Take you, for instance. If I say to you: 'Let's start out and go to Alaska tomorrow,' the first way you feel is that you'd sure like it a terrible lot if you could go. And you want to say yes. And it ain't no different with girls.

"They look different, but right down under their hides they're just the same as boys, only more so. Well, when she asked herself that question about Charlie Loring, the first thing she did was to say 'yes' to herself. And no sooner did she say yes than she began to think the same way that she'd been talking. It's easy to do that. Don't take much to change a man's mind. If you frown by accident, pretty soon you're beginning to feel mad all the way through. But if you make yourself smile, pretty soon you're smiling all the way through. So after she'd said yes, pretty soon she was feeling that she was in love with Loring!"

Here Ronicky interrupted with an infusion of spectacular oaths that would have done credit to a mule skinner on a mountain road.

"It was a fool question to ask herself!" he declared.

"If that was the only fool thing that girls do," said Jenkins, "it wouldn't be so bad. But I've knowed it to go on and get worse and worse. Yes, sir, I've known girls to start fooling themselves that way and never wake up out of their dream till they was gray-headed grandmothers. And then all at once they give a start and a shake like Rip van Winkle. 'Why,' says they to themselves, 'I been sleeping; I ain't been living all this!' And they wake up and get ready to live their real lives, but they find that their real lives are just about up, and by the time they find out what they've done with themselves they're ready to die."

He concluded this dark sermon with a shake of his ponderous head, leaning back in his chair until it creaked loudly.

"What difference does it make?" asked Ronicky gloomily. "If they go ahead and marry and all that, because they're sort of hypnotized, what's the real difference between hypnotism and being awake? It gives you the same results!"

"D'you think it does?" asked Al Jenkins with a singular smile. "No, lad! There was Elsie's mother before her. She hypnotized herself and married that skunk Bennett. But the real girl that I knew was never Bennett's wife. No, sir. Things ain't always what they look to be. Inside the shell they's a kernel. What she was, I know. But she wasn't the woman that the world thought she was—the whole damned world, starting right in with Bennett himself! Same way with Elsie, now. She's got a flying start to make a fool of herself. She's picked out a gent and told herself that she's crazy about him. Then along come you, Doone, and shoot him up, so that she's got a chance to get foolisher still about him. Nothing that makes a woman so in love with a man as finding him helpless on her hands. She begins by feeling proud. She winds up by feeling humble. And when she starts pitying him, it's just the same as putting a crown of glory on him. And for that, Doone, you can blame yourself."

Ronicky Doone glowered at him.

"What she does, and what she thinks," he said, "ain't anything to me. I can't control her."

"But you can start wishing," said Al Jenkins, "that you'd shoot him dead. That would have been better for Elsie Bennett."

"I dunno," said Ronicky gloomily. "Ain't he good enough?"

"Answer that for yourself," said Jenkins. "What d'you thing about Blondy?"

"I dunno what to think," said Ronicky.

Al Jenkins sat quiet and rubbed his chin with his fist. "You'll find out after a while," he said. "Oh, you'll find out!"

"What are you aiming at?" asked Ronicky sharply. "You're talking all around a circle, Jenkins."

"I'm just trying to tell you that she ain't got a wedding ring on—yet!"

CHAPTER XXI

THE LIFTED SHUTTER

Why Jenkins should have said this, and particularly why it should have been accompanied by a tremendous wink, Ronicky could not tell. But Jenkins himself seemed to be perfectly satisfied. He changed the subject abruptly, and when he left a little later, he paused at the door.

"The sheriff may be up to see you," he said, "but you can lay to it that I'll see the sheriff before he sees you, so I guess he won't take up much of your time. About the girl——"

Here he paused and studied Ronicky with narrowed eyes.

"You've started your fight," said Jenkins, "and you'll have to keep it up along the same lines. You've started by knocking down the walls around her and getting at her that way. You'll have to keep it up, son, until you've taken her by force. And as soon as you see that I'm right, I guess you'll be coming along to talk to Uncle Al Jenkins. Good-by for a while!"

He turned away but checked himself again.

"There's seven days left," he said. "I'm going to give Bennett seven days' grace to get a new foreman to take Blondy's place. And when that time's up, I'm going to start a drive that'll sweep Bennett's place as clean as the palm of your hand. Get ready to be with me before that time comes, Ronicky!"

With his final advice he left the younger man and sauntered away. Ronicky remained in his room, plunged in his sorrowful reflections and walking hastily up and down. Every now and then he paused, and whenever he paused, it was because a new picture of the face of the girl had started up before him and startled him to a stop. She was beginning to grow into his mind and become a part of him from which he could not rid himself.

In the evening, just after the rim of the sun was down, his meditations were broken in upon by a sudden hubbub in the street of the town, and Ronicky jerked up the window and leaned out to listen.

He could not hear enough to form any connected story. But he gathered by the disjointed exclamations that the good people of Twin Springs were greatly distraught because of a daring and outrageous raid which had recently been made, half a dozen outlaws having scooped up a freight wagon, loaded with all manner of supplies, and taken it away with them into the mountains toward their camp. More than this, they had ridden on down the road, leaving the driver of the wagon bound behind them, and they had come to the very outskirts of Twin Springs, where they had gathered in a large quantity of money from one of the leading citizens of Twin Springs.

Then, leaving their victims bound and gagged, they had stolen away again and were safely gone, leaving behind them no clew except the sound of their voices and the description of their masks. And Twin Springs was literally roaring with rage and excitement. Ronicky caught a little of the drift of the talk from the window of his room. When he went down stairs, eager to mix in anything that would free him from the burden of his own thoughts, he heard the details.

No one blamed the sheriff for failing to apprehend the criminals. It was simply that they had found a secure refuge among the impregnable mountains near Twin Springs. The vital question was whether or not the forces of the entire town would be able to find the robbers and rout them. Ronicky drew the soberest man he could find to one side and learned still more about the men who lived beyond the law.

On the crests of Solomon Mountain, which was really

many mountains rising to one ragged top, the gang had lived for several months now, growing in strength from time to time, as the rumor of their impregnable position spread abroad and drew in recruits of chosen skill. And as their strength of numbers and quality increased, so also did their boldness. At first they had secured their shelter by committing their depredations at a distance. And so long as they did this, the men of Twin Springs were by no means inclined to bother with the formidable little group, but since then they had begun to come nearer and nearer to the town on occasion, and now at last the blow which all had been dreading, had fallen. The Solomon Mountain gang had struck the precincts of Twin Springs itself, and now the honor of the town was pledged to run them down.

When Ronicky inquired why this was a task of such size, he was informed that Solomon Mountain was a literal labyrinth of canyons and sharp-sided gorges, running one into the other and connecting in a thousand unsuspected places by underground tunnels which were mostly natural caves. A little adroit blasting and pick-and-shovel work had opened them up and made them practicable for man and horse. Not only was this a hole-in-the-wall country, where the shrewdest sheriff in the world would be baffled with a posse of a thousand men, but it was also a place where the outlaws had laid up such provisions that they could stand seige and dis-appear into their subterranean resorts for an indefinite period. Moreover, it was possible to take advantage of the broken nature of the ground and the many outlook points so as to keep an advancing force under observa-tion and, drifting just ahead and inside the limits of safety, make life wretched for those who attempted to break through and capture the miscreants.

There were already a score of stories to be told, in spite of the fact that the headquarters on Solomon Mountain was new, of celebrated man hunters who had rushed at the stronghold and broken the teeth of their reputation on its jagged sides and gone back shorn of honor. Ronicky Doone, as he heard these things, looked up from the town to the ragged crest of the peak and then turned back to the hotel, carrying with him the interesting item that re-cruits were added to the gang simply by riding to the top of the mountain in broad daylight and waiting for what would happen to them. No matter where they paused, they would be sure to be looked over by some invisible spy, and, if they proved acceptable, they would be taken into the inner circle.

But Ronicky paid little heed to the story. His interests were too closely attached to the proprietor's room in the hotel. Here the doctor and Elsie Bennett were fighting to save the life of the man he had shot down.

He learned that Blondy, though still living, was still hardly improved. He had come out of the coma, but he had passed into the almost equally dreaded state of delirium, and now the shrill sounds of his ravings at times were clearly audible through the halls of the ramshackle building. Ronicky walked past the room on the rear veranda and paused by the two big windows which opened upon it from Blondy's quarters. And he heard the murmurings of the injured man clearly. The strong manliness had passed out of the voice. It was a whining complaint.

"What have I done that I got to stand for this? Where's old Bennett? Why ain't he standing his share? Where's the girl? Where's Elsie? Why ain't she helping—why—"

Ronicky felt his heart leap into his throat and swell there to choking. A great sense of wretchedness swept over him. With his bullet he had not only struck down a strong man, but, worse than this, he had destroyed his pride.

A cool-toned, pleasant voice broke in on the rough current of the raving: "I'm here, Charlie. I'm here, dear. There's nothing to worry about; you're only having bad dreams now. Don't you see? You're only having bad dreams now!"

He looked through the door, feeling like a miserable spy, and he saw her sitting by the bed. The lamp had been lighted, as the dusk of the evening increased. And now it was so placed that, while the man on the bed was left veiled in the darkness, a mild radiance fell upon Elsie Bennett. Her hand was on the forehead of Blondy. She was looking down to him with a smile. And at the tenderness in her voice, in her smile, Ronicky felt his pulse leap again.

What lucky star had Charlie Loring been born under? He reverted to what wise old Al Jenkins had said and shook his head. Wise Jenkins might be, but in this case he was mistaken. With all his heart and soul she loved the man she had chosen, or else Ronicky felt that there was no such thing as true and faithful love of woman for man.

He listened, with a guilty and tortured happiness in hearing her, until she rose from the bed and went to the doctor. The latter sat near the lamp with a newspaper shaken out before him, the very picture of indifferent ease. He bent his head and looked up at the girl over the rim of his glasses, still keeping his paper spread out.

"Doctor," she was saying, "is that the true man that I'm hearing talk over there? Can I believe what he's saying about himself and about other people?"

There was a rustling of the bedclothes, as Charlie Loring stirred his nervous arms.

"If I can only get it over with in a rush," he was saying in a mutter. "If I can only get at him and kill him— shoot him down before I got to stand up to them eyes of his—them clear, straight-looking eyes!"

Here the girl caught her breath in something between a sob and a gasp of horror, and the sound apparently broke into the delirious mind of the man, for his talking ceased.

"Does it mean that he was really afraid of Ronicky Doone?" asked the girl faintly. "Oh, doctor, tell me true!"

The doctor lowered his paper, cleared his throat, scratched his head. In short he had not the slightest idea what to answer.

"It might be true, and then again it mightn't," he said. "The mind turns a lot of corners from the truth in a delirium, sometimes. But then again a man will tell the naked truth."

"It can't be the truth here," sighed Elsie Bennett. "Don't you see? He's saying to face Ronicky Doone! And that would mean that he—that he had not told the truth about how he offered to fight Ronicky in the barn at our place. But he said that Ronicky was afraid—that Ronicky crawled and begged to get out of it and——"

"Miss Bennett," said the doctor, "they say that Ronicky Doone was able to face Charlie Loring fairly well today. At least he shot with a steady hand. We have evidence yonder on the bed for that."

"But that may have been shame."

"Shame?"

"Oh, don't you see? In private, with no one to see, Ronicky Doone may have shrunk from Charlie. And Ronicky Doone impressed me as a man who might. He

123

is proud—he is terribly proud. But perhaps it is only the pride that makes him want to appear brave to the crowd. He doesn't care at all what any one man thinks."

"What gave you such an insight into the character of Doone?"

"I saw him. I talked with him."

"H'm!" said the doctor in heavy disapproval.

They were speaking very softly, lest their voices should disturb the wounded man, and Ronicky listened with a strange fascination to the changing emotions so subtly expressed by the voice of the girl, fear, sorrow, horror, all in a murmur hardly louder than a whisper.

"And now this terror that keeps coming back to Charlie in his delirium—"

"Well," asked the doctor bluntly, "what if he is afraid of Ronicky Doone? I understand that a lot of men have feared that young man."

Ronicky guessed that she shivered at this.

"But that would mean—" She paused and did not complete her sentence.

Ronicky waited in a bitter suspense. Would she see the truth?

"No," she cried at length, "it isn't right. I won't believe him against himself. It was no lie that he told to us when he carried Ronicky Doone into the house. And I'll wait till he is well and able to talk for himself before I think of it again!"

"That sounds sensible," said the doctor. "That sounds mighty sensible."

With a sigh Ronicky stole back through the gathering shadows and then stepped from the veranda onto the ground. He felt a shutter had been lifted, and he had seen his future course as it must be.

CHAPTER XXII

RONICKY DECIDES

What that course must be he dared not, however, reveal to himself in a single flash of comprehension. It was too much for his mind to grasp at one stretch. There were results involved which spun out before him in a dizzy succession. He could not see exactly where they would lead him.

But step by step he went down the trail until he decided that it was time to put his thoughts into the realization of action. He went straight into the front of the hotel, found Al Jenkins, as usual, with a dense group rotating around him, and drew him to one side.

"Mr. Jenkins," he said, "you've been sort of hard on me once, but, take you all in all, you've been pretty square, Jenkins, or at least you've tried to be square, and so—"

"Wait!" said the big man.

And laying his mighty grip upon the shoulder of Ronicky he fairly swept him through the night outside, pungent with dust raised by a horse which had just pounded by at a canter.

"When a man begins like you just done," chuckled Al Jenkins, "the best thing to do is to dodge him and get him to think of something else as quick as you can. I can't get you to thinking of something else, but as least I can get you out here by ourselves. Now, Ronicky, you were getting all ready to tell me a piece of bad news. Do you have to tell me still?"

"It won't mean much to you," said Ronicky, "but what I have to say is that I've made up my mind. I thought at first that I was going to be able to get out of Twin Springs without taking any sides in the fight that was going on. But now I see that everything I do has brought me in deeper and deeper. And now I've picked my side in the fight, and I'm sorry to say that I'm against you!"

There was a grunt from Jenkins, an absurdly realistic imitation of the sound a man makes when he has received a heavy body blow.

"But", he protested, "you can't mean it, Ronicky. You're crazy about the girl."

"I never said that," said Ronicky.

"Sure you didn't," agreed Jenkins. "But I say you're wild about her. Well, if you fight on her side, you'll be fighting on the same side with Blondy Loring. And that means you'll be fighting his fight. Don't you see that now that he's down and out she's got to stay with him, and that her loyalty wouldn't let her desert Blondy for anybody else—that little fool!"

"I see all that," said Ronicky gloomily. "But the point is—I've made up my mind!"

Jenkins was silent a moment, and then he laid his hand kindly on Ronicky's shoulder.

"My boy," said he, "if you were like the main run of the young gents that I meet nowadays, I'd let you go and say nothing about it. You ain't going to make me or break me. But I'll take time out to tell you that if you buck up against me, you'd better be bucking up against a stone wall. Understand?"

"I know," admitted Ronicky. "I've imagined a good lot of things about you, Jenkins. I know you put on your gloves when you begin to work. I know that you've got all the odds on your side."

"Hang it!" exploded the rancher. "I half begin to think that that's why you're against me. You got a sneaking idea that because Bennett is the under dog you ought to help him. Is that it?"

"That hound!" said Ronicky. "I tell you straight I ain't wasting any thoughts on him."

Jenkins sighed and began to speak.

"When we meet up," he said, "remember that I'll be bound on a blood trail—if it has to be one. But no matter what I have to climb over to get to the end of it, I'm going to smash Bennett before I'm through. Is that clear? And when you and me smash together head-on, I got an idea that you'll be the one that falls. Keep all them things in mind, son, before you make up your mind for good and all. Will you?"

"Thanks," said Ronicky. "I'll have my own gloves on."

"You realize that you'll be all alone? You know that there ain't a real man on the whole Bennett place? You realize that the old man is going busted, anyway, because he's up to the ears in debt? And you realize that I've got every decent man in the country right behind me?"

"I know all that."

"Then," said Jenkins, "God help you. Good-by and good luck!"

He caught the hand of Ronicky in a great pressure, turned on his heel, and before he reached the veranda steps Ronicky heard him humming again. Then Ronicky himself started around the corner of the building. He paused a moment as he passed the spot where he had stood to confront Charlie Loring earlier that day. Where would the result of the firing of that shot some time place him?

In the shed, he saddled the bay mare and led her out. He left her near the front of the hotel, went to his room, made his pack quickly and deftly, and came down again. A moment later he was galloping through the night on the back of Lou and facing a strange future, indeed.

Knowing the lay of the land better now, he bore off to the right until he reached the road running up the valley to the Bennett place, and on this smooth going the mare made excellent time, never checked her pace until the buildings of the ranch rolled up into his view.

Ronicky dismounted at the side of the ranch house and knocked at the door.

"Come in!" called a voice which he recognized as belonging to the rancher.

He opened the door and stood in the presence of Steve Bennett. His effect was magical. It brought Bennett jumping out of his chair and placed him in a straddle-legged position in front of the fireplace, his gaunt right hand clutching at the butt of his revolver.

Whatever the other faults of the father of Elsie Bennett,

cowardice was not one of them. A fire burned up in his buried eyes, and color flared in his cheeks, while he set his teeth and stood ready to fight and kill, or be killed, for apparently he took it for granted that this must be the reason for Ronicky's coming.

But the latter kicked the door shut behind him. He dared not expose himself by turning aside for an instant from the malignant face of the other.

"Now," said Ronicky, "we can talk."

"Aye, we can. About what, though?

"About Charlie Loring."

"I know all that. But mind yourself, Doone. I got four of my men in yonder room. If I call 'em—"

"Don't lie. I know that you ain't got a man in the house except yourself."

"And what if that were the truth? I ain't as old as I look. I could give you a game that would warm up your face before you saw the finish of Steve Bennett, lad!"

Ronicky nodded, grinning a fierce appreciation. He liked the hardy fellow better than he could ever have dreamed he might like him.

"About Loring," he began saying. "I've come to tell you that Loring ain't dead yet."

"I knew that. I figure that I'd have heard Elsie wailing and crying for him if he was. And the devil knows how long he'll be lying yonder and my girl with him. There ain't a soul here to do the cooking that—"

Ronicky stopped him with a gesture and an ugly look. Such cold indifference to the welfare of his champion was more than the cow-puncher could stand. But he presently restored himself and leaned against the wall, watching the rancher closely all the time.

"Sit down," said Bennettt, "now that you're here."

"I'll stand up for a while," said Ronicky. "I like the feel of a wall behind me. It has a sort of an honest way about it."

He looked Bennett straight in the eyes as he spoke, but he relaxed his vigilance enough to start rolling a cigarette.

"First of all," said Ronicky, "you got a week to get ready in. Jenkins is giving you that much time before he comes after you."

The upper lip of Bennett lifted. Otherwise, he made no sign that he understood.

"A week is a long time," he said at length. "By that

time I'll be ready to run his dirty gang of cutthroats off the range."

"How?" asked Ronicky.

"Are you asking me to tell you? All I got to say is that I can get the men for it."

"You can't," said Ronicky. "There ain't enough fighting men in the mountains that would hire under you to fight against Al Jenkins."

A single deep-voiced curse was the reply of Bennett.

"That," said Ronicky, "is why I've come out here."

"Get finished with your chatter," said Bennett. "I hate your infernal croaking, but, if you're bound to talk, I suppose that I got to listen. Blaze away and finish up."

He lighted a cigarette of his own making and closed his eyes as he inhaled the smoke. His face at once assumed the appearance of great age and deathly thinness. Then, opening his eyes as he blew forth the smoke, he was looking out to Ronicky through a thin veil, and for the moment Ronicky caught the impression—a very ghost of an impression—of a startlingly handsome face, poetic, unusual. That was the face of the man who had married the mother of Elsie Bennett.

Had Jenkins been right? Had she wakened in her age to find out the truth concerning the man she had married? Ronicky could only hope, for her own sake and the sake of her daughter, that she had remained blind to the end.

"Well?" Bennett was urging him. "Are you going to talk? Or are you going to stand there the rest of the night like a buzzard looking at a dead cow?"

"Bennett," said Ronicky, "suppose a real man was to offer to work for you, what sort of terms would you make with him?"

"A real man?" asked Bennett, but at the suggestion a flare of fire altered his eyes.

"I mean a man that's square and a man that's not afraid to fight for himself and his boss."

Bennett threw himself back in the chair with a grim laugh.

"They don't come that way any more," he said. "When I was your age we'd all have risked our lives for the sake of one hoof of the scrawniest yearling on the boss' range. We took it for granted. He paid us to look out for his interests. But nowadays it's different. You can't get men."

"Not if you underpay 'em, underfeed 'em and treat

'em like a lot of dogs. Real men won't work for you then, that's dead sure."

"Well," snarled Bennett, anxiety and anger combining to bring his tone to a singularly piercing whine, "what's up?"

"Bennett, I'll come out here, if you can hit up the right terms with me."

Steve Bennett gasped, glared with a wild hope, and then sank back into his chair, from which he had half risen, with something between a growl and a groan.

"This is some of Al Jenkins' work," he vowed. "He's sent you out here to get a job so that you can dig the ground from under me, and when he's ready he can—"

"Stop that kind of talk," said Ronicky. "It just peeves me and it don't bring you no place in particular, Bennett."

The rancher shrugged his bony shoulders.

"I say again," said Ronicky, "I'll work on your place for you."

Bennett merely stared. Not at Ronicky's face, but in a grim effort to get at his secret mind.

"It's the girl!" he exclaimed suddenly. "She's got enough of her mother in her for that. It's Elsie that's bringing you."

He chuckled and twisted one hand inside the other, as though he were trying to warm them. And more and more the wonder grew in Ronicky that beautiful Elsie Bennett could be the daughter of this man.

"No matter what's bringing me," said Ronicky, "I'm here to hit up a bargain with you. I'll run your place until you're through with the fight with Jenkins. I'll do that, if you'll give me full swing and let me run everything. I'll do it, if you'll let me hire your men and fire 'em, just as I see fit. Does that sound good to you at all, Bennett?"

The rancher, breathing hard, stepped up from his chair and elevated his tall form by the table. He glowered at Ronicky like a famine-stricken wretch who sees food, but fears that it is poisoned.

"How would I know that you ain't from Jenkins?" he asked. "How would I know that you ain't out here to arrange so's he can scoop up the last of my cattle—the unhung robber!—and get off clean and free with it? How am I to know that?"

"I dunno," said Ronicky, "unless you read my mind. But you got no other chance, Bennett. It's up to you to do this or go under. You got no real men on your ranch. You—"

"A lot of cowards—a lot of yallarlivered—"

"Then let me fire them and get a new set."

"You can't. You can't pick up a crew in Twin Springs—not for my ranch. Jenkins, curse him, with his bought men and his bought lies—he's seen to that! He'll be singed for it! Oh, he'll burn for it."

In the strength of his malice he literally gnashed his teeth, and then he brought his attention back to Ronicky Doone. He stalked slowly forward. He laid a gaunt, cold hand upon Ronicky's shoulder.

"Ah," he said, "you got an honest face, Doone. You got an honest face, after all!"

Ronicky struck his hand away with an irresistible outbreak of disgust. For he was remembering how Bennett had stood over him on the evening when big Blondy carried him into this very room and denounced him.

"I don't want your lies," said Ronicky. "You and me might as well come out in the clear quick, Bennett. I ain't doing this to please you, none. And I ain't doing it for your money, because you ain't got none. But I want your promise to let me go straight ahead and run things. Will you do that?"

"And take a chance of getting the house burned down right from over my head, so far as I know?"

He was fairly shaken by dread and temptation combined.

"And take that chance, yes," admitted Ronicky.

It seemed that this admission that he had no proof of good faith to offer made a great impression upon the other. For his face brightened at once.

"I was always a good gambler," he said. "I've gambled on life and death. And why shouldn't I gamble on this ranch that never brought me luck?"

He turned to a cabinet, drew out a bottle, and placed two glasses upon the table.

"I ain't drinking," said Ronicky in return to the questioning glance. "I don't drink when I got hard work ahead."

"Then," said the old man, "I'll drink to myself. It'll give me heart for the chance that I'm taking."

And he poured the little glass full and tossed it off, and then he leaned back against the wall, watching Ronicky with blurred eyes of pleasure, as the alcohol burned home in him.

CHAPTER XXIII

RONICKY'S FIRST MOVE

This, then, was the father of Elsie Bennett. It made Ronicky think of some graceful and lovely orchid rooted in decay. Yet, on a day, no doubt, the mind and the body of Bennett had been far other than it now was. He must have been handsome, strong, vivacious. And such a man as that had married the mother of the girl. The betrayal of Al Jenkins, in the first place, must have begun to undermine his nature. That was the seed of poison which spread until now he was only a ghost of his old self, a ghost in very fact. The long years of failure had put their mark on him. They had made him into a vicious-minded, cruel-witted fellow, such as now leered at Ronicky.

"And now," asked the rancher, "where d'you begin?"

"With sleep," said Ronicky. "Where's a bed for me?"

The old man broke into his harsh laughter, still rubbing his hands with glee and still unable to work any warmth into the bony fingers.

"Sleep?" he asked. "Aye, that's the best place for a beginning, and that's the usual place for an ending, too! Yes, that's where they all end up. I'm close to it. But the rest will finish the same way. You—Loring—Elsie—you'll all end up in a sleep!"

This he muttered to himself, some words audible, others mere indistinct murmurs. And in the meantime he picked up the lamp and went toward the door of the room behind him, walking back into the shadows which finally rushed across it, as the rancher passed into the hall.

He climbed the stairs with Ronicky behind him, thinking sharply back to that other night when he had climbed the same stairs behind the same lamp bearer, with manacles on his wrists. At the head of the stair Bennett stepped aside, allowed him to climb to the top, and then went to the door of the room where Ronicky had been a prisoner, and, pushing it open, turned to him with an evil grin of enjoyment.

It seemed to Ronicky, as he stared into the flat wall of darkness which the lamplight failed to penetrate, that a ghost of himself must still be within, so vivid was his recollection of his waiting in the place for the morning. Now Bennett went on down the hall and took Ronicky to an end room. It was very dingy. The curtains at the window, even, seemed worn and rubbed by age. Here the rancher put the light down and bade his guest farewell for the night. But he paused again at the door still grinning. Then he shook a long forefinger at Ronicky.

"I ain't asking no more questions," he said. "You notice that, Ronicky Doone. I ain't asking what might be in your head, or what your motives could be. No, sir, all I'm doing is waiting—and waiting—waiting to see how things turn out, eh?"

Then he turned and walked off into the darkness of the hall, still muttering to himself and occasionally breaking into a chuckle, a strange and conversational effect that made the body of Ronicky lose some warmth. He harkened to the steps of the rancher going down the stairs slowly, but surely. No one would ever have dreamed that he was walking without a light, to listen to that unfumbling step.

For a time Ronicky sat on the edge of the bed, pondering on the place where he found himself, on the events which were around him, behind and before. And it was like walking in a dream, so unreal was it. When he closed his eyes for a moment he half expected that when he opened them he would find himself back on the veranda of the hotel in Twin Springs, sunning himself lazily, with only his head in the shadow, while some one announced again that Blondy Loring was coming to town.

But when he did open his eyes his glance fell upon the bureau on the far side of the room, with a silver brush upon it, and on either side of the brush was a dainty little bottle of perfume, while still farther on either side—

Suddenly Ronicky sprang up with a stifled oath. He looked around him again. He noted the bright color of the curtain, no matter how faded from the original. He glanced down to the flowered rug beside the bed. He turned to the bed itself and the stainless white of the spread which covered it.

"Lord above," said Ronicky, "he's given me her room!"

And all at once he felt like rushing out into the hall and shouting curses down at the old man and demanding a different place. But what difference did it make? And, after all, perhaps there was no other place for him to sleep in the house on that particular night. Besides, why should he feel like an eavesdropper, an interloper, because he was in the room?

Nevertheless, he did feel that way. Something pressed on his mind from every side. It was shouting out at him now—something of which he had been totally unaware when he first came into the apartment. There were photographs on the wall, photographs of young men and girls. And there was a chest of some dark wood under the window, and upon it lay a dress of dull red. It was her room. A faint perfume had been unnoticeable before. Now it drifted to him clearly. It was like sight of her face, sound of her voice. It brought her bodily within the walls.

Ronicky sat down again gingerly on the bed. How completely the sense of her had wiped out the rest of the world! And when he slept that night she still was walking and talking in his dreams.

In the morning he wakened with the knowledge that only six days remained in which he was to build up the power to foil big Al Jenkins. Six days to meet and counterbalance a strength which had been slowly accumulating for the past years in Twin Springs, nourished by the wealth and by the personality of the rancher. And yet Ronicky Doone, glancing out of the window at the red sky of the dawn, merely tugged his belt tight and shrugged his shoulders.

He was whistling when he went down to breakfast and looked over the cow-punchers who came into the dining room. They were an odd lot and a bad lot. Four sad-faced, underfed, ragged men as ever he had seen, ate their meal in the midst of complete gloom. They were nameless hobos of the range, poor, broken-spirited men who had failed in every other place and had at last drifted to this last resort, knowing perfectly well that they could remain here only because there were no others to replace them.

But what most interested Ronicky was the figure of old Bennett sitting at the head of the table, with a grand manner. He was amiable, smooth-tongued, courteous to these wrecks who worked as cow-punchers on his ranch, selling him out at every turn, as all knew, to Al Jenkins. Ronicky had expected to see fire poured every moment upon the punchers. But he gradually came to the solution of the problem. Only with such as these was Steve Bennett able to act in the grand manner. And therefore he was making the most of the opportunity. Only one voice was heard—the voice of Bennett narrating, and then the polite chuckles and the nods and the grins and sympathetic exclamations, as those rags of humanity jibed in with the master of the pay roll, applauding exactly where applause was expected and needed.

Ronicky watched them in increasing disgust. After breakfast he was drawn to one side by old Bennett.

"Are you going to fire them now?" he asked eagerly. "Are you going to run 'em all off this morning?"

His eagerness was horrible to Ronicky. Here the rancher had been playing the part of the amiable host the one moment, and the next he was ready to knife his late guests.

"Let 'em stay," said Ronicky. "Let 'em be where they are. They can do the work, or not do it, for the next six days. End of that time I hope that I'll be coming back with some way of helping out."

"You're leaving now?" asked Bennett sharply.

"D'you think I'm enough, all by myself, to stop Jenkins and his gang?" asked Ronicky scornfully.

The other nodded and drew back, and from that moment until the time Ronicky left the house the rancher watched him with ratty eyes of suspicion. Up to that moment, perhaps, he had been hoping against hope that Ronicky actually intended to help him. But now he was sure that it was only a bluff.

And Ronicky gladly heard the door slam behind him

as he went out to Lou. He saddled the bay mare at once and rode her out from the barn and onto the road, or rather the wagon trail, which led up the valley toward the ranch. Then, after surveying the landscape carelessly, he picked out as his goal no less a target than the ragged summits of Mount Solomon, and toward this he directed Lou in all her eagerness of morning freshness.

CHAPTER XXIV

CURLY'S CAPTURE

The way wound off from the main floor of the valley after a time, and he headed into a narrow gorge forested closely on either side and with only an open runway of a dozen feet in the center, worn there by the sudden floods which tore down the side of the mountain during the heavy rains. Here the trees closed in on either hand, their branches intertwining across the blue sky above him. He rode under a continually changing pattern too busy with the irregularities of the ground underfoot, however, to pay much heed to what was above him or on either side. And that was the reason, perhaps, that he encountered the danger which almost immediately befell him.

It came unheralded. There was only a faint whisper in the air behind him, such a hissing as a branch makes when it sways through the wind. Yet that noise was sufficient to make Ronicky Doone whirl in his saddle. He was in time to see the open noose of rope hovering above his head, and at the far end of the noose was a man just on the verge of starting out from the edge of the trees, from the shelter of which he had made his cast.

Ronicky saw him in the flash of time that it took him to whirl. But the next moment the rope had whipped down, and his arms were pinned to his sides. His right hand, the fingers of which were just in the act of curling around the butt of his revolver, was paralyzed at the root of its strength. And at the same moment the forward swing of Lou, checked too late by the shout of Ronicky, snapped the rope taut, and Ronicky was lifted from the saddle as cleanly as in the days of old an expert spearsman hurled his foeman over the croup in full career.

It might have broken his neck, that fall. But he unstrung his limbs in mid-air, so to speak, relaxing himself so that every muscle was soft. And he landed on that cushioning of muscle which is the natural pad against shocks at the back of the neck. The impetus of that rolling fall swung him onto his feet again, but still he was helpless.

In the air before him and above him the rope became a living thing. It twisted and writhed and coiled, and every twist was a new bond laid about the struggling form of Ronicky Doone. In five seconds he was trussed securely and sat helpless on the ground, looking up into the face of his captor.

That captor was no other than the celebrated Ananias of Twin Springs, Curly. The usual calm of Curly was gone. The mist of thoughtfulness was gone from his eyes, which sparkled with joy. And he stood with his hands planted on his hips, the fingers of one hand still gripping the end of the rope which he had used with such dexterity.

Both he and his captive were panting from the brief struggle.

"You!" said Ronicky, disgusted beyond measure that the victor should prove this man of all men—this creator of myths.

"Me!" said the other.

"This is the second time," said Ronicky. "I sure got to write you down in my books, Curly. First you tell me the lie about Blondy. And now you—"

Rage choked him.

But the attitude of Curly was one of conscious and easy virtue.

"I done this to make up for the other," he said.

"What?" cried Ronicky.

"Sure," said Curly. "I make it a rule never to have no fallings out with no gun fighters. When I seen how you just wished your gat out of the leather and pumped that slug into Blondy before I could have thought about

138

shooting, I said to myself right there that you were a gent that I'd never have no trouble with if I could help it!"

Ronicky stared at him, helpless with amazement.

"I don't foller you," he gasped. "I sure don't function fast enough for my brain to keep up with you, Curly! Here you—"

He stopped again. Lou came back to him anxiously and snuffed at his dust covered shoulder. And he directed her to stand back with a savage jerk of his head. She obeyed, while Curly swore with admiration at her trained docility.

"I never seen her equal!" he declared.

"They don't grow hosses as fine as that in these parts! But to come back to you and me, Ronicky. Can I trust you if I take that rope off of you?"

"Would you trust me if I gave you my word?" asked Ronicky, very curious.

"Sure," answered Curly cheerfully. "I'd trust you to the end of the earth if you just gave me the word to!"

"H'm," said Ronicky, some of his original fury leaving him. "And how do you work this out, Curly? I ain't going to give you my word, so you can leave the rope around me. But how do you work it out that roping me and jerking me off my hoss was doing me a favor? Leaving out that there was nine chances out of ten that you'd break my neck, how do you work it out?"

"Nine chances out of ten with some folks," admitted Curly. "But not with you. I could tell after watching you take two steps that there was no more chance of throwing you on your head than there would be of throwing a cat. You'd twist around and manage to land right."

"H'm," said Ronicky again, and still he studied big Curly intently. "Go on," he said. "Al Jenkins sent you out to get me out of the way, I guess?"

"He didn't," said the surprising fellow. "He told me to keep away from you less'n I wanted to get hurt, and hurt bad." He added: "The plan is for Al and his men to get together in a flock and herd you into a corner, and then make you give up by force of numbers."

"Get me to take water, eh?" asked Ronicky.

"Which simply means," said Curly, "that they had figured on wiping you off the face of the earth and putting up a stone to show where you made your last appearance, as they say about the lady singer. But I

139

took to thinking things over, Ronicky. I seen as how if there was a crowd, I'd have to be in it. And if there was any shooting at you, you'd be doing some shooting back. And if you done some shooting back, you'd pick out somebody you wasn't partial to for a target. And if you done that, I'd stand a pretty good show of getting into the center of the stage, you see?"

"I see," said Ronicky.

"So what I thought would be better," said Curly, "was for me to go out where you and me could have our little party all over by ourselves. When I heard that you'd gone out to old Bennett's, I climbed on my hoss about daybreak and sloped out here and got onto the top of a hill—you see that round topped feller over yonder—so's I could get a good look at the Bennett house. I had my glasses here along with me, and when you come out, I clamped these glasses onto the house and made out quick that it was you. Then I waited until I seen you going down the valley. That made me lose hope for a while. I thought you were aiming at Twin Springs again. But pretty soon I seen you head in for the gulley.

"I slid over here ahead of you and just got planted comfortable when you come by, and here you are!"

He stopped with a grin of satisfaction.

"All right," said Ronicky. "I suppose you start herding me back for Twin Springs now? It'll make you pretty much of a big gun, Curly, to go down the street with me marching in front, and you with a gat on me from behind!"

Curly merely shook his head.

"You don't get the way I'm drifting," he said. "Suppose I was to do that! Why, the minute you got loose of me you'd be a whooping for my insides!"

"I didn't mean Twin Springs. I mean Al Jenkins' headquarters."

"That wouldn't do, neither. Al ain't a murderer, Ronicky. No, sir. What I'm doing is looking out for my own hide. I'm going to run this little game all my own way, and you won't be able to guess how until you see my cards!"

He concluded by asking Ronicky to rise; and, having disarmed his captive, he mounted his horse, retaining one end of the rope, and allowed the bay mare to follow as she would, knowing that she would not leave her master. Straight down the gulley they proceeded for a short distance, and then turned, at Curly's suggestion, up a side path.

Never in his life had Ronicky been placed in so humiliating a position. Driven like a bull on a rope, with the driver, goading him from behind, he fairly trembled with desire to turn and fling himself at Curly.

But the latter dissuaded him by a comment which he made almost as soon as that shameful journey began.

"I'm praying for two things, Ronicky," he said. "The first is that you don't try to side-step into one of them bushes alongside the road, because if you did, I'd have to start in shooting. The second is that nobody goes by and sees me this way and you that way. Because if they did, I'd know that it meant the same thing. I'd have to kill you, or else you'd kill me when you got loose."

"And do you think that it makes any difference?" asked Ronicky, black with rage. "D'you think that I'll go around spreading good news about you anyway, Curly?"

"Wait and see," said Curly. "Wait and see!"

After a time they turned out from the path, plunged through the forest for three hundred yards, and then came suddenly into view of a little clearing and a small cabin in the midst of it.

"Here we are," said Curly. "Here's home!"

He explained casually, while he put up the horses and consigned Ronicky to a comfortable place in the house. He had found the cabin during one of his rides in the vicinity of Twin Springs, a ride that started in a drunken condition and led him by unknown routes until he arrived, out of the midst of the forest, upon this shack. There he slept, and when he wakened in the morning he took note of the place. The shack itself was then a mere wreck of a place, but he had been fond of it simply because it was unknown to any other man. Five or six years before, some one had started the clearing and built the home, but the undertaking had been quickly abandoned, and now the place was forgotten by the rest of the world. But Curly had been enchanted by the very secrecy of this uncharted home. He spent his spare time from that moment in making expeditions to the shack and bringing it slowly to a state of repair.

"So that if I ever fell foul of the law," he explained to Ronicky now, "I could just simply fade out and nobody would ever find me again."

With that introduction they settled down in the house.

CHAPTER XXV

WATCHFUL WAITING

It had been fitted up comfortably enough, and Ronicky could have looked forward without dread to a stay of a few days in the cabin had it not been that the time was wearing on and that he was needed to help in the fight against Al Jenkins for the sake of Elsie Bennett. The purpose of Curly became apparent almost at once. Curly would win the undying gratitude of Al Jenkins by removing from the scene of battle the chief man among the enemy, until the ruin of Bennett had been accomplished. Then he could turn Ronicky loose.

"And when I turn you loose," said Curly, "you may be tolerable mad, but you ain't going to be raving to kill, because you'll have lived here with me for quite a spell before that happens, and a gent like you, that ain't plumb unreasonable, can't hang out with another gent like me, that ain't plumb poisonous, without getting to sort of see that he ain't all bad. You'll be sort of used to me before I turn you loose, Ronicky. All I got to do in the meantime is to see that you don't turn a trick on me and take me by surprise."

Ronicky made no answer. In his heart of hearts he felt that what he wanted to do most in all the world was to have this man under the cover of his gun and make him beg for mercy. But again he told himself that he must resign himself to patience, for surely the time would quickly come when he could free himself from his bonds. He might burn them in two. He might find an opportunity to get a knife edge against them and shear them apart. Any of these opportunities was most likely to come his way before he had been twenty-four hours in the house.

But twenty-four hours dragged themselves along, and still no chance had been shown to him. He had reckoned without his host. Several times he had a few minutes to himself when Curly was outside tending to the horses in the little shed, but, before he could accomplish anything of importance, Curly was always back in the one room of the shack. And neither knife nor fire was ever exposed.

In the meantime Ronicky's hands were kept behind his back, saving for a few moments every day when he was allowed to exercise the stiffening muscles. And each day was an eternity to Ronicky. The first, the second, the third sunset followed. Finally he knew that within twenty-four hours Al Jenkins would loose his men against poor Bennett, and there would be an end of the war. His ranch swept clean of cattle, Bennett would be the victim of the first of his creditors who chose to foreclose upon him. And that meant dire poverty for Elsie Bennett.

More than this, it meant that his own promise to the rancher was going for nothing. It meant that all his force was being bottled and made useless by Curly, the shift-less, careless, good-natured liar. He writhed in an agony of humiliation and rage when he thought of this.

But though he hounded himself with savage energy all the day, striving to come to some sort of solution of the problem, he could find none. And so the morning as last dawned above him, and he was twenty-four hours from the finish still held fast in Curly's grasp.

Curly himself had not yet wakened. He lay sleeping, heavily snoring. Indeed, it was this snoring which had wakened Ronicky before his usual hour. He hunched himself up awkwardly, bracing his shoulders against the wall and taking no care to keep from waking the sleeper. What difference did it make? The more trouble he could inflict upon Curly the better, for he was beginning to realize that, in spite of all his early vows of undying vengeance, Curly had been right. Their life together had made Ronicky so familiar with the jovial, carefree fellow that he could not hate him.

He looked across the room, in this dull morning light, and saw Curly prone on his back in his blankets. His mouth was open and his features were relaxed in utter sleep. It suddenly came to Ronicky that this was by no means the face which he was accustomed to associating with the voice of Curly. The eyes were surrounded by great hollows; the checks were somewhat fallen; there were lines about the mouth. Altogether it was a face expressing great exhaustion.

And another thing occurred to Ronicky as strange. What he had first noticed during his captivity was that his captor never slept soundly. The least stir on Ronicky's part had always been sufficient to open the eyes of Curly. At first Ronicky had taken it for granted that Curly was simply a marvelously light sleeper by nature. But now, as he stared at the worn face of the cow-puncher, another explanation was suggested to him—that it was only by the immense effort of his will that Curley had been able to keep guard during his sleep. He had filled his mind so full of the determination to watch Ronicky that there was a subconscious mind forever on guard and warning him the instant that Ronicky made a move, day or night.

This was the meaning, also, of the great quantities of coffee which Curly had been drinking. In every possible manner he had been filing his nerves to the point of highest sensibility. But gradually his strength had been giving way, and though for five days he had been strung on a hair trigger, now he had given way and was sleeping like one stunned by a blow.

All of this Ronicky noted without at first taking any comfort to himself. But, as he worked himself to his sitting posture and then continued by climbing to his feet, he was given a thrill of sudden hope by the sight of the eyes of the sleeper, still closed. He took a step. The floor creaked heavily beneath him. And still the snoring of the other continued uninterrupted.

What this liberty of the moment could gain for him he could not tell. There was no manner of escaping from the cabin. The window was too small for him to work his way through it. The door was heavily bolted and locked, and there was no way for him to get the key unless he could reach under the shoulders of the sleeper who slept upon the guns and the key.

Nothing in the cabin showed any sign of life. There was nothing to catch the light of the increasing day except the chimney of the lantern. But even this gave Ronicky his first hope, combined as the sight of it was, with the heavy sleep of Curly. ·

He went to the side of the cabin. On a small shelf there was a bunch of sulphur matches. He worked off one of the matches with his teeth. Then, using his teeth again, he lifted the lantern from its peg to the floor. He knelt with his back to it, and by careful manipulation he managed to work off the chimney. Once the glass squeaked against one of the guards, but the sleeper still slept.

Then he crouched still more, picked up the matches, and went across the room to the stove. He turned his back to it and strove to scratch a match. But the process, which was so simple when he had a free hand, now proved strangely difficult. He could give no easy, smooth flexion of hand and wrist to make the match travel swiftly over a surface and by the friction ignite the head. The match broke under his hand, and he had to cross the room and work off another match with his teeth.

He returned to the stove. The surface of this was at once smooth and rough enough to give him a promise of igniting the match. Finally it succeeded. The flame spurted, and Ronicky hurried back toward the lantern. But his haste set up a current of air in which the match went out.

Again he returned and repeated the performance; an agony of suspense was growing in him every moment. For now the light of the day was increasing rapidly, and at any moment that light might pry open the eyes of the sleeper.

This time he succeeded in igniting the wick of the lantern. No sooner did the flame rise from it than he knelt again and thrust into the fire the stout rope which bound his wrists together.

It was no easy task. He swung his wrists as far as he could to one side and then twisted his head until his neck threatened to break. But still it was hard to keep the rope accurately above the flame. And when at last it did remain long enough in the flame to begin to burn, there was an immediate complication.

For it sent up a strong, pungent smoke, and Ronicky

glanced in alarm at big Curly. It was utterly impossible that he should continue to sleep very much longer in an atmosphere such as this was now becoming.

And to give point to his dread, Curly coughed heavily, raised himself upon his elbow, and then turned and began snoring again!

Ronicky, warned back to his work by the sear of the flame against his wrist, as he watched Curly, thrust the rope into the fire once more, and now he heard a light crackling. For the fire was eating into the heart of the stout rope, and the strands were parting, one by one, though there was still strength enough in what remained to have held a horse.

There was still another complication. Not only did the fire eat straight up through the rope, but it began, as well, to spread sidewise and it threatened to eat into his flesh, also, in a very few seconds.

He could only wait, with the perspiration pouring out on his forehead. Presently more strands of the rope parted with a light snap, but at the same time the volume of the smoke increased, and there was a sneeze from the bunk where Curly was sleeping. Ronicky dared not look. He twisted his head still farther, turned still more, and peered at the burning rope. The fire was edging to his skin, and though the central part of the rope between his wrists was a glowing, blackening mass, he could not tell whether or not the fire had reached the heart of the rope.

In the meantime there was a creaking of the bunk, and Ronicky turned his head in time to see the hands of Curly raised toward his face, where he was slowly rubbing his eyes. Was the cow-puncher about to waken? Or was this simply a motion in his sleep? Or would the rubbing work some of the stinging smoke from the rope into his eyes?

Slowly Curly sat up on the bunk, turned, and directed his dull, sleep-hazy eyes toward Ronicky. At the same time, while he frowned, unable to comprehend, the fire touched both the wrists of Ronicky, and he jumped to his feet, unable to restrain the start under the spur of that pain.

"Hell!" cried Curly, and reached for his gun.

At the same instant, under the tug of his tightened muscles, the ropes which bound the wrists of Ronicky parted. He was free to fight!

CHAPTER XXVI

FREE AND AWAY

No, it was only a false sense and promise of freedom, for, as Curly reached for the gun, and Ronicky leaped forward, his arms swung at his sides, dead weights. The binds had been on them so long that, for the time at least, the blood flowed too sluggishly in them. They were paralyzed.

He changed his mind and his purpose as he lurched forward. He had intended to lash out with his fists. But that would never do. He would not have been able to hit the mark, and if he did he would have no force. Instead of striking with his fist he used his whole body as a projectile. He sprang from the floor and, hurling himself forward, swung in mid-air a little to one side, presenting a hard shoulder with all of his driving weight behind it. And with this he crashed into the body of Curly, half raised from the bunk and half turned to reach for his gun.

The big man was driven with a crash against the side of the shack. Such was the force that the board on which they struck bulged out. Ronicky struck for the head of the other, but his hand was limp and helpless!

With a groan of rage he sprang back, just as Curly, the

gun having slipped from his grip in the surprise of that attack, turned with a bellow of rage and fear and determination to grapple with his far slighter opponent.

By a scant inch Ronicky evaded that grip. And Curly, following his lunge blindly, tumbled off the bunk and rolled on the floor. He struck the legs of Ronicky. Down they went. Down they went together, and Curly, with a single turn, was on top, pinioning the body of Ronicky against the floor with his great bulk.

So suddenly awakened from sleep, no doubt his mind was not yet half recovered. He was still in a dream, a nightmare. And the yell with which Curly realized his position of advantage and prepared to take advantage of it had no human quality in it. It was simply a brute roar of fury.

His fists were heavy and strong enough, but they were not the weapons he had in mind. He reached, instead, for the last billet of firewood which he had cut the night before and which was now beside the stove. This he gripped, heaved up and prepared to strike. The blow would have dashed out the brains of Ronicky.

He had no power to interpose. Blood was coursing tinglingly through his arms again, as he fought, but still their old strength had not returned. But he struck up, and the red-hot fuming rope end which was attached to his wrist jabbed into the face of Curly. At once there was a shriek of pain. Again Ronicky struck with that red-hot weapon, and a shower of sparks was thrown off, as it ground into the flesh of Curly's face.

Dropping the billet of wood, he reeled back to his feet with a scream of horror and pain. For the moment he was blinded. That moment sufficed Ronicky to regain his own feet and tear the rope ends from his scorched wrists. Now, free at last from all bondage and with the power returned to his arms, he could face the other with his full strength.

But Curly was no longer a mere man; he was a huge maniac. His sleep-deadened mind had been startled into wakefulness. Then in a moment he had been struck by pain and fear, and for the moment at least his reason was unhinged. His blackened face contorted with his fury and he made straight at Ronicky, his great hands outstretched. Ronicky dived under those reaching arms and struck into the body and up to the face of the monster, with all his might.

It was like striking a falling wall. Curly still came on. Ronicky dodged and struck again. This time Curly was staggered, for the blow had caught him squarely on the point of the chin, but one shake of his head drove the haze away from his mind, and the next instant his grip was on Ronicky's shirt.

Ronicky whirled in terror. The cloth parted and ripped away in the fingers of Curly. Ronicky was free, but he found himself cornered. There was no chance to dodge. Straight at him came Curly, shouting wildly in exultation and fury. Ronicky dropped to his knees, hoping that the rush would carry the big man straight over him and stun him against the wall. At the same time his right hand closed on cold metal, and he jerked the fallen revolver from beneath the bunk.

His first hope was only partially true. Curly crashed against the wall, but he was not stunned. The next instant his weight dropped upon Ronicky, pinning the latter to the floor. In two seconds of fierce struggling Ronicky was flattened, and a great hand was tearing for a grip at his throat.

And even then he did not use the muzzle of the gun. But, reversing his hold to the barrel, he smashed the heavy, steel-bound butt of the weapon into the face of his foe. He saw a crimson stain start across the forehead of Curly, and then the whole bulk of the other became a limp burden from which he easily rolled.

Ronicky looked down at the sprawling, senseless figure in alarm. It seemed impossible that one blow should have robbed the big frame of its strength. Then, alarmed by the red stream which was trickling down the face of the injured man, he knelt and listened to the breast. The heart beat strong and steadily, though slow, and Ronicky knew that it was only the stunned condition of a moment from which Curly would recover in five minutes. There was no need of staying to help him.

It was better to leave before he recovered, and so avoid the necessity of either binding the big fellow or else continuing the battle. He reached for the key beneath the blankets on the bunk, found it almost at once, and then hurried for the door.

Once outside he lost no time. Lou was hastily saddled, and then, swinging into the stirrups, he started across the clearing. He had not passed over half the distance when he heard a sort of strangled shout behind him and he saw Curly coming in pursuit.

Never in his life had Ronicky seen so terrible a figure. The face was blackened by the charred rope end, and yet it was covered with crimson from the blow with the revolver's butt. His features were convulsed by the frenzy of rage and pain—surely a temporary madness—and his great arms were outflung.

Even Loring himself might well have turned and fled at the sight of this raging demon temporarily clad in human flesh. And Ronicky blessed the speed of Lou and clapped her on the flank.

Her answer was a gallop that sent him rushing among the trees, while the wild shouting of Curly died away in the distance behind them. In a few minutes more Ronicky Doone was safe and free again on the trail up the narrow gorge which led toward the ragged crests of Solomon Mountain.

He was free, and his work lay clear before him. But there was one great difference; whereas he had had six whole days in which to accomplish his ends before, he now had a mere twenty-four hours. And there was the pain in his blackened wrists to tell him what manner of men he had to match and beat in that space of time. Perhaps it was the bulldog in him, rather than the reasoning man, that made him simply thrust out his jaw and urge Lou on up the trail to the mountain.

CHAPTER XXVII

THE MAN WITH THE MUSTACHES

He had never had a very definite plan. With the greater part of a week before him, he had felt that no finely drawn plan was needed. But he must first of all learn the all-important fact: was Blondy Loring still alive, or was he dead from the effects of the wound? Was he, Ronicky Doone, a murderer—no matter under what mitigating circumstances—or was he merely a man who had struck down another while rightfully defending himself from violence?

But this news he could learn, no doubt, as well at the top of Solomon Mountain as in Twin Springs itself. So he kept steadily on his way.

It was the bright, hot middle of the morning before Lou came to a sweating halt on the first thing which approached level land at the crest, and Ronicky looked about him with interest. He had heard often of this mountaintop, but it was the first time he had ever seen Solomon Mountain.

It was a rather small, very high plateau, so far as he could make out. Some great outcropping of the rock-fold had thrust up a great prominence here. The top of that table-land had been scored and worn away, not in the symmetrical shape of a single top, but in a hundred small summits, carved in a fantastic manner, with a hundred different patterns drawn freely out of the brain of the carver. Twisting passages ran in every direction. On either hand he could choose half a dozen different courses to run in any way he wished to travel. No wonder, he thought to himself, that men living beyond the law had chosen to live here. For here they could not be cornered by a thousand men. It would take more than that to watch the exits.

Ronicky continued down the first passage that opened before him, shivering a little as he looked around him. The sides went sheer up on either hand to ragged edges above him. Five hundred men could be in hiding among the rocks, within a radius of a hundred feet, and while they watched his every movement, he could not see a thing. A child could have destroyed the greatest giant that ever walked through the pages of fable, in such a place as this pass. It had only to topple a rock loose somewhere above and let it bound down toward the enemy. If the rock missed its mark, it mattered not, for it would also knock loose in its course half a dozen other stones which projected from the slope, and these would volley down with it to crush the stranger.

Here the way widened out into a perfect little amphitheater, with a hundred exits from the pit. Pausing in the very center of the place Ronicky looked around him in amazement; for it was like a gigantic trap, contrived with the labor of a myriad men and during countless years. Suppose that an attacking party should pour into this place, hurrying as they saw the opening before them— they would be lost, condemned to massacre. Ringing those summits in any direction, a few expert marksmen, lying in perfect security for themselves, could demolish hundreds in a few seconds. Or if they tired of bullets and wished to make a quick destruction, there were the rocks here, as everywhere, masses upon masses of rocks which only needed that one be pried loose at the top of a slope in order to send a vast volley of them thundering to the bottom.

So rapped in interest was he by the natural features of the fortifications, that Ronicky Doone allowed himself to be easily surprised by a horseman who wandered into the amphitheater from behind. When Ronicky turned his head he saw a cow-puncher sitting at ease in the saddle, twisted sideways, with one foot out of the stirrup and one hand combing his long mustaches.

Ronicky looked at him with surprise. He was like a man out of a book. This was one of those formidable-appearing punchers who are described so often in books, but whom Ronicky had never seen before in real life.

"How are you, partner?" exclaimed Ronicky.

"Hello," said the other.

"You sure must have velvet on your hoss," said Ronicky.

"Oh, I dunno. You was so darned set on seeing everything in here that I guess you didn't listen particular careful. Wasn't that it?"

"Maybe. I sure can hear him now, plenty loud."

For, as the cow pony on which the other was mounted took a few steps into the arena, each footfall beat up long echoes, riding the overlooking slopes.

"Well," said the stranger, "I dunno what you think about it, but I figure that *I* was sent up hear on a wild-goose chase!"

"You were?" asked Ronicky.

"Yes, sir. I was told that up here the mountain was just plain climbing with outlaws and man-eaters."

"Did you come up hunting 'em?" asked Ronicky, amused.

The other chuckled and nodded. His voice and manner by no means bore out his formidable mustaches. The one was as soft as a child's, and the other was perfectly calm and gentle.

"Anyways," he said, "if I *did* come up here hunting for 'em, it don't seem no ways likely that I'll find none—unless you're one of 'em?"

And here he looked sharply at Ronicky, though with a smile still lingering in the corners of his eyes, as though he were willing to laugh heartily at his own suggestion, as soon as Ronicky gave him the clew.

"Well," said Ronicky, "you can't never tell. I might be. Just my saying no wouldn't prove nothing, I guess."

"I dunno," replied the other, combing his mustaches gravely. "All them that I've ever knowed always get tolerable hot under the collar when they're accused of being crooks."

"That," said Ronicky, "is because most of the stick-up gents and yeggs that you meet wandering around these parts are a ratty low gang. But I guess you're new around here, eh?"

"I'm new, all right," said the other. "I just come in from away out Denver way. I don't just exactly fit in, I find. So I ain't breaking my heart trying to find a job. I'm just spending a little time and money and trying to get used to new ways."

"You've made a long jump," said Ronicky, "all the way from Denver to here!"

"I'm used to long jumps," said the other, and a slight cloud crossed his forehead. "But go on. You was about to tell me that them that hang out up here are not the same lot of yeggs that wander around most places?"

"Sure they ain't," said Ronicky. "Want me to tell you why?"

"Go ahead."

"Well, it's a long ways to the top of this mountain, ain't it?"

"Tolerable long."

"And it takes a lot of muscle and patience to make the trip, don't it?"

"Reasonable much."

"Well, partner, all the yaller-livered crooks I've ever knowed hate work; and all the downright smart ones know that they got to work, for what they get, just the same as them that are living inside of the law. And all these gents that make headquarters on the top of old Mount Solomon—you can lay to it that they're a uppish crew!"

"If it takes work either way," said the man of the whiskers, "why don't they stay where they won't have to climb so far? Why don't they just remain down below and work like the rest of us?"

"Because they like the taking of a chance," said Ronicky. "Speaking personal, I don't give much for a gent that won't take a chance once in a while. And these boys up here—well, they just nacherally figure it out that they can do better by taking this sort of a chance than they can by staying below and playing the game like the rest of us do."

"H'm," said the other, and he scratched his chin.

"You talk pretty convincing," he chuckled after a moment. "You make it look so dog-gone different from what I was thinking that I'm half minded to try to find some of them gents and ask how about joining up with

154

'em. I wonder how it would be best to go about that, eh?"

"Why," said Ronicky carelessly, "you wouldn't have to look at all."

The other started.

"What?" he asked.

"Sure you wouldn't," said Ronicky. "Why, these men up here are pretty wise, ain't they? They want new men all the time, don't they? Well, you can lay to it that when a man rides up to the top of Solomon Mountain, he gets a pretty good looking-over!"

"H'm," said the other. "You don't say! You sure talk familiar. Maybe you've had a pal that joined up?"

"No, I'm just using common sense."

"Maybe you think that you and me are being spied on?"

"Maybe."

"They're sizing us up from behind one of them rocks, maybe?"

"Nope, they wouldn't do that. All the looking in the world don't help as much for sizing up a gent as it does to have a couple of words with him and see how he talks. No, sir!"

"What would they do then?"

"Oh, when a man comes up to the top of the mountain, most like they'd send out a man to see him."

"You don't say! Just walk a man right out and let him start in talking to you?"

"No, they'd probably put him onto a hoss and let him ride out."

"What would he say?"

"Oh, they's a big enough pile of things that he could say, partner. Just anything to start up the conversation. But of course they'd have to pretend to be plumb innocent. Just happened to be riding up on the top of the mountain, you see?"

"Like me, say, or you?"

"That's right," said Ronicky. "And to ease the conversation along he'd probably say that he come from some place a long ways off—Denver, maybe."

The other laughed, but his eye was sober.

"Well," asked Ronicky suddenly, "what have you decided about me, partner? Will I do for a try?"

CHAPTER XXVIII

SOLOMON MOUNTAIN MEN

While he was not at all sure, Ronicky took the chance and faced it out with the most perfect assurance. The wink which he gave the stranger was a marvel of confidence exchanged. It invited a confession better than spoken words. But the man of the long mustaches regarded him with a dull and wondering eye.

"I dunno what you're talking about," he said.

"All right," answered Ronicky. "If you feel that way about it, of course I ain't the man to bother you none. Let's talk about something else—Denver, say."

The other said nothing, but he continued to regard Ronicky with eyes which were so steady that they would have been impertinent had they not been so misted over with unconcern.

"Denver?" he asked. "Why, sure. I'm always glad to talk about Denver. Know any other folks from Denver?"

"Plenty," said Ronicky.

"Let's hear. Maybe we got some mutual friends."

"Maybe we have. There was 'Pete the Blacksmith.' Did you know him?"

"Didn't hang out with the blacksmiths much."

"He got his name from the way he could handle a drill," said Ronicky, staring closely at the other.

"I ain't a miner either," said he of the mustaches.

"There was 'Lefty Joe', too," said Ronicky. "I think you must have heard of him."

He was inventing names as well as he could, such names as yeggs might have, the one with the other. But still the man of the mustaches shook his head.

"Never knowed a Lefty Joe in Denver," he said.

"Well," said Ronicky, determined to make one desperate rally and beat down the reserve of the other, "you ought to have knowed him. He's a first-class inside man. I've seen him do everything from the making of soup to the making of the mold and the running of the soup in it."

He of the mustaches stopped combing them for a moment.

"Look here," said Ronicky, "I ain't a fool. Loosen up and talk. What's your monica?"

And like light from a great distance, a smile began to spread over the hardy features of the other. It increased finally to a rather sad-faced grin which was apparently the nearest approach to mirth of which the man was capable. A pressure of his knees brought his cow pony close to Lou. He stretched out his hand.

"Put it there," he said. "I thought at first you were four-flushing. But I see you ain't. I'm 'Montana Charlie.' Maybe we've met up before some place I disremember, or was I so bad that you just read right through me?"

"Bad actor?" asked Ronicky, eager to make sure that the pride of his new companion should not be injured. "I should say not. Matter of fact you were so smooth, Charlie, that I began to think that I was all wrong about you. But I *have* seen you somewhere. I disremember where. Were you working with 'Mississippi Fatty' three years back?"

"Nope, because three years back I was playing a lone hand and doing pretty well with it, at that. This here is the first time that I've ever throwed in with a gang. But I got sort of lonesome and decided that I needed a change. So that's why I'm down here with the boys on Solomon Mountain. What do you think of it?"

"Slick as grass," said Ronicky. "Of course I've heard about it a pile. But this is my first trip up, and it sure looks better than anything that they've said about it, and that means a lot. Eh?"

"Yep, that means a lot. We been breaking the heart of

one sheriff a month, on the average, ever since we got together here. But what's your name, partner?"

Ronicky Doone reflected swiftly. Should he give them his true name? That name was too clearly known by this time as that of a cow-puncher. Ronicky Doone was no name by which a lawbreaker would travel. On the other hand it was possible that some one might have seen him in Twin Springs. In that case he would be known. He summed up the chances. It was very possible that to assume a new name would be fatal. If they had seen him and known him in Twin Springs, then the fact that he had changed his name would be heavy evidence against him. But if he did not assume a name the chances were great that he would never see the interior dens of Mount Solomon. And that was the purpose for which he had taken this ride. Moreover it might very well be that no one from the mountain had been in Twin Springs while he was there. While they, no doubt, got daily news of everything that happened in the town, there was also no doubt that this news must be relayed to them. He determined then to run the risk and give a false name.

"I'm 'Texas Slim,'" he said. "Maybe where you and me bumped into each other away back was out in that direction."

"Maybe it was," agreed Montana Charlie. "I've sure hunted the old Lone Star from one end to the other and got some fat pickings."

"Sure," replied Ronicky, nodding.

"Well," went on Montana, "let's get down below. And what did you think of my make-up—tell me straight!"

He fumbled at his face. The long mustaches disappeared. And at the same time it even seemed to Ronicky that some of the wrinkles of age, which doubtless only his imagination had furnished, had disappeared at the same moment. He found himself staring at the face of a man not more than thirty years old. His eyes were keen, and, as he straightened out of his lazy slouch on the horse, never had Ronicky seen the very heart of a man changed so quickly. Montana Charlie had become in a second or two a young man fairly alive with energy, and he sat in his saddle, laughing at Ronicky's bewilderment.

"You ought to be on the stage," Ronicky assured him. "You sure know how to make up!"

Montana Charlie was as happy as a child over the effect which he had produced.

"I pretty near come to laughing," he said, "when you said that you'd met me in some place before."

"Maybe I have, though," said Ronicky. "And maybe it was just the sound of your voice or something like that that made me recognize you."

In the meantime Montana Charlie was leading the way to the side and through a narrow passage. Ronicky turned to listen to the echoes which went chiming high above them, and when he faced the front again, the other had disappeared. He stared around him bewildered, until there was a burst of laughter immediately before him, and presently Montana Charlie appeared again from around the corner of an immense boulder.

"You see what sort of a place we got up here," he said. "We could make a posse so sick and dizzy that it'd never find itself again after it chased us for ten full minutes. Look here!"

He beckoned Ronicky to him and showed behind the rock the opening of a high and narrow passage. It was hardly noticeable from either end of the boulder, but it was of sufficient size for horse and man to disappear into it. Montana led through the opening and checked his horse again just inside the entrance.

"If you got any doubts about belonging up here," he said gravely, "you better come no farther, Texas. Because them that get inside of here on a bluff, sure are made sorry for it before they get out again!"

But Ronicky, having committed himself to the adventure, would not draw back again. He waved Montana on with a laugh, and the two presently rode out of the narrow passage, turned to the right into a spacious hall formed by a great cleft in the rock, with air and light filtering through in plenty from fissures above, and followed this hall until it widened suddenly into a large chamber, where Ronicky found himself in the presence of half a dozen lolling figures.

They showed their self-assurance by regarding him with more or less indifference.

"Here he is," exclaimed Montana Charlie. "Here's the man, boys, that 'Whitey' reported down to us. And he's one of the right kind—one of our kind. He's Texas Slim. Anybody here know him?"

The six men represented six silences. They sat up now, however, abandoning their occupations of the moment, whether this were tinkering with guns, or the repair of worn clothes, or the mending of bridles and saddle straps. They regarded Ronicky with the most solemn attention. And he in turn looked back to them with an eager regard.

He had traveled far and wide, but never had he seen such an assemblage. Tall and short and thick and lean, there were men of every complexion and size, so it seemed, in that meager half dozen. And each man by himself was a separate and interesting study. Weatherbeaten, sharp of eyes, hard of jaw, each was formidable in his own way. There could be no mistaking them. These were either soldiers for the law or soldiers against it. A child could have guessed as much at the first glance.

Nobody, it seemed, knew Texas Slim. So there was a little pause which took Ronicky's breath, though he managed to maintain a smile of indifference and meet their questioning glances, one by one.

"I was down Texas way last year," said a beetle-browed individual at the farther end of the rock cavern, "and I've been down there off and on for the last seven years. I never heard tell of no Texas Slim."

"Sure you didn't," said Montana Charlie. "In Texas they don't call each other 'Tex.'"

And this appropriate remark drew a hearty burst of laughter from the crowd.

Laughter after all is our best introduction. In a trice all was good humor among them. Furthermore they liked Ronicky Doone for the manner in which he bore himself.

"All man and a yard wide," they decided that he was. And they came up and shook hands with him, one by one, giving their names a little solemnly. For an introduction among their kind was a solemn matter. It meant to a certain extent the acceptance of the other as a companion, and by that acceptance it meant that they were intrusting their safety in his hands.

Ronicky Doone was equally grave. And he knew that now a single false step would ruin him. He could only pray that his time on Solomon Mountain need not be long.

CHAPTER XXIX

THE DOCTOR SPEAKS TO BLONDY

In the meantime the six days had been filled with a bitter fight for life and against death in the hotel at Twin Springs. For there the doctor and Elsie Bennett were struggling for the life of Charlie Loring, and through the first four days he hung literally between life and death, the balance turning first one way and then the next.

But on the fifth day there was a turn for the better, and on the sixth Blondy opened his eyes, and for the first time they were cleared of delirium and gleamed with intelligence again. The girl, leaning above him, studied sadly and gladly, in strange mixture, the features which showed how near death had been to the sick man. They were sadly hollowed and worn. The square jaw was now lean and pointing. The flesh drew back, leaving the nose sharp and high and pulling the corners of the mouth into a sullen expression of discontent. His unshaven beard covered his face, and his hair would not be subdued to any regular shape, but was continually put on end by the turning and twisting of the wounded man.

Now he looked up at the girl searchingly, and then

with a frown of disappointment. "Elsie?" he asked, half in wonder and half, she thought, in disgust.

"Yes," she answered and patted his hand reassuringly.

She forced a steady, almost careless smile. He would cling to her hand and pour out a tale of gratitude to her. And she must endure the tide of thanks and accept it as a mere nothing. But what was this he was saying?

"You ain't the same. You're different. Why, Elsie, you look ten years older!"

She shrank away from the bed, still managing to continue a ghost of her smile, but it was a wan ghost indeed! And here the doctor stepped in between them. He had proved himself a fine and faithful type, this doctor. There was no money in the case for him, saving that first money which Ronicky Doone had thrust into the pocket of his coat. But he had stayed steadily by the bed and had even outdone Elsie Bennett in the rigors of his watching and nursing. For, whereas her strength had twice given out and forced her to sleep, the doctor seemed to need no rest. Day by day he would sit in the corner, and though he nodded a little from time to time, yet he was never soundly asleep for any long period, and it was never hard to rouse him when he was needed.

Between them they had brought the wounded man through. And now there was the authority of a long and close companionship in the familiar manner in which the doctor pushed the girl away from the bed, parting her hand from the hand of Charlie Loring.

"You go lie down," he commanded.

"But Charlie——" she began.

"No matter about Charlie right now. You need sleep."

"I could sleep while——"

"You go try. If you can't sleep, black is white."

She wavered.

"But I want to talk to her!" said Charlie.

She was resolute again.

"You see how it is, doctor? He needs me still. I must stay here until——"

"Until he's delirious again? I tell you, you got to go and sleep! Go this moment, Elsie!"

She backed away toward the cot on the far side of the room. But still she was reluctant, uneasy, and she glanced frowningly from the doctor to the patient.

"All right," said Charlie Loring, with the petulance

which so often goes with the sick bed. "All right, I'll lie here and wait till she wakes up, I suppose."

"Doctor!" cried the girl. "It isn't safe for me to leave him when——"

"When fiddlesticks," said the doctor brutally. "I don't want him bothered. I have a reason. You lie down!"

He advanced toward her almost threateningly, and she reluctantly sat down on the couch and then reclined, under his further threat, to one side.

"Close your eyes," said the doctor, setting his teeth a little, as the great, purple-shadowed eyes stared up at him, puzzled.

She obeyed.

"But I can't sleep," she insisted. "I know that I can't sleep."

"I'm not asking you to sleep," said the doctor. "I'm just asking you to close your eyes. Will you do that? Just keep them closed for ten minutes. You'll find it a curious experiment in relaxing."

"For ten minutes," sighed the girl. "All right, then, for just ten minutes I'll do as you say. But the moment Charlie needs anything I'll——"

Her voice had gone haltingly to the close of this phrase, but now she stopped altogether. The next word trembled for an instant on her lips, and then her whole body seemed to settle and melt. The features relaxed. Her head fell back a little into the pillow, her breast rose slowly with a long breath, and one hand slipped from the edge of the couch, and the arm dangled toward the floor. The doctor crossed hastily to her and, raising the arm, replaced it beside her, palm up, in the attitude of the greatest rest.

"She's sort of tuckered out, ain't she?" asked the wounded man.

"Shut up!" said the doctor, whirling fiercely on his patient.

Charlie Loring started and blinked under the shock of that speech.

"You—you can't talk like that to me!" he gasped. "You—you'll start me bleeding again!"

"Hell!" said the doctor. "I hardly care if you bleed to death. But if you keep on talking loud enough to disturb her, I'll——" He finished the sentence with a most unprofessionally ugly glance at the other, and Loring was astonished.

163

Charlie was only dimly conscious that, during a long, faintly remembered period, he had been cared for as though he were an infant. This harsh, fierce tone of the doctor, as though he had been guilty of some crime, astonished him.

"Tuckered out!" exclaimed the doctor. "I should say she is. And then you tell her that she looks ten years older!"

He began to tramp fiercely up and down the room, wrath fairly dripping from him, his fists clenching and relaxing in swift successions. At length he came back and faced his patient again.

"Blondy," he said, "I've got a couple of things to say to you. I'm not like a lot of doctors. There are some that think a man when he's sick and delirious never shows anything that's on his mind. But I'm different from that sort of a doctor. I believe there's a certain element of truth in delirious ravings!"

As he said this he saw that Blondy Loring contracted in every muscle and cast a sharp glance at him, as though he wished at a single fierce effort to pierce through to the full meaning of the doctor.

"What's up with you now?" he asked, a little hoarse with his emotion. "What's bothering you now, doc?"

And there was something of a challenge and also something of a plea in what he said.

"I'm not going to tell you," said the doctor. "I can't tell you that—I don't think that it would be professional honesty to tell you in your sane moments of the things which you have said during delirious moments."

Perspiration issued bright and gleaming upon the forehead of the other, his lips worked, as he glared at the doctor.

Suddenly he was half whispering: "Come around here; come around here where I can get a good look at you, will you?"

The doctor obeyed without a murmur. Then the wasted hand of Blondy reached up and gripped at his.

"What the dickens are you driving at?" asked Blondy. "What do you mean by the things that you overheard me say? What did I say?"

"I've already told you that I couldn't tell you now," said the doctor, "much as I'd like to!"

"You're trying to bluff me about something," said

Blondy, but his nervousness belied his attempted smile of indifference.

"I'm not trying to bluff you," said the doctor. "I wouldn't talk to you now except that I see your fever is nearly gone, and it's worth risking a relapse just to straighten out your relations with the girl a little!"

"Eh?" grunted the other.

"I mean what I say!"

"Are you interfering between Miss Bennett and me?"

"Don't talk that way," said the doctor, and he raised a hand in protest. "It makes me tired to hear you, Blondy. Look here: Everything that I've heard, the girl has heard —and more!"

Again there was that guilty start from Charlie Loring.

"About what?" he gasped.

"Everything, Blondy. Everything!" said the merciless doctor. "We know all about you now from A to Z!"

Blondy winced and closed his eyes. The gray pallor which overspread his face made the sick pallor of the moment before seem the color of hearty youth.

"Tell me everything you know!" he said at last.

"You seem sort of cut up about even guessing at what we know," said the doctor sternly.

"Well," gasped Blondy, "everybody has something on his conscience, in one shape or another. They all got something. How would *you* like to have folks know everything that ever went on in your brain, doc?"

"Why," said the doctor, "I might blush, my son, but I should never tremble!"

"Tremble?"

"That's what I said—tremble! Which is what you would do, Blondy, if we were to tell what we know."

"I don't believe it," murmured Charlie Loring savagely. "I've got nothing against me—much!"

"Nothing much?" echoed the doctor. "Do you call this nothing much?"

He leaned and whispered in the ear of the youth.

Then he stepped back and saw in the wide eyes of the sick man a great terror. But almost immediately the fear vanished, and in its place there was a contemptuous unconcern.

"Nobody would believe you if you was to tell that," said Charlie Loring. "Besides, what sort of proof can you rake up against me, doc?"

"Doesn't that sound like enough?" asked the doctor grimly. "Then listen to this."

This time he remained bowed at the ear of Loring, whispering for some time. And, as he reached the end of each sentence, he would half straighten, and then, observing upon the face of the wounded man an expression as of one who had just been struck a brutal blow, he would lean hastily down again and strike once more. Until finally Charlie Loring went crimson and then white and pressed both of his trembling hands across his face.

When Charlie covered his face, the doctor, as though satisfied, stepped back and left Loring to digest the substance of those whispers, while he walked back and forth through the room. And there was a sort of strut to his stride, as the pace of one who has done a good deed. Yet it seemed a very cruel thing that he had done to poor Charlie Loring, Blondy the big puncher of the Bennett Ranch.

He turned again to his patient and this time saw that Blondy had turned his head so as to observe him, and in the eyes of the patient there was a consuming, a withering hatred. It made the doctor start, and then, shrugging his shoulders, he cast the horror from him.

Again he went to Blondy.

"I'll tell you the crowning hell of all your case, Loring," he said. "I'll tell you at once. It's this: the girl wanted to marry you before because she thought that you were a sort of a knight that had just stepped out of the pages of one of the old fool books that she'd been reading. And now she wants to marry you to save you from yourself!"

He made a gesture, calling heaven to witness the prodigious absurdity of this. And then he strode up and down the room through two or three turns.

"It's ghastly! It's positively ghastly!" he declared to the world at large and to Blondy Loring in particular. Then he paused beside the bed and shook his forefinger at the sufferer.

"But you can bet your bottom dollar that matters will go no farther than this!" he vowed. "You can lay your last cent on that, Loring. And the reason that I'm telling you all of the things that I know about you is so that you will be in my power—and *know* that you are in my power!"

He looked down thoughtfully.

166

"If you tell what you know," said Loring, "you break your oath which you took when you became a doctor."

The doctor glanced up hastily and, as he did so, saw the face of Blondy suddenly convulsed to a wolfish ferocity. A veritable devil had peered out for the instant, as from behind a mask.

"Break my oath?" asked the doctor sadly. "That, Loring, is something I never expected that I could do. But my honor as a doctor is worth less than the soul of this girl. Never dream, Loring, that I'll let it be thrown away on you!"

Loring raised his hand in sudden surrender and closed his eyes as though physically, mentally he had given way under the sudden strain. But it was a false surrender.

"You'll try nothing like that?" asked the doctor.

"Nothing like that," whispered Charlie Loring.

But his mind was ceaselessly revolving the problem. There was some way of evading the danger from the doctor, and he would find that way.

CHAPTER XXX

NEWS FROM TWIN SPRINGS

Almost at once Ronicky Doone found himself adopted by the man who had first met up with him. He was drawn out from the main chamber where, for that day, at least, the outlaws of Mount Solomon had established their headquarters, and he was taken into a small adjoining room or rather cave, where Montana Charlie had taken up his own quarters on this date.

But Ronicky noted that there were no permanent features of furniture in the cave. Indeed it would be difficult in the extreme to bring up such luxuries to the top of Mount Solomon. Moreover if they led a shifting life, moving here and there, the probabilities were that they could not possibly carry their conveniences with them. Montana Charlie soon explained the whole matter in detail.

The originator of the scheme of making Mount Solomon a stronghold for his kind, had drawn up a complete plan by which it should operate. And one of the first things which he laid down as an inviolable rule was that there should be no articles of furniture either brought up the mountains or made at the top.

The idea was that such things would tend to fix the life of the citizens of Mount Solomon in the furnished caves, whereas, ideally, they should be constantly wandering. Moving from cave to cave they could leave fewer traces of habitation. And, also, if they lived on what they carried on their horses up the slope, they would not be tempted to stay too long on the crest. Ronicky was surprised by this point in the rules and their purposes. But the point was readily explained.

"This," said Montana Charlie, "is just sort of a camping place for overnight. It ain't a place for gents to hang out when they are flush and want to spend their money. It's just a place where they can duck to when the whole land is hot on their trail; and it's the sort of a place where they can come to meet up with some of their pals, and here they can fix up their layouts for their next jobs. But nobody, not even the best, can lay up here for more than one week. If a gent comes in on a Sunday, he has to go out some time before midnight the next Sunday. And that's the way it works all the time."

"But who sees to it that the rules are kept?" asked Ronicky.

"Why, the majority," said Montana cheerfully. "You see this is a real democracy, partner! Or, rather, it's like a club. We elect our members."

"Am I elected then?" asked Ronicky.

"Nope, only part way. I brought you in. That means that you can stay with us in this one hang-out. But before you can begin to circulate around, you got to be taken around by somebody else. Any two can elect you, and it takes more'n half to keep you out on a vote."

Ronicky nodded, surprised at the wisdom of these arrangements which provided for the safety of all.

"Who fixed up these rules?" he asked at length.

"Who d'you think?" asked the other. "Why, it was 'Kit' himself."

He said this as one delivering a master stroke, and Ronicky managed to muster enough surprise to suit the occasion.

"Kit?" he echoed. "Not Kit!"

"Yep, Christopher was the boy that done it. There was some up to that time that figured that Kit was just good for gun plays and that sort of thing. But when he planned how the boys was to use Mount Solomon, we changed our minds about him."

"What does he get out of it?" asked Ronicky. "Does

169

he get the right to dig out a part of the profits of everybody that hangs out here regular?"

"Nope, he don't. The surprising thing is that Kit don't ask for a darn thing except one. And that one thing is that he's to be allowed to stay here just as much as he pleases. And even that he don't use as much as he might!"

Ronicky sketched for the satisfaction of his imagination the picture of an all-wise and deep-seeing crook who had seen the possibilities of the mountain and had planned to gather around him for his own protection as well as for theirs a host of expert fighters. There were always enough men present, Charlie told him, to insure the presence of two or three guards who, posted upon a few prominent places on the tops of the ridges, could keep an easy survey sweeping across the sides and make sure that no unwanted stranger climbed toward the top.

And when a man was observed climbing, glasses were at once focused on him. If he were recognized as a friend, he was, of course, allowed to come on at his pleasure. But if he were not so recognized, he was surveyed as a possibility. It might be that he would prove to be some man of the law. And in that case he would find the top of the mountain totally deserted in appearance, while spies watched him from covert. Or, if he seemed a promising youth, a man would be sent out, as Montana Charlie had been sent, to encounter him and examine him cautiously. Conducted in this fashion and adhering strictly to the rules which had been laid down by the celebrated gun fighter, Christopher, the "club" on top of Mount Solomon gave promise of flourishing for an indefinite period. The beautiful part of its organization was that it depended upon no central head who, knowing things and having a power which none of the others possessed, could make or break the rest by his guidance. This was a group which produced its leader from among its own numbers. This was fortunate, for Christopher had been absent for months.

These details Ronicky listened to with the greatest interest. He was only surprised by the name of the leader, Christopher. This was his first incursion in these lands, but he had heard in the north of an outlaw of that name. However there was no atmosphere of celebrity attaching to the name of Christopher, surely not enough to make him the accepted founder of such an institution as this.

Perhaps this was the first "great" thing which he had done, and from what Montana Charlie had said Ronicky gathered that this must be the case.

Here the narrative of Montana broke off sharply, and canting his head to one side he listened to the voice of a man who had just entered the larger rock-chamber and was greeted with a rumble of voices from the outlaws.

"It's Cook," said Montana, raising himself eagerly. "It's old Cook himself. He's come in with the news, I guess. It must be something pretty important."

"Where's he come from?" asked Ronicky carelessly.

"From Twin Springs," was the answer, and Ronicky caught his breath sharply.

What an irony of Fate it was that his entry had been so successful, only to have his exit blocked by a man who would be sure to know all about the shooting of Blondy Loring? He could only hug one faint hope to his bosom, and that was that Cook had gone to Twin Springs after the shooting took place, so that he had not seen Ronicky himself.

"And he'll have some news about Kit," said Montana Charlie. "He'll know how the old man is coming along, and he will be able to tell us whether Kit is going to be able to get back on his feet or not."

"Christopher is sick?" asked Ronicky.

"Sure! Don't you know that? Ain't you been in Twin Springs?"

Ronicky made no answer, fearing to expose his ignorance. Luckily at that moment, while Montana Charlie was waiting for his response, the newly arrived man in the other part of the cave began to speak, and Montana was instantly all ears, putting away the gun belt he had been repairing, in order to listen.

"He's doing fine," said Cook. "He ain't on his feet. Matter of fact he's a considerable long distance from being on his feet. But the girl is treating him fine. Never leaves him night or day."

"It's about time she should pay some attention to him," answered another, "after all the months that he's been working for her old man and waiting for his pay."

"Well," said Cook, "you can lay to it that she's paying him back all that he ever done for her father and her. The doctor says that without her he'd never have been able to pull Kit through. Poor Kit! I had a look at him the other

171

day. Couldn't get near to look at him before. But the doctor finally let me open the door and take a squint at him. What I seen would have made your head spin. You remember him with the complexion of a girl in a high wind? Well, he's as pale as ashes, all you can see of him, except that he's got a faded yaller beard over the most of his face. He's mighty thin, and he looks plumb played out."

"I know," said another. "I know that look that comes onto a gent after he's been pretty near to dying. There's a sort of a shadow lying all over him. Like he didn't care much what he'd been near to. Sort of dull-like. Ain't that the way that Christopher looks now?"

"Not a bit," said Cook. "He had an eye that was on fire. He give me a look and a signal to come nearer the minute he clapped his eyes onto me. But when I tried to come in the doctor shuts me out.

" 'I just wanted to show you that he's better and that his head is cleared,' said the doc. 'Now run along and tell the rest of his friends that he's all right.'

"And so I couldn't do nothing but what he said. I went out and told everybody, and everybody seemed mighty glad to hear. Yes, sir, you wouldn't never think that Christopher would have many friends in a place like Twin Springs. But gents that would run a mile if you just whispered the name of C. L. Christopher into their ear, now smile and - grin and want to know all about Charlie Loring!"

This brought a chuckle of amusement from the crowd, but Ronicky Doone sat with his head bowed toward the ground. It had burst upon him like a shell exploding. The tall fair-haired youth who had impressed him so favorably in Twin Springs, when he had ridden into the town, was no other than the known desperado and youthful bandit, Christopher. He had apparently made no effort to disguise himself beyond taking the first two of his real names, and so he had made himself known as Charlie Loring instead of Charlie L. Christopher.

The consummate boldness of it stunned Ronicky. And still his brain refused to grasp the whole truth. He found points which stuck in his crop, so to speak. What, for instance, could have induced such a man as Christopher to accept employment as a cow-puncher on a ranch? Yet was that not answered by the beauty of Elsie Bennett?

Yes, for her sake he had played the game and striven to pose as an honest man.

Swift confirmation was coming from the round of talk in the next apartment of the cave.

"I'm glad he's out of it," said one. "But after all he's only got what was coming to him for being such a fool and trying to live two lives instead of one. Ain't I right, boys?"

"Maybe," they answered, "but that don't keep us from being sorry. Besides," said one, "you got to admire him for the way he worked things. Think of him riding down to drag Doone's hoss out of the river that day!"

"Yes," said another, "that's something that I never could make out. Why did he make that play about the hoss?"

"So's folks would never be able to make a guess about what he really was," said another. "He wanted to make 'em think—even when he thought that he was running away from a bunch that were riding to get him for murder—that he was the honest young gent who was plumb drove against his will into shooting to kill. He knowed quick that if he made that play to save the hoss, while he was running for his life, that no jury in the mountains would ever hang him. Besides, the news of that must sure have made the girl's heart start beating quick."

"But this Ronicky Doone," said another. "How come that he was able to beat the chief to the draw?"

"Because he waited and kept right on waiting until Kit's nerve begin to rub thin. He held off and held off until Kit got nervous. And you know what he is then. He ain't half of a man. He needs to act right on the spur of the moment. And some day somebody else that knows how the trick is done, is going to wait out on Kit until his nerve is gone, and then he'll kill him plumb easy."

"H'm," said a companion. "That sounds easy, but I'd hate to be taking the chance."

And the general chuckle confirmed this last opinion.

"Let's go out and get some more news out of Cook," said Montana cheerfully. "That's sure good news about Kit being on the way to getting well, eh?"

"Yes," replied Ronicky and rose reluctantly to his feet.

He had come to the test. Would Cook know him as the conqueror of Blondy Loring Christopher? If so, his lease on life was short indeed! Yet he could do nothing other than follow his companion.

CHAPTER XXXI

A DOUBLE DILEMMA

In the meantime in the hotel at Twin Springs the doctor rested content. He had, he felt, effectually tied the hands of his patient, and now he had only to sit back and watch the recovery of the body of a man whose mind, he knew, was irretrievably damned.

For out of the ravings of Blondy Loring, both he and the girl had learned the truth, that the seemingly lighthearted, harmless cow-puncher was in reality the dreaded outlaw, Christopher. And this was the truth which he had whispered into the ear of Blondy to paralyze the resistance of the big wounded fellow.

It had been a hard task for the girl to be convinced. No matter what damning details dropped from the lips of Blondy during his sickness she would not believe that he could be guilty. Though the entire facts about a robbery were given in a fairly consecutive story by Blondy, yet she declared that he might have heard the story from some other person, and so he had repeated them with the peculiar vividness which any tale receives when it drops from the lips of a delirious person.

It was only when tale after tale was told in part or in the whole, by exact description or by inference, that she began to be shaken in her belief. And whereas at first she had beaten down all of the doctor's attempted arguments by simply saying: "Look at his face! How can you believe such things of him?"—she at last changed her attitude.

Her attitude, in short, was altered to one which was most difficult for the doctor to combat. Instead of pointing to him, as she had done in the first place, and demanding who could believe wrong of a man with a face so nobly chiseled, she now pointed to him and demanded to know who could possibly believe that evil was ineradicably planted in his soul?

When this question was first asked in a trembling voice and with shining eyes, the doctor was too dumfounded to answer.

"I don't know about it. I'm not the sky pilot of the town," he said. "Evil in his soul? Well, since it is nothing that can be cut out with a knife, or rooted out with medicine, I can't pretend to argue about it. I won't answer you."

"Because you have a blind prejudice against him," said the girl hotly. "But I tell you, doctor, there is something in instinct, and instinct tells me——"

Here the doctor threw up both hands and groaned.

"Instinct!" he said. "That's the last resort of my dear wife. And I've learned not to run against that wall of rock. If you've come to the question of instinct, this is no longer an argument. But go on, and I'll try to listen calmly."

"I knew you would act in this manner," said Elsie Bennett sadly. "You wouldn't understand how, the first moment I laid eyes on him, I said to myself that there was something he needed, and which I could give him."

"H'm," said the doctor.

"It was instinct!" cried Elsie Bennett. "And though my faith was shaken for a little while by—by—by what we've found out——"

"By the fact that we now know Blondy Loring is the thief, hypocrite, and murderer, Charlie Christopher?"

The array of unbeautiful words jolted at her shrewdly and made her head come up by jerks and stole her color away.

"You don't know everything!" she managed to exclaim faintly.

"Do you?" demanded the doctor.

"What temptations may have been in his path, and how he may have been forced by circumstances——"

"Forced? Bah!" said the brutal doctor. "I tell you, my dear girl, that every one knows the story of Christopher. And every one knows that he was given a good education—good enough so that he should have been able to know right from wrong, anyway! But he was spoiled, and he got into the habit of wanting his own way. So when his father died and left Christopher without any money, the boy went bad. He got at the point of a gun what he used to get from his father. And that's all there is to it. He went from bad to worse. And now here he is!"

"From bad to worse!" cried the girl indignantly and skipping over the part of the doctor's remark which appeared to her unanswerable. "From bad to worse! Do you call it worse for him to have worked as he has done for my poor father, without even wages to encourage him or for him to hope for?"

Here the doctor actually burst into laughter, regardless of the sleeping patient.

"Wages? Nonsense! He'd seen you, my dear. He'd seen you, and your pretty face was what he was working for, and any boy I know of would consider the hope of you wages enough!"

This bluntness brought a wonderful crimson up her cheeks. She stared angrily at the doctor, but it was through a mist of tears.

"How dare——" she began and then changed her plan and the point of her remark.

"He has always been the height of courtesy to me," she said.

"I have never denied him good sense," said the doctor.

Here she stamped as one provoked well-nigh beyond endurance.

"It was something in him," she declared, "speaking to something in me."

"If you're in love with him," said the doctor, "I'll stop arguing."

"I'm not in—you have no right—oh, won't you understand?" she cried and threw out her hands in such a fashion that the doctor, who certainly could make no sense at all out of this sentence, nodded and smiled in the kindliest and briskest manner possible.

"Now, my dear, my dear!" said he, and gathering in

both her hands he patted them. "Don't be silly. In the end you will have your own way. You're too pretty for it to be otherwise, and that's the curse of pretty girls—all that I've known."

"I'm not asking anything," said she. "All I want to do is to convince you that I haven't the slightest feeling about Charlie except in so far as I can help him. We have very little in common, he and I."

Here the doctor coughed, and she was instantly angered out of reason.

"You are mocking me?" she asked.

"Tush!" said the doctor. "The neatest little tragedy I've ever had under my eyes is in progress, and do you think that I could mock? No, I am sorry to say that my heart is not as hard as that, and the more's the pity. I should have been a rich man, otherwise!"

"Tragedy?" she asked.

"You are beginning to pity him," said the doctor. "And if that doesn't lead to a tragedy, I confess myself a blind idiot unable to see the width of my hand into the future."

"Pity!" she exclaimed. "I should not dare to say as much as that! But I simply see an opportunity for service. Perhaps I can be the small lever that will pry him out of his old ways and lift him to a higher level where——"

The groan of the doctor ended her discourse.

"Marriage?" he asked.

She flushed still more hotly.

"Why not?"

Here the doctor leaned forward and punched his remarks with a stubby forefinger into the palm of his opposite hand.

"The minute you start to marry him," he said, "I expose the facts about Christopher to the entire world. His wedding ceremony will put a rope around his neck. I tell you, I'm not going to see your life sacrificed!"

And he left the room, while Elsie Bennett sat stark and stiff in her chair and stared after him and studied blankly the panels of the door through which he had disappeared.

This was the conversation which preceded the wakening of the outlaw on the sixth morning, when he looked about him, with a steady pulse, a normal temperature, and a clear eye. In the last long sleep he had advanced to absolute safety so far as the results of that bullet wound were concerned.

He had improved so much that even the talk with the doctor did not throw him back into a fever. To be sure the threats of the honest physician made his pulses jump, but he controlled them with a great effort and managed to establish one of those calms in which the mind works hard, beating back every impulse toward hysteria.

His foolhardiness in venturing out of his stronghold in the mountains and his double safeguard of the outlaw companion seemed now little short of insanity. And yet, when he turned his head and looked toward the girl, where she was sleeping on the couch on the far side of the room, he could not question but that she was a prize worthy of a great risk.

Worthy of a great risk, indeed, but certainly not worth his own life. He gritted his teeth at the thought. He even felt a huge wave of resentment against her rising in him. It was as though she had deliberately tricked him into loving her. In truth there was little room in the heart of Charlie Loring Christopher for love of another; his affection and esteem for himself occupied most of the available space. And though the beauty of Elsie Bennett thrilled him, he had looked forward to a wedding with her rather as a proof of his own daring and a glove thrown in the face of the law-abiding world, than because his happiness would be unassured until she was his. It had been a great adventure. Instead of bullion, there was a girl. And now, like the treasure seeker wrecked on a desert island, he was apt to curse the goal which had induced him to set sail and trust to chance.

She was very beautiful, but she was not beautiful enough to make up for the pain he was undergoing and the downright peril which now threatened him in case he should push forward his schemes concerning the girl.

But one thing worried him terribly. As long as the doctor knew the truth about him, was it not true that the doctor would conceal his knowledge only so long as the outlaw was sick, and as soon as he approached a cure, would not the physician turn over his patient to the hangman?

Any other course than this seemed to Christopher impossible. And this for the simple reason that he would have adopted no other course himself had he been in the doctor's position.

His dilemma then began to grow blacker and blacker. He must provide against the future danger. He must manage in some way to tie the hands of the doctor. And what instrument did he possess with which he could make the doctor his man? Hunting desperately for a solution he turned his head after the fashion worried men have, and his eyes rested upon the girl. They lingered long on her pale, tired face, and the longer he looked the more brightly a fire began to blaze up in them.

He did not see the solution, but he began to see a light which was a hope of help.

CHAPTER XXXII

HELD BY THE OUTLAW

As he stepped from the recess where he had been talking with Montana Charlie, Ronicky Doone took care to hang back, so that the attention of Cook would not be immediately called to him. Luckily for him the talk was now so busy and unceasing that there was no attention paid to him. Not even Montana gained a word; for when he hailed Cook, the new arrival merely waved and went on with his narrative of news.

And Ronicky employed the interval in studying the face of Cook. He could not remember a man with such features in Twin Springs. And he felt a great sense of relief as he made sure of the fact. However his memory for the faces of the men in Twin Springs would not be particularly keen, for most of the time he spent in the village had been passed in lounging in the sunshine and smoking innumerable cigarettes. Moreover there was nothing by which Cook could have been easily remembered. He was simply the usual type of sun-blackened, lean, hard-skinned cow-puncher. He was neither young nor old, big nor small, blond nor dark, but in all things he was average. He would have faded into the background of any crowd.

He was enjoying his prominence of the moment on Mount Solomon, as though this were an unaccustomed thing. But Ronicky ground his teeth, as the talk, by evil chance, swung around and centered upon himself.

"What about this Ronicky Doone?"

Cook replied: "Of course I looked up as much as I could about him. There were a couple of gents in Twin Springs that claimed to know all about him. I talked to them. They said that farther up north, Ronicky Doone had a mighty big name for fighting of any kind. And when I asked 'em some more about him, each of 'em come out with a string of yarns big enough to choke a hoss. That was all good enough, but the main trouble was that the yarns didn't hitch up together at all! Wasn't two alike in either set!"

"Was old Ingram one of them that talked?" asked Montana Charlie.

"Sure he was one."

"He's made up of nothing but lies," said Montana. "I guess maybe both of 'em were just stringing you along a little, eh? They found out that nobody in town knew any facts, so they got a little attention by making up histories of Ronicky Doone, eh?"

"Maybe they done that easy enough," said Cook. "Fact remains that he was good enough to down Christopher."

"Might have been some luck in that," remarked another. "Which reminds me of a time down near the Rio Grande when——"

The talk veered away from the subject of Ronicky Doone as quickly as it had focused upon him, and he was duly grateful. He began edging more deeply into the shadow by the wall of the cave, where the light from the fissure above fell dim and uncertain. In this light, unless Cook were entirely sure of his man, he would probably go unrecognized. And before he stirred out of that shadow, who could tell but that Cook might be called off on a mission of some sort that would carry him away from Mount Solomon?

So he sat down and literally made himself small while he waited. In half an hour he saw Cook rise and stretch.

"I got to be drifting on," he said. "I took up too much time in Twin Springs the way it was, and now I got to ride."

Ronicky felt a thrill of gratification and an odd fear commingled. For was it not too good to be true that

Cook was actually leaving? They were all bidding Cook good-by, waving and calling. Ronicky waved with the rest to make himself less conspicuous than he might have been had he remained motionless.

But the instant he spoke, the head of Cook snapped toward him. And Ronicky knew that he was lost. That sudden turning of the head, that brightening and hardening of the eyes, recalled him to some face which he had seen at the moment of his encounter with Blondy Loring. Whether he had seen the man at a window or an open door, or merely on the far side of the street, he could not tell. But during the moments when he was facing Loring and waiting for the bark of the dog, all his senses had been raised to a new level of keen alertness. He had seen as though all objects were outlined in fire.

And now he recalled that face of Cook in fiery vividness. Cook had seen him shoot down Blondy. Cook had heard him speak. Would he come back now to further investigate the voice which had sounded familiarly upon his ear?

Cook stood with his legs braced, his thumbs hooked into his belt, glaring into the shadow. Apparently in the distance he mistook Ronicky for another companion.

Now he laughed, saying: "That was funny. Just for a minute I took 'Hank,' yonder, for—well, I won't say who. But it was plumb funny what a trick my ear played on me. So long, boys."

He waved again, and, as Ronicky's panic-stricken heart stopped its thunder and relapsed into a steadier beating, Cook turned on his heel and disappeared in the passage which led out toward the daylight. Here a red-shirted man arose from a sitting posture to his heels and loosed a stentorian roar: "Cook!"

"Well?" called Cook.

"Come back here!"

"What do you want?" he asked with a curse.

But in spite of his curses Cook reappeared.

"Who'd you call Hank?" asked the red-shirted man. "Hank ain't here. He left yesterday."

"What?"

Ronicky found himself freezing to the rigidity of the stone against which his shoulders leaned. Then Cook strode toward him, and Cook's right hand was held dangerously near to his holster.

Ronicky began to estimate chances. He could do one

of two things: He could stay where he was and start shooting from the little niche into which he had squeezed himself to take advantage of the shadow, or else he could plunge for the opening of the passage which led out of the cave. In the former case the chances were ten to one against him. In the latter case the chances of taking so many and such men by surprise were almost equally small.

He decided to do neither, but sat perfectly still; and now Cook halted two paces away, with an oath that rang up and down the cave.

"It's Doone!" he called. "It's Ronicky Doone! What is he doing here?"

There was a shout from the others. In an instant a solid semicircle of men hemmed in Ronicky, and each of them was perilously prepared for shooting. Ronicky rolled up to his feet slowly, so that they could watch his every motion, and he confronted them with his arms folded high, for in this fashion they were most clearly able to see that his hands were kept well away from his revolver.

"I'm Ronicky Doone," he said quietly, "and I guess I've jammed into a sort of a mess."

He could see that they were too unutterably amazed at his presence to make head or tail of him.

"D'you mind," he asked, "if I try to tell you just why I've come up here?"

They were falling back a little, as he stepped out where the light fell clearly upon his face. Now they studied him with scowls of the most intense interest, and he looked gradually from one to another until he had surveyed the entire group as he spoke.

"I'll tell you what," he said. "A shooting is a pile easier to think about than it is to do. I thought that shooting up Blondy would be plumb satisfactory, but when I seen him drop it made me sick. And when I heard how the Bennett place would go bust with Blondy off of it, it made me a lot sicker. On top of that I seen the girl, and she made me sicker still!"

He sighed and went on: "I made up my mind that, even if I'd pushed Blondy off the stage for a while, I'd try to keep his work from going smash all around. So I went out to the Bennett place to see what I could do. And the first and last thing I seen that I had to do was to get men, plenty of men, fighting men, to stave off

Al Jenkins when he starts to clean up the ranch and rustle off the cows. And I made up my mind that I'd take a chance. I'd go up to Mount Solomon, try to play the part of being one of you gents, and finally get half a dozen of you to come down and spend a week's vacation just riding the range for Bennett! Well, I was held up for the most part of the week by a lot of bad luck. And now I've got roped by Cook, and I guess a plan that looked a sort of crazy to start with is sure turning out crazy all around! But I've told you the straight of this yarn so's you can know just where to figure me."

He stepped back again and leaned once more against the rock wall. For a moment the outlaws were bewildered. Then Cook, edged back toward the exit by the necessity of his sudden departure, spoke before he left.

"Boys," he said, "go easy on believing a yarn like that. It sounds too saintly to be true. And just put this inside of your heads: if the gents in Twin Springs ever wake up to the fact that the man they got on the sick bed down there is Christopher, it may come in pretty handy to us and to Christopher if we have somebody up here that we could trade in for him. Ain't that reasonable? Keep the gent that knocked Blondy over, for them, and if they're men they'll trade even Christopher to see that no harm comes to Doone. Anyway keep thinking about that hard and fast. I got to go!"

He disappeared. But he had fired a shot which, it seemed, was to sink the ship of Ronicky's hopes. The certainty of Cook was all they needed.

Quickly they rehearsed the possibilities. They dared not turn him loose at once and let him go. He had learned too much about the men and the ways of Mount Solomon. And yet if they kept him as an exchange, he would carry an even greater knowledge away with him when he left.

They decided that the only thing to do was to follow the advice of Cook and keep Ronicky Doone a secure prisoner until they were assured that Christopher was back on his feet and safely out of the town.

"And when Kit is up on his feet and back among us once more," suggested the man in the red shirt, "we don't have to worry none about what to do with Doone. Because maybe Kit will have a couple of suggestions about that, all out of his own head!"

This suggestion brought an ominous laugh, and Ronicky saw that he was fettered again. To be restrained by big Curly had been bad enough. But to be a captive in the hands of all these fighters was a thousand times worse. Five seconds later they had his gun, and he was more helpless than the rope of Curly had rendered him.

CHAPTER XXXIII

LORING LIES

The hope which had glowed in the eyes of Blondy Christopher, as he lay in his bed and stared at the girl, continued until it was a flame. He spoke her name softly. She did not respond at once, but the complete relaxation of her features and her body changed. He spoke again, and her eyes were suddenly open.

She sat up on the couch, swaying slightly from side to side, still drugged by unsatisfied needs of sleep, white with exhaustion, and rendered to the eye of Blondy far from beautiful by the disarray of her hair. She had to pucker her brows into a frown before she could focus her misted glance upon him. But then she smiled instantly.

"How she loves me!" thought Blondy. "How she loves me—the little fool!"

A tolerant warmth filled him. He stretched out his hand to her with a great pity and scorn. And she stood by the bed holding that big hand to which the strength was so rapidly returning. Indeed, so swiftly was his vigor coming back that it made him grind his teeth to think that he could not leap up on his feet and break through these foolish bonds which held him. But, no; instead of that he must lean upon a weak woman for help and turn to her for his aid.

In the meantime he looked curiously into her face. He must know how far he could go with her, and he must learn it quickly. And yet he must not press her too soon. The color had sprung back into her cheek at a single step, as she stood looking down upon him. And one or two dexterous touches had done wonders for the disarrayed hair. Her eyes, too, were cleared, and all in all she was not easily recognizable for the girl at whom he had been staring the moment before, as she lay on the couch.

He placed his other hand over hers, pressing it lightly, but she warned him back and made him lie in a more composed position. He must be careful, she declared. If he moved with unnecessary violence he might start a hemorrhage which would kill him in a few moments. But he merely laughed at her, and he could see that his recklessness pleased her.

A great idea dawned in his brain, as he lay there looking up to her smile. If she could smile upon him, though she knew all that the doctor knew about him, her faith must be indestructible.

"I've been walking in a sort of a cloud," he told her, gathering the gloomiest possible expression to his face. "Seems to me like I've been living in a solid block of night, d'you know?"

"You've been delirious," she said gently. "But you're better, much better now. Did you want something? You called me?"

"I want something, yes," he said slowly, looking down, as though it was hard to face her. "I—I want a listener. I've got to talk to you, Elsie."

"About nothing that will excite you!"

"It won't excite me. It's something that I've got to talk *off* my mind. You see?"

She nodded.

"And you're the only one that I dare tell it to!"

At this she grew more serious than before, but she was by no means afraid to hear. Straightway he plunged into the narration. He had had to make up his mind on the spur of the moment, and he had to invent as he went. He must cling as closely as possible to the truth, the truth which he had revealed during his delirium.

187

But he must qualify the brutal facts of his life so far that the girl would see them in a new light.

After all it was a simple tale which he told her. He merely dragged in an imaginary person and then built all the guilt of his career around the newcomer. There was one thing which must be explained away before all else, and that was the act of highway robbery with which his career had begun.

"It all started one evening," he said to the girl. "There was a friend of mine called, but even now I can't tell you what his name was. Only, he was the best friend I had, I thought. He came to me, scared stiff and looking for help. Seems that he was hard up against it for money, and the reason was that he'd taken a lot of coin out of the safe where——"

He stopped with a sharp click of his teeth and frowned.

"I'm afraid I'm talking too much."

"Oh, I'll remember nothing," said the girl. "It's all sealed and forgotten, as far as I am concerned."

"Well, I sure trust you, Elsie," said the outlaw, with a quiet pretense of trust which almost convinced himself. "Anyway my partner was sure a gone goose if he didn't get five hundred. And there was no way he could get it except from me. But I didn't have a cent. I'd been raised expecting to have enough to live easy on without even lifting a hand. But there was a crash, and I got nothing. Well, I sat by myself thinking things over. There was my best friend nearly wild for the want of a miserable five hundred, and me with my hands tied, you might say. Well, Elsie, I'm one that takes the wants of his friends to heart more than he takes his own."

"I believe it, Charlie," she cried. "I do believe it, indeed!"

And the thrill in her voice trickled pleasantly into his consciousness and filled his eyes with a moisture of self-esteem, self-pity.

"Anyway," went on Blondy Christopher with a short gesture, as though he refused to dwell upon his own virtues at any great length, "anyway I left the house and went out to walk and to try to think of some way to raise five hundred. I went to everybody I knew, but it seemed that they didn't know me well enough to give me that money."

"The hard-hearted wretches!" cried Elsie.

"And finally, as I was drifting along on the edge of

the town, I seen old William Lucas walking out there. He went with his head down and his hands stuck in the hollow of his back, like he was afraid that he would break in two if he didn't hold himself together. I thought back about all I'd heard of Lucas. There was a man that could let me have a thousand times five hundred, if he was a mind. He always went with a couple of thousand dollars in his wallet, lest he should come across a good chance of picking something up mighty good and cheap for ready cash. And how had he got his money? By pressing in on them that worked hard and honest, but that couldn't quite meet the interest that the old hound got out of them. All along his way of life he'd left wrecks behind him. Big men had killed themselves, women had busted their hearts, and kids had starved, just because old Lucas wanted to squeeze out a few more dollars. I thought about all that, Elsie, when I seen him. And it made me bitter. D'you know how bitter a gent can feel about a thing like that?"

"But no matter how you felt," she cried, "you surely wouldn't have hurt a helpless old man like that to get some money away from him?"

"Hurt him?" Charlie laughed. Here, at least, he was telling the truth, and he rejoiced in the memory of the encounter. "Didn't I say that he always carried a couple of thousand along with him? Well, do you think that old skinflint would have gone out with all that money and nothing but his own withered-up hands to protect it? You don't know Lucas! No, sir, he never stirred that he didn't have a couple of big nephews of his along, regular bulldogs they were! They'd as soon shoot a man down as a dog. They'd both had their killings to their credit. Anyway, when I looked at them three, I said to myself that it sure wouldn't be harming the world none if I took from Lucas five hundred dollars to save my best friend. So I fixed up a mask out of my handkerchief and——"

"Oh, Charlie!"

"It was for my friend, I tell you!"

"I know, but—go on, go on!"

"I slipped around in front of 'em, jumped out, and stuck 'em up."

"You did what?"

"Shoved my gun under their noses and asked them to put their hands up. The old man was yaller. He

189

stuck his hands up quick enough, but his two nephews just let out growls like a coupla of bulldogs. They both dived to the side and went for their guns."

Here he paused significantly, while the girl trembled with excitement.

"When the smoke cleared away," said Charlie sadly, "they was both on the ground, and I was still on my feet, and the old man was begging for mercy!"

"You—you didn't hurt him?"

"Hurt an old man like him? Of course not! I just took his wallet and went on my way!"

"And the two—the two—they—they weren't dead, Charlie?"

"But they weren't dead," said Charlie. "They were hurt considerable, because a forty-five slug ain't exactly a needle going through a gent. But they both got well, and I paid their doctor bills!"

The last was a grace note in the way of a lie of which he had not thought until the spur of the moment, but the effect of it was completely to convince the girl. Instantly she was all flushed with pleasure.

"Oh, that was a fine thing to do, Charlie! And your friend? Your money saved him?"

"He turned straight and never touched the coin of other folks afterward," lied Charlie Christopher calmly. "A month later he was married to one of the finest girls you ever laid eyes on. They got twin boys and a little girl now."

Elsie gasped, and Charlie looked sharply at her. Had he piled this on a little too thick? He had not. Starry-eyed she was looking into the dim future.

"But that's something that I got no right to think about," said Charlie gloomily. "It's the one thing that I want more'n anything else—that's kids of my own. I take to 'em nacheral, but I can never have one!"

"Why not? Oh, why not, Charlie?"

"Because of the life I led," said Charlie. "What I done when I held up Lucas was only a start. I was seen and recognized. And after that, no matter how hard I tried to go straight, they wouldn't let me. If I went into a town and started to work quiet and honest, pretty soon somebody would drift into town that had heard of me, and then I'd have to get out. They hunted me the way they'd hunt a wolf. Nobody in the whole range of the mountains ever done anything real bad that wasn't blamed onto me. Why, sometimes I've heard crimes laid up to me so thick and so horrible, that I almost got to believing that I done them myself."

"Yes, yes!" she said eagerly. "I can see perfectly how that might be."

"Not that I didn't do enough," said the outlaw sadly. "Yes, I got so that I didn't care what become of me. They hated me; they were hunting me. So I just hit back at 'em. What I needed I took, and I took it at the point of a gun, simply because I didn't have a chance to make money by honest work."

"I believe it!" she cried. She made a gesture to show that a vast burden was falling from her heart. "Oh, Charlie, I've known all this before—all about the terrible things you've done. You told of them when you were delirious; one by one you told about them—horrible things that you've done, or planned to do. But that's in the past. That's forgotten. All the things you've done were in other places. And people don't know your face. You can stay here in Twin Springs when you're well, or on our ranch—if we still have it!"

"On your ranch?" asked Charlie softly, and he drew at her hand until she was close to him. "Elsie, it's the love of you that kept me on your ranch, do you know that? And if I'm ever a good man again, it'd be the love of you that has made me. Elsie, do you care even half of a little bit for me?"

He expected her to wince with joy, grow crimson, and pale in turn. Instead, to his profound astonishment, she simply pressed his hand gently and looked down at him with a peculiar, brooding quiet in her eyes which reminded him of the look of motherhood.

"Poor Charlie!" she said. "Do you really care as much as that?"

It amazed and shocked him. Was she pitying *him*?

"I wish—I profoundly wish," she was saying, "that I could say I love you. But love is something made up of fire and wonder. Isn't it?"

"Book talk," said Charlie, hoarse with shame and anger.

"And in real life, too. But I haven't it in me, Charlie, the thing that makes you red in the face and white about the lips. I have no emotion as intense as that for you."

She was attributing the color of his anger to love. He could have laughed in her face, had he dared!

"But at least I respect you, I see the possibilities of a

fine manhood in you, Charlie. And if I could help you to realize your possibilities—why, what more could any woman wish for in her life? If I could be a true helpmate to you—do you understand what I am trying to say, Charlie?"

He cast his hand across his eyes as though to hide his emotion, and his emotion was a raging shame. She was daring to talk down to him—to Charlie Christopher—to the adored of a hundred pretty girls, in a hundred scattered towns through the mountains. He wanted to cut at her with scornful jests and throw her loving-kindness back in her face. But, instead, he must lie there and endure it all for fear of death. And it was almost worse than death to Charlie, this trial of pride!

She was continuing, her voice the soul of gentleness: "But even if I wish to help you in all that a woman can help a man, even if I should be your wife, Charlie, and should try to bring more happiness into this wild, strong life of yours—I couldn't stir to help you. The doctor knows all that I know! And he hates you so much that if he thought we were to be married, he would expose you and turn you over to the law!"

Even as she spoke, Charlie saw the loophole through which he must escape if he escaped at all. And he sprang at the chance.

"The doctor? That old fool!"

"Fool? He saved your life, Charlie!"

"Of course! And he's a good man, Elsie, but the trouble is that he thinks I'm worse than I am. However, as much as he hates me, he loves you. And if once you and I were man and wife, do you think that he'd even dream of accusing me? No, no! He would never do it! He'd rather die first, Elsie!"

She pondered on what he said for a moment. "If we were actually married—if we were man and wife." Then the whole idea came home to her.

But he was continuing with his persuasion.

"Besides, Elsie, I can't trust him the way it is. As soon as I get a little better he may turn me over to the sheriff. I got no guarantee. But if you and I were married, he'd grind his teeth maybe, but he'd have to give up and give in! He'd feel like cursing me, but he wouldn't betray me. Ain't that clear?"

It was almost too clear. For the moment she looked at him doubtfully. This was strangely like cowardice. This was strangely like shielding himself behind her. But in an instant, as he smiled at her in his excitement, she forgot the ugly suspicion. He was brave, if ever a man were brave. Besides, what he suggested was dangerously intriguing. It meant marriage by stealth. It would be an undoing of the stern old doctor's precautions. It only needed that they should take him by surprise, or render him helpless for a few short moments.

She knew the minister who would come to her in no matter what situation, and at her will he would perform the ceremony. And she thought of nothing else—just the excitement and the opportunity, as she felt it to be, of helping Charlie Christopher. But that she was binding herself for life to a man she did not love and whose past was black with crime—this slipped out of her thoughts.

Charlie, lying tense in the bed, knew by the dawning radiance in her face that she was swinging around to the acceptance of his proposal.

CHAPTER XXXIV

RONICKY PREVAILS

THE men of Mount Solomon took the story which Ronicky Doone had told them as a joke. Had they detected anything overcunning in the narrative which he presented for their inspection, they might have resented the attempt to pull the wool over their eyes. But the truth, exactly as he told it, seemed so entirely absurd that they laughed heartily, and still more heartily whenever they thought of it.

And afterward, when they found that he was quite willing to be laughed at, and even would smile with them, they liked him for it and accepted him as a whole-hearted good fellow. For he had proved both courage and fighting skill in downing Christopher, and this adventure onto Mount Solomon was only an excess of foolhardiness.

They even began to banter him about his good intentions in riding to Mount Solomon and posing as a recruit for the band, all for the sake of leading some half dozen fighters down to mask the batteries of terrible Al Jenkins.

"Maybe," they suggested, "you're kind of fond of Charlie and hate to see his work wasted on the Bennett place."

"That's just it," said Ronicky.

And they roared with laughter at the thought of it.
"And why," they asked, "are you so thick with Charlie?"
"He saved my hoss," said Ronicky.

This brought fresh laughter. Everything he said seemed to amuse them. They threw back their heads and shouted with pleasure at the thought of a man venturing his neck to repay the saving of a horse. For horses in their minds were simply the tough, ugly little cow ponies of the Western mountains.

Ronicky cut their laughter short. With a low whistle he brought a short neigh of response, and then out of the entrance passage flashed the bay mare and came straight to him, dancing eagerly and tossing her head at the strangers. Her beauty brought a volley of admiration and curses from the outlaws. To them such speed as her shapely body and strong legs represented, might mean the difference between freedom and imprisonment, or life and death. And then a wave of Ronicky's hand sent her back to her original hiding place.

There was no need of words. The sight of the mare had been enough to convince them of the importance of the action whereby Christopher had drawn her from the very grip of death. And they looked at Ronicky with a renewed respect and interest.

But they went back in their banter to another subject: the pretense of Ronicky that he would attempt to persuade them to go down and ride herd for Steve Bennett.

"How would you go about persuading a gent to leave off a free life and the ability to do what he wants, in order to go down there and be the slave of another man?" they asked.

Ronicky's answer was ready.

"You sure got a lot of fine freedom up here," he said. "Living in a hole like rats and sitting on stones—that's a fine freedom, gents. But I'd rather be a slave and live easy, while I'm living. We're a long time dead."

This pointed remark brought something of a growl from them.

"You'd have us leave off and work on cows, eh? Twelve hours a day running the doggies?"

"How many hours do you work at your jobs that you got now?" he asked them.

"Only when we feel like it!" They answered him in a chorus. Evidently this was one point which they relished most.

"Sure," said Ronicky, "you only work when you feel like it, but it seems to me that you must feel like it all the time. There's old Cook. He just come in from a hard trail, and he had to go right out again. He didn't have time to do much more'n say hello. But didn't he want to stay here? Sure he did, only he was due a long ways off, and if he misses connections at the other end of that ride he'll have to turn around and come clear back, living on hope most of the way, going and coming. I sure don't cotton to that sort of a life, boys, because, take me by and large, you'll find me a lazy cuss! I like the ease of punching cows."

They regarded him almost agape. Such reasoning was beyond them, although the bitter truth of the last remark he had made was bearing in on the mind of every one of them. They, all of them, had ridden their trails which had no ending, and they had turned back from a lost goal, hungry and weary and hopeless.

"Besides, the odds are too big," said Ronicky, continuing a monologue which was addressed to himself as much as to them—for he seemed to be merely thinking aloud. "You boys against the rest of the world. Nobody can beat that game forever."

In protest they shrugged their shoulders.

"Freedom," said Ronicky, "you ain't got. And a chance for a lazy life you sure ain't got. What else is on your side of the fence, boys?"

"Money," said the red-shirted man hotly. "We got some coin to spend, now and then. That's more'n the cowpunchers have!"

"Well," said Ronicky, "how much are you ahead of the game?"

"I've been rich, pretty near," said the other reminiscently. He rocked back on the big stone on which he was sitting and, clasping his knee in his hands, gazed intently into his past. "There was a month right after a little job that me and Turk Ralston done in Nevada, when we was rolling in loot. Yep, we sure had lots of the kale. I had close to twenty-five thousand on me then!"

There was a little murmur that passed around the circle. All eyes turned upon Ronicky. Certainly he was answered this time. Ronicky himself took off his hat and waved it to the other.

"If you got twenty-five thousand," he said, "you sure have a lot more'n I'll ever get out of cow-punching."

"Oh, I didn't mean that I have it now," said the other. And he shivered a little as he spoke. The joy went out of his face, and a wintry darkness took its place. "Nope, right after that, Ralston, the dog, double-crossed me and turned me over to the sheriff. And the sheriff got the loot and me with it. I got five years for that!"

"All right," said Ronicky. "That sort of changes things. I was envying you a lot a while back, but I feel a little different right now. You have twenty-five thousand to look at for a month, and then you paid for it by busting rocks for five years for nothing. Is that right?"

He of the red shirt moistened his lips with the tip of his tongue and cast an ugly look at Ronicky. He did not like to have the glory of that twenty-five-thousand-dollar haul besmirched so rudely.

"It's more'n you'll ever put your finger on, son," he said sharply.

"Sure it is," said Ronicky, "because I can't figure on paying a price as high as that for money. Not for one month's worth of money! You see, I like my freedom too well!"

There was a moment of silence, while the outlaws reflected darkly upon these remarks. It seemed that they were being backed up against the wall, and yet they felt that there must be some escape.

"Now, there's Bud, yonder," said he of the red shirt at last. "He ain't ever spent a day in jail in his life. There's freedom for you!"

At once the case of Bud was taken up with acclaim.

"Yep, let's have any of the cow-punchers, beginning with yourself, stand up and say that they've led as free a life as Bud has led!"

Ronicky looked closely at Bud. He was a very tall, very thin man. Eternal melancholy sat upon his eyes. His cheek were drawn famine-thin. And there was a faint and uncertain spot of color in each cheek, although the rest of his face was deathly white. Even as Ronicky looked at him, Bud coughed, a racking cough that tore his frame.

"All right," said Ronicky with deadly solemnity. "I guess Bud may have lived a free life. But there's other ways of paying for freedom than in a prison. I wish Bud all the freedom he can get and the best time!"

Plainly he had guessed the grim secret of Bud and a heavy silence fell on the circle.

"In the whole bunch of you," asked Ronicky suddenly, "is there just one that's got a thousand dollars?"

The silence was an eloquent answer in the negative.

"Among the whole bunch of you," demanded Ronicky, "is there a one that ain't paid for his times when he was flush, by months of prison and hard riding in all kinds of weather, and being hounded here and there through the mountains, till you had to keep your eyes peeled on every bush that you passed? Is there a one of you that doesn't have to look extra hard when a new man comes into the room, because that new gent may be somebody that you fell foul of?"

He paused abruptly from the tirade and found that one and all were watching him, with haunted eyes of dread. It seemed that he was speaking for each man in words which revealed his own peril most intimately.

Finally he of the red shirt, but in a harsh, choked voice, said: "Well, Ronicky, I dunno where you aim to drive with all this chatter. You sure don't expect that we'd go down onto Bennett's Ranch and really ride herd for you."

"Why not?" asked Ronicky sharply.

"Why—thunder! Us? They'd have us hung inside of ten days at the most!"

"Why would they? You boys ain't been operating around here. Nine chance out of ten they won't be a soul around that'll know you at all."

"Go into slavery?" asked one.

"Why not try it for a week—or for a day?" asked Ronicky. "There's nobody to make you do anything longer than you want to."

The novelty of the idea began to appeal to them suddenly.

"Why, boys," said the tall man, Bud, raising his great length and looking hungrily at Ronicky, "if I could get to a real, honest-Injun bed for one night, I figure that it might do me some good, eh?"

"It'd be sort of fun to sing to the doggies, too," said another reflectively.

"And as he says, we don't have to stay."

"But what about keeping him here for a hostage until Christopher is in the clear?"

"Tell that idea to your hat. He ain't going to blow on Kit. He's got too much sense. He knows that if he starts anything like that he'll have the whole mob of us after

198

him, and he sure ain't lining out any sort of a future like that for himself!"

Ronicky Doone said not a word. He was looking down at his watch. It was still only a little after noon, and there was time if they acted at once!

CHAPTER XXXV

RONICKY'S TRIUMPH

THE greatest day of Al Jenkins' life had come. He sat his horse on the tallest hill near his house, and he could look across more than the mere ground. What he was seeing was his entire past life reduced to pictures. Just below him was the small house where he had begun his struggle. It was a battered and sadly worn house. Once it had represented almost an ideal to him, because it had been around that house that he had grouped his hopes for a home. He remembered when he had planted the small orchard to the left of the house, and the line of trees which was to fence in the drive out to the main road up the valley.

All of these things he had done in the flush of youth, when both he and young Steve Bennett had been fighting fiercely for the hand of the same girl. Far, far away to his right, buried from sight among the hills, was the old Bennett house. It had gone to rack and ruin long since; it had not been lived in for twenty years, for Bennett married a home as well as a wife. Yonder thin streak of blue against the brown hillside told of the big house. This, also, was falling to pieces in the Bennett régime. They were doomed to be destroyers, so it seemed. But in the old days that big house, of which the rising smoke was telling, had been the show place of the mountains.

It was for the sake of the big house and the big property, as much as for the girl, Al could not help but feel, that Steve Bennett had betrayed him. Had it been for love alone, Al vowed that he could have forgiven his lucky rival for his success, but he had always felt that love for the girl was only one small part of it.

He turned his glance back to the little house in the hollow beneath him. Certainly it had not been her wealth that had been the loadstone to him. It was not the thought of the big ranch and what he could have done with it, that made his heart heavy as lead. It was she who might have made his life a heaven upon earth!

It was with a sharp pang that he stared down on the house. He could remember the planting of every one of those trees, he felt. They would tempt her eye, he had felt at the time. He would make this so smiling a home that she could not but cast a longing glance toward it.

The orchard was withered now. Only a few withered, writhen trunks, here and there, told of the labor that had made it and the hopes that had been planted with it. The paint, too, which he had plastered on the house with such a devout joyousness, was long since peeled and cracked away, and it left the boards a sturdy and weathered brown. It was a symbol of the changes in his whole life, he told himself.

He had started out the gayest and gentlest of men. And now long experience, bitter disappointments, had taught him that no man was to be trusted outside of his interests. He might reproach himself for his lack of faith in his fellow men, but no amount of self-reproaching could change his mental furniture. And it seemed to Al Jenkins that he sat his horse in the midst of a desert. There was no joy in it; there was no joy in his life. At least there was no pleasure other than the pleasure of great power. He was the strongest man in that district, he assured himself. No one could stand up against him. As for Steve Bennett, there was no real war with him now. There was no suspense other than that which he himself had provided by delaying the destruction of the other for a few days. He could have struck as soon as Blondy Loring was shot down. But he had delayed those six days to give poor Bennett a chance to fight against the inevitable. Inevitable the conclusion certainly must be!

There was only the shadowy form of Ronicky Doone, that strange youth who had forwarded his plans an immense step by removing the formidable and active Blondy, only to turn around and swear that he intended to do his best for Bennett. Ronicky Doone, to be sure, had loomed large in his mind's eye for a few days. But now that the week was almost lapsed, Al Jenkins was beginning to consign Ronicky's threats and promises to the region of the thin and shadowy spirits. Ronicky had made a few boasts and then ridden off and left Al to digest them the rest of his life.

Besides, what could one man do to stop him?

Al Jenkins turned his head. Beside him and behind him there were three stalwarts, chosen men of war in case of need. And yonder, scattered at different points through the mountains on the Bennett ranch, there were twenty more picked men, ready for any sort of trouble. These were the ones who were about to close in upon the rancher and scoop his ranges clean of cattle. How could one man block schemes as widely extended as these?

And there was more, much more to be said. For behind him stood arrayed a solid body of public opinion which would back him against any odds and against all foes. Truly he was well fortified. He looked back of him to the very crest of the hill. At that highest point there was a great pile of wood. It was a truly imposing mass, which had been collected for weeks and months, no one being able to understand its purpose. And now it had been recently finished off, to the complete wonder of Al's men, with a thick crown of green wood and foliage.

They could not understand, but a torch applied to that heap of wood would send a vast smoke column standing stiffly into the air, and the sight of that smoke column would warn every one of the score of men scattered among the hills, that the time to begin the drive had come; and they would set to work just as in the old days that same Steve Bennett had launched a brutal host against him and swept his smaller ranch clean.

No wonder that Al Jenkins delayed in applying the torch. For he was in the position of Jove. At his nod the lightning flew. But it would only fly once; and he lingered, delaying the stroke for the joy of balancing the destruction in the palm of his hand.

But at last he made up his mind that the time had come past delay. His men must be safely in their appointed places for the beginning of the round-up. The cowardly crew of cow-punchers who had been working for Bennett before, had been seen to leave the ranch long ago, warned of the impending blow. All the stage was set for the catastrophe. In the meantime the sun had reached the late afternoon, and already its light was beginning to turn yellow and give a less biting brilliance, a less withering blast of heat.

He turned to give the signal which would sweep Steve Bennett into pauperism, and then he delayed the signal for yet another moment. For his eye had caught an advancing group of horsemen who had just wound into view on the valley road. He lowered the hand which he was about to wave, as he called to "Freckles" to light the match that would start the fire. For there was something in the manner of riding in that group and in the group itself, that arrested his attention.

In the first place there were eight men, which was a larger number than generally gathered together going to and from a ranch. In the second place they rode well bunched together and went along at a steady gait as though they were in a businesslike mood and had a distinct destination just before them.

And above all, as they drew nearer, a rather small bay horse, which even in the distance showed the utmost delicacy and beauty of line, flashed into the lead and then turned suddenly into the very driveway which led to Al Jenkins' house!

Jenkins forgot all about the high-built bonfire behind him. He uttered an exclamation of the keenest wonder and interest.

"It's Ronicky Doone!" he cried. "It's Ronicky Doone, boys, and if I ain't mistaken, he's here to raise trouble with me!"

The announcement caused a burst of consternation. The defeat of Blondy Loring in the center of Twin Springs had been spectacular enough to impress even the dullest minds and the least apprehensive spirits. But the sight of such a man, riding at the head of seven followers who, so far as was known, might be men of his own caliber, was a thunderbolt to their plans and their confidence. They packed in close around the rancher and waited eagerly for his decision.

Immediately they grew nervous when he did not give a command for them to turn the heads of their horses and start traveling in the opposite direction. Especially now that the advancing party swarmed around the house, apparently found at once that there was no one in it, and then straightened out for the place where Jenkins and his smaller party waited.

Freckles voiced the opinion of the others.

"If Ronicky Doone is working for Bennett," he said, "and if he's got us, eight to four, don't it seem sort of nacheral and wise for us to vamoose, chief?"

But Al Jenkins waved the thought aside.

"If Blondy Loring on his little bunch of gray lightning couldn't ride away from that bay mare, what chance do you think we'd have with our hosses? No, if he wants to talk to us, let him come up here and talk. I'm going to stay right here, but the rest of you can do what you want to do."

They made no reply, but, reigning their horses back, they prepared to wait for the attack.

It came with a rush and a swirl. Up the hill dashed the eight in a scattered line, but what Al Jenkins looked at was not the row of horses, stretching in a hard gallop up the slope, but the riders who spurred them on. He thought that he had never seen seven such formidable characters. There was a wide-shouldered man in a red shirt riding right behind Ronicky Doone, an ugly man, the ugliest that Al Jenkins could remember encountering. And he had a purposeful manner about him that suggested great readiness with weapons. At one end of the line there was a man famine-thin and very tall. And his lean face had the ferocious eagerness of a Lark. And all the other men in between were hardly less impressive. If it came to a show-down, "God pity my men," thought the rancher.

In the meantime he summoned a cheerful smile and rode out a pace or two in the front. Ronicky brought the bay mare to a halt immediately before him.

He had expected a triumphant defiance in the manner of the fighting youth. He was agreeably surprised when Ronicky came to him with a smile and an outstretched hand. They shook hands to the mutual bewilderment of the opposing parties, both of which were glowering darkly at one another.

"I'm mighty glad to see you again," said Ronicky.

"We're lined up on the wrong sides in this party, it looks like, but I'm aiming to play clean and fair, Mr. Jenkins!"

Al Jenkins was so relieved that he broke into laughter and smote Ronicky a tremendous blow on the shoulder.

"I've never yet worked crooked," he said, "and I ain't going to begin. But what you driving at, Ronicky?"

The explanation of Ronicky was brief and wholly to the point.

"I've come down with some partners of mine," he said, "to give things a look around these parts. We aim to be friends of Steve Bennett, all of us. And being friends of his. we thought maybe you might like to know that we was around in this neighborhood."

"Sure." said Al Jenkins, falling at once into the spirit of this talk. "I'm a public-spirited man, son, and I'm always interested in the folks that call on my neighbors. You're going to stay with Steve Bennett for a while?"

"Sure! We're his new hands. Me and the boys figured that maybe he'd be losing some of his hands before long, and that he'd want to take on a few more."

"Right." replied Al Jenkins. "His whole gang quit just this morning. But I didn't know that he ever used a crowd as big as eight, outside of a rush season?"

"But this," said Ronicky, "*is* a rush season with Bennett, though I suppose that you'd never guess it."

The innuendoes were hugely to the taste of the cow-punchers on both sides, and they grinned at each other with a mutual understanding. Now Ronicky and Al Jenkins drew to one side.

"It means that your game is called off, Jenkins," said Ronicky. "These boys of mine may not be as many as the ones that you've got working for you. But they got something better than numbers—they got good steady hands and quick trigger fingers. Look 'em over, Jenkins. And, besides, they're better than they look!"

"In one sense I suppose that they are," said Jenkins gloomily. His good humor was rapidly vanishing, as he saw the chance for action on this day removed. Then he added with a touch of malice: "I'd like to have the history of every one of that gang. I think it might be interesting to people—particularly to the sheriff!"

"Sure it would be," said Ronicky. "It would be mighty interesting. But it would be awful hard on the gent that started out to collect the news. And he'd waste a pile of hossflesh doing it. I hope you ain't aiming at that right away?"

Jenkins sighed.

"Right now," he said, "it looks like I got to postpone the deal. You know what I mean. But sooner or later, it don't make no difference, Bennett has got to go down. You won't have your friends with you all the time! You won't even be here all the time yourself, Ronicky!"

Ronicky nodded.

"I'm only asking a fighting chance for the girl," he said.

"So's her father can gamble it away?" asked Jenkins.

"I'll tend to him," said Ronicky. "Don't you be worrying about that. And in the meantime, Jenkins, I know that I've got the upper hand. You can beat Bennett and me together next month; but this month him and me have the upper hand. Is that clear?"

"Clear," admitted Jenkins through his teeth. "Son, does it come into your head that one of these days I may make you sweat for interfering?"

"I've sweated already over this job," admitted Ronicky frankly. "And I guess that I'll sweat again. Good-by, Jenkins. Here's the last thing I got to say: if your men should happen to be riding promiscuous around on the Bennett place in the next few days, my boys are apt to be going around with rifles all ready to shoot quick—they're as nervous as that!"

And he swung Lou around.

CHAPTER XXXVI

SKINNY'S STORY

WHAT does it all mean?" asked the dazed followers of Al Jenkins, gaping after Ronicky and his men, as the wild riders plunged down the slope toward the house again.

"It means," said Al Jenkins savagely, "that I've been beat at the last minute by a kid half my age. It means that I've been a blockhead and fool not to jump Bennett a week ago when I had him down and out. I've waited too long. I've tried to give him a sporting chance to fight for his life, and now I'm dynamited by this man of powder and lightning! Look at him go!"

There was a gloomy admiration mingled with his anger, as he saw Ronicky dart out to the head of his men, the beautiful bay mare running smoothly as flowing water.

"And now maybe it'll take me another year of waiting till I get Bennett rounded up."

As for Ronicky Doone, riding at the head of his little band, he felt singing and laughter overflowing in his heart. Truly the story of these past six days had been a crowded narrative, and now he was coming to the reward of honest labor, and that reward was sweet in the prospect. He could go to Elsie Bennett and say to her:

"Here is your father preserved, your ranch retained, and all is well for a little longer. The great Al Jenkins has been foiled!" What would she say in reply? He did not guess; that part was a happy blur.

Just as evening fell, he and his men hurried up the trail toward the Bennett place.

"That pile of wood was to make the smoke that was to start the drive," Ronicky declared confidently to the outlaws. "And as long as we don't see that behind us, we're safe enough, and there's no big cause for hurry. He won't try anything to-day. And if he does, there'll be a fight. I guess you boys ain't unwilling?"

They grinned broadly at the thought. Unwilling? Unwilling to take part in a fight in which they would not have the banded powers of the law against them, but in which they would be defending a man's legal rights against the aggressions of another? Such a battle would be after their inmost wishes.

Above all they were delighted by the thought that they were fighting the battle of their leader, and that while he lay helpless in Twin Springs, feeling that all of his work in the name of Bennett had been in vain, they, his men from Mount Solomon, were fighting his fight unknown to him.

"But what beats me," said the tall man who was usually known as "Bud," though "Skinny" was also a favorite name, "what beats me is that Kit should waste so much time over a girl like Elsie Bennett. I dunno how his mind works. Or maybe he's getting reformed!"

"Why not?" asked Ronicky. "Why shouldn't he reform and settle down and marry? He's not known in this part of the country. Matter of fact, his face doesn't seem to be well known in any part!"

But Skinny merely shook his head.

"Sure," he said. "It would be all fine for Blondy to settle down with a wife. But in the first place he ain't the kind that settles down."

"How do you know?" interrupted Ronicky. "She's pretty enough to tame wilder men than Christopher ever was!"

"Is she? I dunno but what she is," said Skinny. Here he paused and looked around so as to bring all eyes upon him. And since they were walking their horses up a steep grade and had plenty of leisure to make their observations, they turned readily to the speaker.

"I dunno but what she *is* pretty enough to tame wilder men than Kit, but the point is that he don't stay tamed very long."

"How do you know?" asked Ronicky, an ugly suspicion beginning to grow in his mind, as he watched the face of the tall man.

"I'll tell you why," said Skinny. "I know because I know that he's already tried this settling-down idea!"

This announcement brought an incredulous roar from the others. What, Christopher married? They could not and would not believe it. But Bud persisted.

It was a full year and a half before, he said, that he and Christopher had been working on a "job" together, and that during their adventure they had encountered a pretty black-eyed girl who made a complete conquest of Blondy. Twelve hours after they met they were married, and he, Skinny, was the witness to the ceremony.

He told the story with so many details that there was no doubting him. He would not have had the imagination to furnish forth the story so completely.

As for Ronicky Doone, while the band of outlaws exclaimed, he was silent, stunned, and thoughtful. Yet it seemed to him that only a kindly Fate had revealed these tidings to him through the lips of Skinny. And a hope, which he had carefully stifled, burst into a blaze of joyous strength.

But what had been the purpose of Blondy Christopher, as it was revealed by the information which Skinny had just given them? Did Blondy really have a big and generous heart? Had the beauty of the girl simply worked upon him like water on a sandy soil and brought forth a surprising fruit? Had his months of labor at the Bennett place been only to help Elsie Bennett by helping her father?

It was a fine thing to think about, but another grim doubt arose in the heart of Ronicky, and he shook his head at the prospect. He could not help doubting the existence of such altruistic virtues in the heart of the big man. What should he do next, therefore, in the light of all that he had heard? He must get to the girl at once and watch over her and keep her safe!

There would be only a brief stay on the Bennett ranch. But here he was abruptly recalled to the way and to the story of Skinny, which had been proceeding all the time, but to which his own thoughts had strongly deafened him.

"And when I got the letter from her," Skinny was saying, "I didn't know what to do. I didn't feel like riding two hundred miles so's a girl could cry on my shoulder and ask me to bring her husband back to her. If Kit was tired of her, that was Kit's business. But after a while I couldn't help remembering her happy face, when she stood up beside Kit and married him and swore she'd stay by him, and he swore he'd stay by her! I got to thinking about that so much that finally I couldn't stand it no longer. And that's why I lit out a couple of weeks ago. I went right down to see Ruth. And what d'you think she done when she seen me? She led me into the next room and showed me a baby asleep in a cradle. And there she picks it up and starts crying over it and telling me how bad she and the baby need Kit.

"It sure put a dent in me to hear the way she went on about it. I done what I could for her, and I promised that I'd sure enough get Kit back to her. So then I hot-footed it back here, but when I landed yesterday I heard all this yarn about Kit being laid up with a slug through the middle of things. Then I started to thinking. I'd sworn to Kit that I'd never tell a soul about him being married, but I figure that the best thing for all the three of them is to tell what I know, so that Kit'll be shamed into going back and taking care of the two of them. The girl would sure do her best to make him happy, and if he's any kind of a man he'd ought to be happy to have a Charlie junior hanging around his house. Am I right, boys?"

They replied with great vehemence that he was, and then a moment of damning silence held the group. Plainly they did not think many favorable things about the conduct of Kit in this affair, and if he had been there he might have learned various strongly worded opinions at first hand.

"It's plumb bad," said the man in the red shirt. "This is something that Kit'll have to fight hard to live down. I never guessed anything as black as this about him!"

And that was the concensus of opinion, as they rattled into the open space beside the Bennett house. Their shout brought a slow opening of the door, and then a shrill cry of joy, as old Bennett cast the door wide and ran out to them.

"Ronicky Doone!" he cried. "You've come back after

all! You've come back after all! And all these gentlemen ready to work for me? But not work first, lads! It's gun -play that I'm needing! They're swarming yonder through the hills! I've gone up and seen 'em. I spotted three with my own eyes, and they got a lot more lying here and there. They got every man of mine off the ranch, and now they're ready for their drive."

He was close to an hysteria of excited joy; he began to stammer thanks, orders, prayers, but Ronicky Doone was giving quiet and efficient directions, sending off his warriors in three directions, two pairs and a group of three. It would go hard with any skulkers who encountered any of that array!

Then Ronicky turned to face the old man alone.

CHAPTER XXXVII

PAVING THE PRIMROSE PATH

THE excitement of the game still kept Elsie Bennett employed. Only the adventure of it was brought home to her mind. In the morning what would people say when they knew that she had married Blondy Loring? And she herself—how strange it would be to know that she was bound for life to him!

She began what she felt was to prove a life of obedience to her husband by letting him lay all the plans; and he made those plans with a cunning which delighted and surprised her. The license had to be obtained, and that was no easy matter to arrange secretly. And after the license had been obtained, there was the necessity of getting the doctor out of the room long enough to permit her friend, the minister, to come in and perform the ceremony.

To accomplish these desirable ends the outlaw gave full directions, going into every detail, and at noon she issued from the hotel to get the license. It entailed a brief and exciting interview with a boy who had gone to the same village school with her, but who assumed a tremendously judicial air when he heard of her business. Finally he was persuaded to move the sanctity of his office to the hotel during the noon hour, and there in the bedroom the necessary questions were asked and answered, and the license was issued.

After that she went in search of the minister. She found the good man walking in his garden, which was in the rear of his house. For the Reverend Philip Walton had brought back from England this purely English taste. The back of his house was turned to the street in Twin Springs, and the front of it faced on a little garden which he had laid out, planted, and cared for in all its growth with his own hands. It was not big enough, to be sure, for a man of any length of stride to pace up and down in with much comfort. But Philip Walton was a very little man, with a very little withered body and legs in proportion, and a stride which had never been very long or very elastic, was now shortened still more by an advancing age. Two things about him remained young: his quick glance and the crispness with which he spoke. But though his accent and enunciation were as brisk as ever, the voice was sadly inclined to crack, and the glance, no matter though it were as quick as ever in its birdlike suddenness of movement, was filmed over.

He was a tremendously cheerful little man. Nothing could dull and diminish his good humor. His family history was one of continued tragedy. A poverty-stricken and work-laden childhood had passed into an early manhood of heartbreaking study, and this was lightened by only the briefest of romances which terminated, a month after his wedding, in the death of his wife. But from that moment on a curse seemed to hang over his relations, until eventually he was left the last of his clan. Yet, when he heard the quick step of the girl, he turned to face her with a smile as gay as her own and an impulsive movement of his hand in greeting.

Under the shade of the arbor she sat down beside him. It was hardly large enough to accommodate them both, and there she told him her great news. He listened gravely, eagerly; and when she had concluded, he shook his head.

"When I was a boy," he began, unheeding the sigh with which she greeted this introduction to a story, "I had an uncle who was fond of saying: 'That which begins in the shadow is apt to end in the shadow: if you want your plants to live and flourish, put them in the sun!' And that, Elsie, is what I have done in my garden. And that, child,

213

is what I strongly advise that you do with your life. Keep in the sun. Never do things in the shadow."

"You've heard so many evil things about him," said Elsie, "that you're prejudiced against poor Charlie. Confess that that's it!"

But still he shook his head, smiling at her.

"I don't listen to evil gossip," he said. "Such stuff doesn't stay in my mind. Because, you see, I have hardly sufficient space to crowd in all the pleasant things I know. But aside from all that—and I'm afraid it's a rather foolish reason—I'm standing against you here simply because you wish to do this thing in such secrecy. That is all! You don't want any one to know. I must come to you and marry you and promise not to tell a soul until you say that I may. You say that this will not be for long. But how do I know? To-morrow you may change your mind. You may come begging that I still delay telling the world my great news. And you know that I never can resist you when you seriously want me, Elsie!"

She smiled kindly at him.

"But," he said, "a marriage under the rose—I don't know anything in the world that could be more distasteful to me. Will you believe me, my dear, and will you try to think on my side of the question a little bit?"

She promised that she would, and no sooner had she promised than she began to attack him again with such an array of arguments that poor Mr. Philip Walton held his withered little hands over his ears and shook his head and laughed at her.

"Of course I shall go there when you wish me to," he said. "I am protesting merely to make an honorable surrender possible, and so that I may reserve the right to say I told you so, later on! When do you need me?"

"Just after dark——" she began.

And here he interrupted: "It's in actual shadow, then? Ah, Elsie, it isn't fair to the rest of us. We've been waiting all these years in the hope that eventually we should see you walk up the aisle in the church and——"

He stopped and shook his head again.

"But I'll come there to-night as you wish, and if an old man's honest blessing can help you to happiness, you shall have it, my dear. You shall have it!"

And so she left him. But when she reached the street on the way back to the hotel, she found that she was not happy at all. Indeed a darkness had fallen upon her spirit. And this with a blessing hardly yet silent in her ears! But it was simply because the old man had brought such an air of solemnity to the occasion. And now Elsie began to remember that weddings were times of tears and sad thought as well as of merriment and laughter. A wedding was the death of a name, the death of an old life, and the beginning of a new.

So she said to herself as she went slowly onward. But the happiness was taken out of her heart. Moreover, now that two of the steps had been taken, there seemed no great need for anxiety about the third. This was the step which was most important of all, and in the eyes of Blondy it would be the most difficult for her to accomplish. But he did not know her power.

On the outskirts of the town, where it began to run into the western hills, she stopped before a small cottage set well back from the street, and at her coming a tall, brown-faced, long-shanked boy in the awkward age of fifteen, rose and uncoiled his length to greet her. His grin abashed and diminished all the other features of his face.

Why a cousin of her own should look like this she could not tell, though she had often asked that question of an uncommunicative Providence. But from his birth, it seemed, Willie Chalmers had been mostly mouth, so far as his face was concerned, and mostly legs in the rest of his make-up. She could not look beyond the veil of the future and see him a stalwart, fine-looking youth a short three years hence.

"Willie," she asked, "why have you never come to see me all the time I've been at the hotel?"

"I sort of thought," he answered, "that you'd be busy, Elsie. That's why I never come. But I sure enough thought about it a couple of times. How's everything with you been going?"

He advanced toward the gate and faced her, dropping the heel of his right shoe most awkwardly upon the toes of his left and thrusting his hands into bottomless pockets.

So she explained to him, still smiling and watching him during every instant of that smile, that on that very night she would have a tremendous need of him, and she wondered if she could depend on him. Willie was so eager that he swallowed before he could answer. Of course she could use him as she pleased to use him!

"How far is it," she asked, "to the Roger place?"

"About a mile and a half," said Willie.

"And how long would it take a man to ride that far?"

"All depends," said Willie. "If he went like lickety he might get there in five minutes, I suppose."

"It has to be farther then," she said. "But how far is it to the Chalmers' place?"

"That's three mile, I guess."

"Oh, three miles—then it will take twice as long."

"More'n that. His hoss would get pretty tired before it hit the last mile and a half at that clip."

"Well, that's good! Willie, you know the Chalmers boy?"

"Joe Chalmers? Sure, him and me fought every other week last year. I busted his face good for him. Sure I know Joe. Him and me are chums. We're going shooting next month!"

She was too serious to smile at this strange recital of the bases of friendship among the young.

"Willie," she said, "this is to be kept a dead secret, you see?"

His eyes grew very wide.

"Cross my heart to die!" whispered Willie in delight. "I sure won't breathe a word of it to nobody!"

"Then you come running to the hotel to-night at a quarter to eight—mind you, at seven-forty-five sharp! And you come shouting for the doctor!"

"Why for the doctor?"

"Because the Chalmers boy has been thrown from a horse and broken his leg."

"Thrown from a hoss? Why, there ain't a hoss in the world that could throw—oh!"

With this exclamation the light dawned upon Willie in a great and a blinding burst, so that he gasped, choked, and then was silent.

"Will you do it?" she asked.

"Will I do it?" exclaimed Willie. "Didn't that damn doctor—excuse me for swearing, Elsie—pretty near raise me on castor oil?"

CHAPTER XXXVIII

A FORMULA FOR HAPPINESS

PERHAPS the agreement at which Ronicky Doone arrived with the rancher was not large in words, but it was eloquent in substance.

"How come you've lost so much coin?" asked Ronicky when he came to the gist of his argument in the growing twilight before the ranch house.

"By bad luck," said the other sadly. "Nobody in the world, hardly, has had such bad luck as I've had!"

"At what?"

"Cows—men—everything that I count on goes wrong."

"Chiefly cards, though," said Ronicky.

"Eh? The cards? I've had my ups and downs with 'em! Are you feeling up to a small game of stud?"

But Ronicky was shaking his head and grinning scornfully.

"I can see through you like glass, Bennett," he said. "It's the cards that have taken everything away from you. If you and me hit up for an agreement, we got to start right there!"

"Right where?" asked the rancher, dismayed.

"Right at the cards! Bennett, you're through. You never

lay a bet on the turn of a card again so long as you live. Understand?"

Steve Bennett gasped a protest, but Ronicky raised his hand to silence the older man.

"These boys I brung down here," he said, "will be plumb happy to work for you and to clean up on Jenkins' men. But the minute I give 'em the word they'll be against you and for Jenkins. And the first time that I hear of you putting up some stakes I'm going to send word to the boys. Is that clear, and does that go?"

Bennett swallowed and nodded sadly.

"I was thinking of keeping 'em amused," he began.

"You keep 'em amused," said Ronicky, "by starting your chink to cooking the best dinner that he ever turned out. That's the best way to keep them amused. And don't mind it if they make a mite of racket. They're that kind."

Again Bennett could only mutely agree with the terms laid down by the dictator.

"I'm going to slide off to Twin Springs," said Ronicky. "But tell the boys that I'm coming back to-night. There ain't going to be no trouble and no shooting scrapes come out of this little party. Everything is going to be plumb quiet, but to-morrow morning early I'm going to be back on the job, rounding up all the chances for a fight with Jenkins' gang. But I think we've got 'em beat!"

"We have!" shouted Bennett savagely. "We've beat 'em, and when I see him again, the skunk, I'm going to tell him just what I——"

But Ronicky had no desire to hear more of this meaningless boasting. He turned Lou with a twist of his body and, waving farewell to Bennett, galloped down the valley toward the little town.

It was completely dark before he had covered more than half of the distance. In the shadows of the full night he swung down the street of Twin Springs, the bay mare rocking along as tirelessly as when he began the long run of that day's journeying. And so he came to the hotel.

But he did not choose to enter from the front. There might be too much talk, too much comment from the other men of the town. It seemed far better to Ronicky to send Lou between the two buildings next to the hotel and so around to the rear of the place. Here he dismounted and slipped up onto the veranda.

There he paused, recalling the picture which he had last

seen from that veranda, looking through the big window into the room where Blondy Loring lay. Now, stepping close to the outside edge, so that the boards would not creak under his weight, he stole softly on.

As he went he heard a regular murmuring from the room—the low, low voice of the girl—the voices of two men—but all was kept so indistinct that he could not understand a syllable of it until he came opposite the window, and then a single glance was more eloquent with meaning than a thousand words.

For there sat Elsie Bennett, wonderfully beautiful in an old yellow dress, with little flowers worked obscurely upon it in pastel shades, her blonde hair done low upon her forehead and upon her neck, her face quite pale with emotion that seemed to Ronicky to be fear. But with all her heart and soul she seemed to be driving herself forward.

Beside her lay Blondy Loring, one hand stretched out from the bed and holding her hand. Over them stood a man reading from a book, a little man, with a high light thrown from the lamp on the back of his very bald head, and the light also shining in the aureole of misty hair which floated around the edge of the bald spot.

And now the voice of Blondy, repeating the words of the minister, rose in a deep, heavy volume: "With this ring I thee wed!" And then the pale face of the girl was bowed over Blondy to kiss him.

One step took Ronicky to the window, and another carried him over the low ledge and into the room. At the very shadow of his coming Elsie Bennett had started back. In vain Blondy strove to detain her with his big arm. She slipped out of his grasp and stood back against the farther wall, gasping, while the minister turned agape to face the intruder. Blondy was barely able to turn his head to view Ronicky.

"You're too late for the fun, son," he sneered at Ronicky. "I'm sorry you didn't come for the rest of the show!"

"I've come to give it the last send-off, though," said Ronicky grimly. "I've come to bring you good news."

"What news?"

"A son has been born to your wife, and she's sent for you—she needs you, Christopher!"

He could not tell that this last name was already known to the girl. But it was not the name which struck

219

her dumb; it was that first horrible message. Little Philip Walton reached her in time to lower her into a chair, where she sat nearly fainting and staring at Ronicky with uncomprehending eyes.

Ronicky stepped to the bed and towered over the cringing, trembling outlaw. All the courage had gone out of the body of the bold Christopher, like the water out of a squeezed sponge.

"I'm going to get you safe out of this," said Ronicky Doone. "But when you're safe and well, I'm going to run you down and kill you, you hound. At first I thought you were a sort of hero, and then I took you for a wolf of a man, Blondy, but finally I seen that all you were was just a miserable, sneaking coyote. And that's the way I'm going to hound you, and I'm going to kill you in the end! But the time ain't come yet. I'm not going to let the law finish you. I want to leave that for myself!"

And to crown the horror, when the girl finally looked at her pseudo husband, she found him shaking and quivering and begging like a whipped dog. She got up from the chair, cold and perfectly calm, and walked straight to Ronicky and took his hand in both of hers.

"I've been a great fool," she said, "and you've saved me from myself!"

So she turned and left the room, as quietly as though she were slipping out to let the patient get his rest undisturbed.

"Ah," said the minister, "what a woman she is! And what a God's blessing, young man, that you came when you did. Now let's find the sheriff!"

But from that resolution Ronicky carefully dissuaded him in a long argument which lasted until the light burned low and until Christopher was nearly dead with fear and shame on the bed. Then the minister gave in, and he took Ronicky home with him.

At the gate they parted.

"It's made me young again." said the minister, "listening to you talk. It's made me young again. But what I continually wonder at, Ronicky Doone, is where you get your reward?"

"Why," said Ronicky, "I've been thinking about that myself. I figure a gent gets his reward when he sees other people happy. As long as I can help other people to their happiness, I don't require no other reward. But I'm going to stay around here and wait."

He added this with a little emphasis, and the minister chuckled.

"I see," he said. "I see perfectly. Yes, I think that would be the best thing to do after all—just wait!"

And he was still chuckling when he went into his house.

But Ronicky went back down the street full of a sad happiness and with his brain full of Elsie Bennett. He could not guess—that night—that she was watching from an upper window of the hotel every step he took that night.

Max Brand is the best-known pen name of Frederick Faust, creator of Dr. Kildare, Destry, and many other fictional characters popular with readers and viewers worldwide. Faust wrote for a variety of audiences in many genres. His enormous output, totaling approximately thirty million words or the equivalent of 530 ordinary books, covered nearly every field: crime, fantasy, historical romance, espionage, Westerns, science fiction, adventure, animal stories, love, war, and fashionable society, big business and big medicine. Eighty motion pictures have been based on his work along with many radio and television programs. For good measure he also published four volumes of poetry. Perhaps no other author has reached more people in more different ways.

Born in Seattle in 1892, orphaned early, Faust grew up in the rural San Joaquin Valley of California. At Berkeley he became a student rebel and one-man literary movement, contributing prodigiously to all campus publications. Denied a degree because of unconventional conduct, he embarked on a series of adventures culminating in New York City where, after a period of near starvation, he received simultaneous recognition as a serious poet and successful popular-prose writer. Later, he traveled widely, making his home in New York. then in Florence, and finally in Los Angeles.

Once the United States entered the Second World War, Faust abandoned his lucrative writing career and his work as a screenwriter to serve as a war correspondent with the infantry in Italy, despite his fifty-one years and a bad heart. He was killed during a night attack on a hilltop village held by the German army. New books based on magazine serials or unpublished manuscripts continue to appear. Alive and dead he has averaged a new one every four months for seventy-five years. In the U.S. alone nine publishers issue his work, plus many more in foreign countries. Yet, only recently have the full dimensions of this extraordinarily versatile and prolific writer come to be recognized and his stature as a protean literary figure in the 20th Century acknowledged. His popularity continues to grow throughout the world.

MAX BRAND
Authentic Western Action
By The World's Most Celebrated Western Writer!

"Brand is a topnotcher!"
—New York Times

The Whispering Outlaw. He is a mystery among frontier bandits—a masked gunman who never shows his true face. When he plans a spree of daring robberies, he recruits a passel of ornery outlaws for a gang. All The Whisperer wants is one chance to strike it rich—all it will take to bring him down is one man who gets too greedy.

_3678-9 $3.99 US/$4.99 CAN

Blackie and Red. Blackie Jason and Red Hardwick are two of the orneriest cayuses ever to run wild on the open range. Nothing can come between them—nothing but a heap of money and a life of ease. With gold in their eyes, Blackie and Red learn a law of the West that no one can forget: Greed has a way of starting trouble, and trouble always ends up with someone dead in the dirt.

_3697-5 $3.99 US/$4.99 CAN

Ronicky Doone. Doone's name is famous throughout the Old West. But Bill Gregg isn't one to let a living legend get in his way, and he'd shoot Doone dead as soon as look at him. But nobody tells Gregg that Doone doesn't enjoy living his hard-riding life unless he takes a chance on losing it once in a while.

_3738-6 $3.99 US/$4.99 CAN

Dorchester Publishing Co., Inc.
65 Commerce Road
Stamford, CT 06902

Please add $1.75 for shipping and handling for the first book and $.50 for each book thereafter. NY, NYC, PA and CT residents, please add appropriate sales tax. No cash, stamps, or C.O.D.s. All orders shipped within 6 weeks via postal service book rate. Canadian orders require $2.00 extra postage and must be paid in U.S. dollars through a U.S. banking facility.

Name_____

Address_____

City _____ State _____Zip_____

I have enclosed $_____in payment for the checked book(s).
Payment <u>must</u> accompany all orders.☐ Please send a free catalog.